South of the
Law Line

South of the Law Line

A Western Trio

WALT COBURN

SAGEBRUSH
Large Print Westerns

First published in Great Britain by ISIS Publishing Ltd.
First published in the United States by Five Star

Published in Large Print 2009 by ISIS Publishing Ltd.,
7 Centremead, Osney Mead, Oxford OX2 0ES
United Kingdom
by arrangement with
Golden West Literary Agency

British Library Cataloguing in Publication Data
Coburn, Walt, 1889–1971
    South of the law line: a western trio. –
    Large print ed. –
    (Sagebrush western series)
    1. Western stories
    2. Large type books
    I. Title II. Coburn, Walt, 1889–1971.
    Riders of the purple III. Coburn, Walt, 1889–1971.
    High jack and low
    813.5'2 [FS]

ISBN 978–0–7531–8247–5 (hb)

Printed and bound in Great Britain by
T. J. International Ltd., Padstow, Cornwall

Additional Copyright Information:

Table of Contents

Riders of the Purple

By 1924, Walt Coburn was a regular contributor of stories to Street & Smith's *Western Story Magazine*, which had a weekly circulation of 2.5 million copies. Jack Kelly, who was the chief editor of Fiction House's pulp magazines, went to Santa Barbara, California, where Coburn was living at the time, and negotiated a contract with Coburn whereby the author was to write a 25,000-word novelette each month for *Action Stories*, a monthly magazine that cost 20¢ when *Western Story Magazine* was priced at 15¢. Coburn was to be paid $100 a week by Fiction House as a guarantee against his income from writing stories and would be given top billing. When Fiction House launched *Lariat Story Magazine* in 1925, Coburn was also asked to contribute Western stories to this magazine. "Riders of the Purple" — an obvious reference to Zane Gray's classic *Riders of the Purple Sage* — appeared in the first issue, dated August, 1925. It was subsequently reprinted by Fiction House as "Crossfire Colts" in *Lariat Story Magazine* (7/43) and, again, as "Crossfire Colts" in *Tops in Western Stories* (Fall, 53), the penultimate issue of this short-lived magazine.

CHAPTER
ONE

Time was when a man could ride from the Rafter T Ranch on the Missouri River to the Bar L Ranch on Milk River and never open a gate or pass through a lane. The distance, as the crow flies, was 100 miles. Just where the Rafter T ended and the Bar L range commenced, no man could say. No signpost or drift fence marked the division. Many a Bar L cow wintered on Rafter T hay, fed to her by a Rafter T cowhand. Every second maverick on the Bar L range was put in the Rafter T iron by the Bar L man who ran across the critter. The owners of these two big cow outfits swapped hay, men, or horses with the same unconcern that two brothers trade hats. The friendship of Pete Carver of the Rafter T and Ike Rutherford of the Bar L was a byword throughout Montana.

Pete Carver was a short, square-built man, quick talking and active as a panther. No better rider ever forked a spoiled horse and his skill with a rope was uncanny. His temper was as quick as his tongue. The indomitable will of the grizzled cowman showed in the jutting squareness of his jaw and the steely coldness of his eyes that glittered from under abnormally bushy iron-gray brows.

Ike Rutherford reminded one of weather-toughened rawhide held together by barb wire. Lean, sinewy, his tanned face interwoven by myriad lines, he stood over six feet with his boots off. Easy and sure of movement, he could, with miraculous ease, go down a taut rope and, in the space of a minute, twist down the bawling, struggling yearling bull at the end of that rope. With equal ease, he was known to "ear down" a striking, fighting bronco. He knew every brand, earmark, and wattle mark between the Canadian line and the Pecos. A beef man *par excellence*, and as quick as a rattler with six-shooter or fist. Hard winters and endless hours in the saddle had whitened his hair. His eyes were of the same sunny blue as Montana's summer skies. A staunch friend and a hard hater was Rutherford. Men either blessed him or cursed him.

These two had come from Texas with the early trail herds, put their money in cows, and helped make cow country history in one of the finest, yet harshest cow countries that men ever rode. With the passing of years, their herds grew until the 100 square miles of their combined ranges were stocked to overflowing with white-face cattle. Then came the fateful day when these two men faced one another in cold, deadly anger and men held their breath as they waited for the crashing roar of lead-spitting guns.

The break came on a raw November morning when the two cattlemen worked the mammoth beef

4

herd on the sagebrush flat beyond the Chinook stockyards. The bitter wind that swept the bleak flat had chilled the men until they seemed frozen in their saddles. The herd had been hard to hold and the nerves of every man who fought the restless steers had been rubbed raw since dawn. At the yards, impatient trainmen beat their mittened hands and swung stiff arms to restore circulation while they waited for the penning of the herd that was to be shipped to Chicago.

Pete and Ike, cutting strays into the discard herd, had been in the saddle since the first streak of lead-gray sky had heralded the dawn. They were the only men who had not slipped back to the mess wagon for a cup of steaming coffee to thaw the chill in their blood. Pete worked a four-year-old roan steer to the edge of the herd and his horse, with a quick practiced dash, shooed the animal into the open. Ike, who had just cut a stray bull out, was turning his horse back into the herd when he saw the roan steer.

"Made a mistake there, Pete!" he called, and cut the roan steer back.

"Mistake, hell," grunted Pete. "Earmarks show it's a Two Bar critter. Split the right, crop the left. Brand's dim but I mind the day that critter was branded, at the Little Warm corral. It's one of Jim Bartlet's steers. That steer's mammy was a brockle-faced two-year-old heifer at the time that roan calf was branded, four years ago. A brockle-faced heifer that I got damn' good reason to know was stole from me by that Bartlet skunk. I'll

5

see him in hell afore I ship ary Two Bar stuff on my train."

"I made a dicker with Bartlet to ship his stuff," argued Ike. "He's payin' five dollars a head fer all we ship. I give him my word to ship his steers. I keeps my word regardless."

"You're fergittin' that this ain't the Bar L wagon that's gathered this herd. This is the Rafter T outfit and I'm runnin' it. And I'll tell a man that as long as I am runnin' my own outfit, I ship what I damn' please an' cuts back ary steer that don't belong. I'm cuttin' that Two Bar steer into the discard herd. I don't aim that you nor ary other human is goin' to keep me from it."

"Cut back that steer into the culls, Pete Carver, and I cuts every damn' Bar L steer I own into that same discard. Ship that roan critter, I tell you, or me 'n' you splits the blankets here and now."

Both men were white with anger. Each held the other's gaze with a steadiness that caused the listening cowpunchers to squirm uneasily in their saddles.

Then Pete Carver whirled his horse and called in a loud, rasping voice to his foreman: "Ride over to the yards and tell that train crew that I'm cancelin' them cars. We ain't shippin' this herd till it's *clean*."

Then he jabbed his horse with the spurs and cut the roan steer into the discard herd.

When Pete Carver shipped, two days later, the herd was straight Rafter T. That night the grizzled little cowman got drunk for the first time in twenty years.

Over at the Chinook House bar, Ike Rutherford was pouring raw whiskey into his stomach. He had been drinking for twenty-four hours.

Each man stayed in the saloon where he was drinking, avoiding the other. Each was surrounded by his own cowpunchers; they drank their drinks and, when the liquor thawed them, made fight talk.

Big Bob McClean, who had been sheriff for two terms, chewed the soggy butt of a cold cigar and cursed methodically. Then he loaded a sawed-off shotgun and crossed the blizzard-swept street to the Chinook House. He held the gun in the crook of his arm when he stepped into the barroom.

"Ike," he said in a voice that was so deadly calm that it threw an ominous hush over the half-drunk crowd, "I want your gun."

"Meanin'?"

"Meanin' that I'm placin' you under arrest. There's a good fire a-goin' over at the jail. Bring a bottle along if you've a mind to."

"Supposin'," asked Rutherford, his eyes narrowing to slits of blue flame, "I won't be arrested, Bob?"

"I ain't never gone after nobody that I didn't git, Ike. I'm plumb old and set in my ways. I'm takin' you, Ike."

Ike Rutherford, drunk as he was, knew that the sheriff spoke the truth. The sheriff's shotgun was cocked. With a shrug, he handed over his .45, butt first. His eyes, normal once more, held the sun of summer skies in their blue depths.

7

"You danged old timber wolf, Bob McClean. Damned if I don't believe you'd turn that there scatter-gun loose on me. Now, what in hell is it all about?"

"I heered you was aimin' to kill old Pete Carver on sight, Ike. I don't aim that you'll do it."

The sheriff locked Ike up in a tiny cell, then hunted out Pete Carver.

"Pete, you're pullin' out fer home," he announced as he stepped alongside the cowman who was buying out the Bloody Heart saloon, drink by drink.

"Huh?"

"Your hoss is out in front, Pete, saddled. You'll make it home by mornin' if you keep goin'."

"What's the joke, Bob?"

"Whatever it is, she's on you, pardner. I'm runnin' you and your men outta town, plain speakin'."

"Because I 'lowed I was goin' after Ike Rutherford's scalp?"

"Suthin' like that, Pete. You put me in office to uphold the law and order of this Chinook town. I'm aimin' not to disappoint them as voted fer me."

"If I give the word, Bob, my boys'll jest nacherally pick you to pieces and sling the hunks out in the snow. You're makin' fight talk."

"And I backs up ary talk I makes, Pete. Mebbyso them drunk cowhands will down me, but you won't be standin' to watch it. This here gun's loaded, and, unless you're drunker'n I figger, you kin see which way she's pointed."

"Where's Rutherford?" snapped Carver.

"In jail."

"Jail?"

"You heard me. He's stayin' there till he's sober enough to ride home. Next week, when you two damn' old fools have come to your senses, you'll kiss and make up. Now git and take your men along."

"Ike Rutherford's in jail, boys." Pete chuckled. "It'll hurt him worse'n shootin' could. Do we quit town or do I make this gun-totin', bad-talkin' sheriff swaller that gun?"

Bob McClean's lips tightened as he read the light of drunken recklessness in the cattleman's eyes.

"Fergit it, Pete," urged his foreman, who was fairly sober and had done his utmost to span the break between the two cowmen. "Let's drag it fer the ranch."

So Pete Carver and his men left town and calamity was averted. But a splendid friendship between the two cattlemen had been ripped apart and there seemed no way of mending the ragged edges.

In the weeks that followed, Bob McClean tried more than once to make peace between them. Cowpunchers on both sides, with the sanction of their wagon bosses, did all in their power to prevent a split in the working of the two ranges that had always been one. Pete Carver, learning of these peaceful overtures, called his foreman into a quiet corner of the big bunkhouse.

"Beginnin' now," said Pete, biting his words till they popped like cracking ice, "I'm firin' ary Rafter T man that speaks to a Bar L waddie on the range or in town. It's up to you to carry out these orders of mine, or, damn you, you're fired here and now. Hear me?"

"Yes, sir."

It was the first and last time that any Rafter T man ever called their employer anything but Pete. The foreman had been startled into addressing him as "sir". Pete took it as flippancy.

A short arm swing that traveled but a scant six inches caught the foreman on the point of the jaw and lifted him off the floor. He was unconscious when he slumped to the pine boards.

"Tell him," said Pete shortly, "when he comes to, that his check's waitin' fer him on his bunk. I'll 'sir' him! He's fired! So're any more of you that's got any funny sayin's that wants voicin'."

When the Rafter T foreman regained consciousness, he rubbed his swollen jaw and grinned. Pete was at the stable, nursing a heavy grouch.

"Fired, eh?" He grinned. "Fired because I said 'sir'. Fired, hell! I done worked fer Pete Carver too danged long to let him fire me thataway. Him nor no other man kin fire a gent that won't quit."

Whereupon he tore up the check and walked to the barn. Pete, forking hay to his horse, whirled at the sound of spur rowels, anticipating trouble. Hay fork in hand, he confronted his foreman.

"Keep your shirt on, Pete." The foreman laughed. "I jest moseyed over from the bunkhouse to strike you fer a tendollar raise. Do I git it or do I work all winter at the wages I bin gittin'?" He rubbed his jaw meaningfully.

"Raise you twenty," growled the hot-tempered little cattleman. "You might go to work for that Rutherford polecat, otherwise."

The foreman shook his head. The incident was closed.

"Looks to me like we was due fer a hard winter, Pete. What you aim to do about feedin' the hell-slue of Bar L stuff that'll need hay to pull through?"

"We'll feed 'em, of course," growled Pete. "Come spring, we'll work our range clean and git shet of their danged stuff. Every hoof. I'll throw a drift fence across the range and put on line riders to keep Rutherford's stuff back. My quarrel is with Rutherford, son. Not with his pore cows and steers that need hay shoved into 'em. No man kin say that Pete Carver let a Bar L critter starve because they was so plumb unfortunate as to be owned by a danged old bull-headed rannihan that throws down an old-time friend fer a cow-stealin' skunk like Jim Bartlet."

"Durned if I thought Ike Rutherford could be so lowdown, Pete," said the foreman gravely. "I've known sheep folks with more principle."

"What the devil d'you know about it?" snapped Pete. "I'm payin' you top wages to run this cow spread, not to blackguard Ike Rutherford."

"Shore thing, Pete." He moved away to the farther end of the stable before Pete could read the mirth in his eyes.

One week later, the Rafter T foreman met the Bar L foreman in a coulée that afforded some shelter from the snowstorm that was whitening the hills.

"Goshamighty," observed the Rafter T boss, thawing the numbness from his fingers preparatory to rolling a cigarette, "he like to run that danged hay fork through me when I 'lowed that Ike was kinda low-down. Mebbyso there's hopes yet of patchin' the thing up. Sore as Pete is around the horns, I plumb believe he'd kill ary stranger that spoke bad of Ike Rutherford."

The Bar L boss nodded. "Hear the latest news about Ike?"

"Let's have it, feller. Ain't got much time. Pete's a-ridin' thisaway mebby, and, if he ketches me augerin' a Bar L man, he'll like as not shoot my ears off. Gimme the news."

"Ike done bought out Jim Bartlet, lock, stock, and barrel. Then he took his coonskin off and whipped this Bartlet skunk and two, three Two Bar men fer good measure. He come home with two busted knuckles and a black eye, happier'n a Blackfoot squaw with a red blanket."

"Is he weakenin' any?"

"Not him. He's workin' us like he owned us and he's drinkin' some. We done got orders to whup all Rafter T men on sight. He's gonna build a drift fence, come spring."

"Then we'll be poundin' staples and stretchin' wire, side-by-side, pardner. The Rafter T's throwin' up a drift fence from Squaw Butte to the lone cottonwood on Bull Crick."

The two bosses grinned, finished their cigarettes, and parted.

"See you at the drift fence in May, you Rafter T polecat."

"So long till spring, you Bar L coyote."

CHAPTER
TWO

Montana stockmen who survived it still shake their heads and look grave when one mentions the winter of 1886–1887. Bitter disaster swept the cow country like a white-boned hand of death. Blizzard after blizzard whined and howled across the bleak greasewood flats and left them dotted with the bony carcasses of steers. 100,000 wild-eyed steers, drifting with the storm, death glazing their frost-seared eyeballs even before they dropped in their dogged, hopeless trot. Milling, drifting, piling up against the cutbanks until the coulées were filled with their frozen bodies.

Cowpunchers, bundled in wool chaps, coonskins, and mufflers, faced tired mounts into the teeth of that terrible storm and, with heavy hearts, put up a sullen, desperate fight with a heroism that is never to be forgotten so long as men gather and trade tales of the range. No trace of weakening showed on their frost-blackened faces. No word of complaint from lips too stiff to hold a cigarette. If there were some who quit, their pitiful minority is lost in the army of game men who fought their hopeless battle with a grin frozen on their lips. They asked no reward save their $40 a month. And when, as the winter wore on and cattlemen whose herds had numbered thousands were left without a critter to carry their brand, these cowboys worked on, without pay, gathering what stock drifted their way, regardless of what brand marked their tight-stretched hide. God, in His greatness, never made truer, braver men than these laughter-loving, carefree cowboys who without restraint, without question gave the best that was in them. Those who lost their battle with the terrible white death that swept the prairies lay buried in the drifts until the warm Chinook wind should lay the hills bare and brown in the late spring. Their comrades, when they found them, would mark their graves with a pile of boulders, then ride on.

Oh, bury me not on the lone prairieeeee!

The old range song, doleful as a dirge, took on a new significance. Cattle owners were wiped out; cowboys gave their lives; native four-year-old steers died by the thousands. Epic in its devastation was that winter of 1886.

Old Ike Rutherford, gaunt, frost-blackened, unshaven, fought his losing fight and doled out scant forkfuls of priceless hay to the handful of cattle that had not drifted beyond reach with the first driving blizzard.

Each morning he led his men north, into the teeth of the bitter wind, to gather poor cattle and drift home with them at dusk. Hay was scarce. The banks would loan not a penny to buy more. The gaunt, old cowman, fighting on when hope was long since lost, grinned

15

gamely and made a pitiful attempt at being jocular with his men. He fooled no one, not even himself.

Fifty miles south of the Bar L Ranch, Pete Carver scowled at the long-staggering stream of gaunt Bar L steers that poured into the brakes from the open country.

"Looks like we done ketched everything of Rutherford's except his milk pen stuff," he growled. "How's the hay holdin' out, boys?"

"Not worth a damn. If this storm don't break in a week, we'll have to quit feedin' to save enough hay fer the saddle hosses. There's a million dead cattle at the head of the brakes. A million, Pete, or I'm a sheepherder. The boys cut open a cow that had jest died. Skinnier than a barbed-wire fence. Willow branches thicker'n a man's fist in the pore critter's paunch. I was as fer as the forks of Cottonwood huntin' fer a sign of that Wyoming boy that didn't git back the night of the bad wind."

"Find him?" asked Pete in a listless tone.

"Found his hoss at the foot of a shale cliff. Dug fer two hours in the drifts but nary trace of the boy. Either he'd quit his hoss and was afoot when the hoss went over the bank in the dark, else he's too deep buried. I marked the place so's we could find it, once the snow goes. It's . . . it's hell, Pete."

"Hell 'n' then some. How's the stuff in the brakes along Rock Crick?"

"Still pawin' to feed. Good shelter in these badlands, Pete. Brush thick, too, and there's wuss cow feed than buckbrush and willows."

Pete nodded, grinning twistedly. "Yeah. Barbed wire or sawdust is wuss. Still, we'll save enough to make a showin' in the spring. That's better'n some cowmen'll do."

"Ike Rutherford," put in the foreman, "will be wiped out, plumb."

"Except fer what's drifted in on us. Which, by the looks of the string the boys is hazin' into the sheds yonder, is about ten million head. Ain't there no end to them damn' Bar L scarecrows? Me short-handed and no hay, a-wastin' time and feed and men on a outfit that turned down a real friend fer a damn' skunk of a cow thief! I'd orter've lined my sights on his skinny brisket and pulled the trigger!"

"Easy enough to let them Bar L steers drift across the river to yon side, cuttin' back the Rafter Ts as the herd passes the pole gate," suggested the foreman.

"Son, don't read no brands when you pass out the hay. It'll shore make old Ike Rutherford happy to see them cattle, come spring."

"*Hmmm.* Thought you was all but ready to swap shots with him, Pete?"

"Was. Still am, dang his ornery old hide. But that ain't no cause fer me wantin' to see him broke and huntin' work next spring."

So it came about that many a Bar L steer, thanks to Pete Carver, was kept alive through these bitter days on Rafter T feed.

Hay ran low until Pete gave orders to feed only the horses. Snowplows broke the crusted drifts for the trailing skeletons that followed, bawling, in their wake.

Men worked like fiends from daybreak till long past dark to save the lives of the cattle that huddled in pitiful misery in the low-roofed sheds, gnawing at the bark on the logs, pulling the brush thatch from the roof.

Every Rafter T rider carried a carbine and a belt full of shells, for the wolves and coyotes were growing bolder every day. Each man had orders to shoot any cow or steer that was too far gone to save, and sprinkle the meat with strychnine. Thus the animals were humanely disposed of and the poison would perhaps kill a wolf that, alive, would pull down a cow that otherwise might live through the winter. In this matter of cow shooting, the cowpunchers were ordered to disregard brands. If the animal needed killing, it was killed regardless of what brand it wore. These were days of drastic measures.

CHAPTER
THREE

Fifteen miles down the river from Carver's ranch, a cluster of log cabins squatted on the high bank of the river. Above the door of one of these cabins was a rudely lettered sign. SALOON it read.

Here a smoky lamp burned far into the night. In the smoke-laden, whiskey-fumed saloon, unshaved, roughly garbed men played cards or traded stories to the tune of a squeaky fiddle. Trappers, for the most part, with a sprinkling of cowpunchers, half-breed woodcutters, and an occasional tin-horn gambler who had been run out of town for crooked dealing. Sometimes a nameless, hard-eyed man drifted in from the lonely cabin where he was wintering. Silent, bearded, his right hand never straying more than a few inches from his gun, he would buy his quart or gallon of moonshine whiskey, pay for it, and depart.

A half-breed would trade a load of pitch wood for a gallon of vile liquor and stay perhaps until the jug was empty, then linger on until his credit was no longer good. A wolf pelt or beaver hide bought a quart for the trapper. The tin-horn played solitaire in a far corner and, like a spider in its web waiting for the fly, would bide his time until some man with a craving for poker drifted in.

The squeaky fiddle in the grimy hands of its half-breed owner droned out such tunes as the "Red River Jig" and "Hell Among the Yearlin's".

To this saloon at the Rocky Point crossing came Jim Bartlet and two of his men. In Bartlet's pocket was a roll of banknotes. In his heart a black hatred for the big cow outfits, the Rafter T and Bar L in particular. His face was not yet healed from the beating he had suffered at the hands of Ike Rutherford.

Tall, heavy-framed, with the flat features of a bulldog, he saw the world through closely set pig-like eyes of pale gray color. Burly of build, swaggering of manner, he was a braggart who usually was able to prove his boasts. Most men feared his strength and brutality and let him alone. Other men, such as Rutherford, Carver, and Bob McClean, held the swashbuckling bully in contempt.

While it had never been actually proven that Jim Bartlet was a cattle rustler, it remained a mystery how he had built a sizable herd from a few head of cows in so short a time. There were a score of others like him, fringing on the big ranges and fattening their herds with cattle stolen from the larger outfits. Hard riders, heavy drinkers, quick with a gun or lariat. They knew brands and every possible way of changing a brand by blanket, plucking, or working it with pitch. Sleeper-marking some, hair-branding others, they gathered other men's calves and moved the animals to their home ranches. Sometimes they drove a long nail into

20

the cow's foot so to lame her that she could not follow. Other cows, whose calves they stole, they roped, threw, and sewed up the poor animals' eyelids or filled the eyes full of sand. An adept at these inhuman practices was Jim Bartlet.

Drinking, gambling, fighting, he spent his days at the Rocky Point Saloon. Always he made his boast of what he had done and what he intended doing to Ike Rutherford and Pete Carver.

"They done run me outta my place," he bawled to his drunken audience. "Damn 'em! Might as well try to run a timber wolf off by throwin' rocks at 'im, eh, boys? I'll git 'em both, hear me? This winter is gonna bust that Rutherford skunk. Me, Jim Bartlet, is gonna finish the job. And when that Pete Carver heaves in sight, he'd better come a-shootin'. I'm mean, I am. A fightin', snappin' wolf, hear me? Drink up, gents."

Night after night, Bartlet and his two men drank until they could no longer stand up to the pine bar. Daytimes they rode into the rough hills and left the saloonkeeper to wonder what manner of devilment they were up to. They bought many cartridges at the little trading post across the river. They carried butcher knives. Each night when they returned to the saloon, they would wash frozen blood from their lariats.

"The wolves," Bartlet would chuckle when drink had warmed him, "is shore a-killin' off a heap of Bar L and Rafter T stuff. And lemme tell you suthin', gents. That Pete Carver is shore a tricky jasper. He's a-killin' off Rutherford's cattle. Me 'n' the boys seen him and his men a-killin' 'em and poisonin' the carcasses. I kin show you no less'n a hundred head of big native steers either shot or with their throats cut. I'm ridin' to Chinook to get the sheriff tomorrow. Drinks is on me fer the evenin', boys. Licker up. And lemme tell you suthin' more. It ain't only Rutherford cattle that's bein' killed off to leave more feed fer Rafter T stuff. No, sir. I kin show you ten other brands on dead critters that Carver and his men has killed. Brands that belongs to the little fellers like I was afore Rutherford forced me out and 'lowed he'd run me outta the country. Wait till the sheriff gits here, that's all."

The following day Jim Bartlet left for Chinook. It was a long ride, and, during the three days it took him to cover the trail, the man suffered terribly. Only the determination to revenge himself on the men who he hated kept him from turning back to the crossing.

After a ravenous meal and several drinks, Bartlet sought out Bob McClean in his office. There he spent an hour in telling his story.

"And you figger I'll make that ride" — Bob smiled mirthlessly — "in weather like this on the say-so of a man of your reputation? You're either drunk, Bartlet, or you done gone loco. Yonder's the door you come in. It works both ways. Will you walk out or git carried out?"

"Meanin' you won't go down there to see about this cattle killin' that's goin' on?"

"You guessed it fust time, Bartlet."

"If I go to the district attorney and swear out a warrant fer Pete Carver, you *gotta* serve it!" blustered Bartlet.

22

"Jest what right, mister, have *you* got to swear out ary warrant? You don't own a single head of cattle. Ike Rutherford, accordin' to your story, is the man that's loser. I jest can't somehow see no picture of Ike swearin' out a warrant for Pete Carver. Not if the hull damned Bar L herd was layin' dead in front of Pete's house. Git outta here, you damned loud-mouthed polecat."

Jim Bartlet stiffened, his hand poised above his gun butt.

"Pull it, Bartlet," invited McClean. "You'll be drilled afore you git it clear of the scabbard. If I was so yaller as to let coyotes like you run a whizzer on me, I'd've bin dead years ago. Git!"

"All right, McClean," sneered Bartlet, "I'm goin'. But I'm comin' back with a fist full of warrants and I'm seein' that you serve 'em."

Half an hour later, Jim Bartlet left town. He was gone a week. When he returned, he was accompanied by five men. Each one of these owned upwards of fifty head of cattle on the edge of the Bar L and Rafter T ranges. A grim-lipped, hard-eyed lot, they swarmed into the office of the district attorney.

The district attorney was a young man, fresh from law school, who had been back slapped and hand shaken into accepting this office that older, wiser lawyers were wont to decline firmly and with sarcastic thanks. It was an honor that carried too much grief for the pay involved. This young man who held the office was fired with zeal and still cherished many of his university ideals. Secretly he cherished the great hope

23

of reforming Chinook and making of the cow town a city that he could write East about and modestly tell of its reformation under his rule. A worthy ambition, truly. He did not know that this great hope of his was one of Chinook's standing jokes.

Now, as he leaned back in his chair, twirling a pencil and jotting down occasional notations, he nodded gravely as the loquacious Bartlet poured forth a tale of justice blinded by prejudice, of the iron rule of the cattle barons, the gross injustice done the struggling ranchers of lesser means and smaller herds.

"Sheriff McClean refuses to serve the warrants, Mister Bartlet?"

"He shore does. Carver and Rutherford has got him buffaloed. He's scared of their money. Them and outfits like 'em put McClean in office. They kin push him out and he knows it. What we wants is a square deal, mister. We ain't gittin' it. I sold out to Rutherford at the point of a six-gun and I got witnesses to prove it."

He did not add that Ike had given him an over-generous price for cattle he had stolen.

"You are ready to swear to the truth of your accusations, Mister Bartlet?"

The title of "mister" gave Jim Bartlet an air of importance.

"I kin take you to the spot where the dead animals lays," he boasted. "I got two witnesses to prove what I says. We seen Pete Carver kill the critters."

"What was his object in killing the cows?"

"They was eatin' his grass, mister. No use foolin' with McClean. Wire up to Helena fer a stock inspector

24

that'll do his duty that he's swore to carry out. Let McClean sit alongside his stove and toast his rheumatism. He's too much of a old woman. Slower'n molasses."

"He is an odd old chap," admitted the young attorney, recalling past incidents when Bob McClean had not been overly enthusiastic about carrying out his wishes. "Don't know but what you've made a wise suggestion. I'll wire Helena and get a man here who will look at the matter from an unbiased viewpoint. Drop in tomorrow morning and I think I'll have news for you."

In response to the district attorney's wire, a stock inspector arrived on the midnight train. There was a session behind closed doors in the office of the district attorney. For once, Jim Bartlet had not boasted of his plans and Chinook was unaware of what went on. Bob McClean was at the Rutherford ranch on business pertaining to a loan that he had hoped in vain to make in Ike's behalf.

Sunup found the stock inspector with Bartlet and the five cattlemen, on the trail to the Rafter T Ranch. The day was clear but the mercury stood at thirty below zero. In the inspector's pocket was a warrant for the arrest of Pete Carver.

A Rutherford rider happened to meet them as they swung southward along the trail. Jim Bartlet slouched sideways in his saddle to leer crookedly into the cowpuncher's unfriendly eyes.

"You kin tell Ike Rutherford and that settin' hen of a Bob McClean," he instructed the Bar L man, "if you see 'em, that I don't need 'em nor their help to git a square deal in this man's country. Afore this time next week, I'm tackin' Pete Carver's hide on the fence. He'll be lookin' out from between the bars of the jail. Tell your boss and that six-bit sheriff of his'n that they kin go to hell."

Jim Bartlet, with a harsh laugh, spurred his horse into the cowpuncher's mount. Grinning, the other members of the posse followed in the wake of their self-appointed leader. A frown of annoyance clouded the brow of the stock inspector. He was beginning to wonder if he was making a mistake in not conferring with Bob McClean before acting. His instructions from headquarters had been somewhat vague regarding that. The young district attorney had advised against it. Still, he did not like the manner in which Jim Bartlet was pushing matters.

Back on the trail, the scowling Bar L man watched them out of sight, then spurred his horse to a long trot and headed for the home ranch to carry Bartlet's message to Ike Rutherford.

It was dark when he arrived at the Bar L Ranch. The old cattleman and the sheriff were playing seven-up. They looked grave when they learned of the threat to arrest Pete Carver.

"There was a law officer with them jaspers, son?" asked the old sheriff.

"Stock inspector, near as I could figger, Sheriff, a kinda young gent with a good-lookin' rig. Packed a white-handled gun plain and protrudin' like."

"Some damn' glory hunter, Ike," rumbled Bob. "That young D.A. has like as not ribbed him up to thinkin' I'm layin' down on the job. Hell's gonna pop, Ike, if them tinhorns try to drag Pete Carver out of his hole. They'd a heap better tackle a lion bare-handed."

"A heap," agreed Ike. "Dang his pesky old pitcher. Ornery as snake p'izen, is Pete, but them calf-stealin' buzzards is wuss. Only fer that Bartlet houn', me 'n' Pete'd be friends this minute. I swear that, if them short horns hurt Pete Carver, I'll kill 'em all like they were so many rattlers. Tromp 'em out. That hoss of yourn good fer a long ride, Bob?"

"Plenty good, Ike. Figger we better git goin'?"

"Reckon so, Bob. I ain't doin' myself no good by stayin' here and watchin' my stock die off like flies. I need a hard ride and mebbyso a fast scrap to take the sickish feelin' outta my heart."

"I'm plumb glad to see you bury the hatchet, Ike." Bob nodded.

"Uh?" Ike, shrugging into his enormous coonskin, glanced with mild inquiry at the sheriff.

"Right tickled, Ike, to learn you done quit bein' a fool and are ready to shake hands with Pete and call it square."

"Who in tarnation said I was gonna shake hands, Bob McClean?" roared the cowman. "I'd as lief shake hands with a polecat. I'm not throwin' in with danged old fools that turn down a friend that has gone through hell 'n' high water with 'em. Let that sawed-off, bench-legged li'l ol' varmint so much as speak to me and I'll claw his hair off."

"Uhn-huh. Shore thing, Ike," agreed Bob in a soothing tone that held an undercurrent of laughter. "I'll hold your coat whilst you do it, too. Never knew a more ornery, bull-headed old fool than Pete Carver. Dunno but what Jim Bartlet was right about him a-killin' your cattle, Ike. He shore hates you bad."

Ike bit off an end from a ten-inch length of plug and, with a bulging cheek, eyed the sheriff who was scowling as if in deep thought.

"Dang your old speckled hide, Bob McClean," rumbled Ike, the light of mirth dancing in his blue eyes. "Let's git goin'."

Suddenly both men tensed. Motionless, their faces a study in expression, they stood there in the cabin, listening.

A rush of wind from without whined and howled as it swooped through the giant, bare-limbed cottonwoods.

"The Chinook!" croaked Ike hoarsely. "She's done come! The storm's busted!"

With a single stride of his long legs, he was at the door and had flung it open. Bareheaded, he stepped out into the darkness that was filled with the warm wind that meant salvation to the cattlemen. Silently, his eyes fixed on the blanket of stars overhead, he stood there. Darkness hid the dry sobs that shook him. His lips moved soundlessly. Perhaps he prayed.

Bob McClean, standing in the doorway, watched Ike's shadowy form in the illumination from the open doorway that silhouetted the big man who stood beyond its glare. The old sheriff felt a tight sensation in his throat, for he sensed what was in Ike Rutherford's mind. He knew that for the Bar L cowman, the hot Chinook had come too late. The winter had wiped him out.

After a time, Bob went out and laid an arm across the shoulders of his old friend. "Some of your stuff's bound to have drifted into the brakes where Carver's boys'd feed 'em. You'll have some left, Ike."

"I wasn't thinkin' of the cattle, Bob," said Ike quietly. "Four of my boys died this winter a-fightin' to save my cattle. I was thinkin' about them, jest then."

Miles farther south, the warm rush of wind caught the posse under the leadership of Jim Bartlet.

"We gotta keep movin' now, gents," he growled. "That damn' hot wind'll cut these drifts like fire. Coulées'll be swimmin' by mornin'. Travelin'll be nigh impossible in some of the places where we want to ride. The cañons where some of them dead cattle is will be hell-roarin' rivers. Our evidence will be washed plumb away, like as not."

The inspector smiled to himself in the dark. It was a smile of hopeful relief. He was rapidly growing nauseated at the task that lay ahead. Bartlet's bragging, the whiskey bottles that passed to and from the men who he had sworn in as deputies to take his orders but who were plainly bent on taking matters in their own hands. There had even been veiled threats of lynchings, shooting, and wiping out of the Rafter T outfit. All were in various stages of intoxication, all ugly. He was wishing he could slip away in the dark but they kept close watch on him, as if he were a prisoner.

"Inspector," said Bartlet, riding alongside the officer, "this damn' wind may hide them cattle that Carver and his men shot. These brakes is clean impossible to travel when the snow's meltin'. Gotta keep on the ridges or sink outta sight in the soft drifts with water underneath. Now jest supposin' we can't find them dead critters? Have we still got a case again' the Rafter T spread?"

"No case at all, Bartlet, without the evidence."

"The sworn oath of me and my men?"

"Won't be wuth six-bits, Mex."

"*Hmmm*. But if *you* was to see the evidence, your word as a law officer would go big afore a jury, eh?"

"I'd have to see the evidence, Bartlet." The inspector's tone was firm.

"So? Listen, feller. Stick to me and my friends and we'll see you git paid aplenty. Swear on the stand to what I tell you and we makes you a purty present of more money than you ever'll git in a lifetime. Savvy what I'm drivin' at?"

"I think I do, Bartlet." The inspector halted his horse, his hand on his gun. In the darkness, the others surrounded him.

"You're takin' cards in our game?" asked Bartlet.

"Not by a damn' sight!" The officer's gun came from its scabbard, hammer clicking to a full cock.

A dull roar. A crimson flash from Bartlet's gun, pressed close against the inspector's side. The officer's white-handled gun spat flame and one of the riders yelped as the slug ripped open his shoulder. Then the inspector slumped in his saddle and fell, dead before he hit the ground.

"Light a match," commanded Bartlet, "while I frisk him fer his badge and the warrants. From now on, I'm inspector. We'll tie this gent's carcass to his saddle and take him along. It's a case of Judge Lynch fer the Rafter T now, boys. We gotta go through. This jasper, remember, was killed while tryin' to arrest Carver. That's our story. God have mercy on the man that weakens and don't stick to it."

"We're kinda short-handed to tackle that outfit," complained one of the band.

Bartlet grinned. "Short-handed? I reckon not, pardner. My two boys is to meet us at the crossin' with ten, twelve men that kin shoot and keep their mouths shut afterwards. When we swarms down on Carver and his gang, we're outnumberin' 'em three to one. Got that inspector tied on? Good. Let's go. Here's where we clean out the big spreads that's done us dirt."

CHAPTER
FOUR

Only yesterday, the badlands had been quiet as a tomb. White, cold, silent in the grip of the winter. Now, a hundred noises filled the hills. The warm wind, rushing with a swishing roar through the scrub pines. Swift flowing water, cascading from the ridges into the deep cañons, churning, gurgling, swirling through brush and cutting gorges in the drifts. Cattle, by instinct seeking the high points, clattered up the ridges that were already bare of snow. Startled deer crashed through the buckbrush and red willow thickets, escaping the treacherous drifts that were rapidly undermined by melting ice and snow. Slush, mud, and the coulées were filled with torrents of muddy water.

Night came again and the wind still roared in the pine trees. At the Rafter T Ranch, the cowpunchers joshed one another as they stropped their razors preparatory to ridding their frost-seared faces of the winter's beards. One of the men had fished a service-worn harmonica from his war sack and was blowing wheezy tunes on the instrument. The lines of worry were fading from the faces of these men who had fought their fight against the blizzards. Pete Carver was the gayest of the lot. Joking, slapping men on the back, jigging when the harmonica whined "Turkey in the Straw" and "Forty-Seven Bottles". The Chinook had come! Cares and grief of the past months slipped from these riders of the big ranges. Joy, unrestrained and carefree, took its place.

At the saloon at Rocky Point Crossing, twenty men, riding in single file along the riverbank, were lost in the shadows of the giant cottonwoods. They spoke in low tones. Cigarettes glowed like fireflies in the dark. An occasional laugh, short and grating, cut through the low-toned banter. A moon rose above the ragged ridge and its white light fell on the butts of carbines and six-shooters.

In the lead of these men, breaking trail through melting snow, rode Jim Bartlet. Half drunk, he slouched in his saddle, bulking big in the moonlight. Fast-emptying whiskey bottles passed from hand to hand. Always the toast was the same.

"To hell with the Rafter T!"

To the north, other riders traveled the treacherous trails. Ike Rutherford and Sheriff Bob McClean, armed and riding in grim silence, pushed their leg-weary mounts southward along the trail. The slush splattered them, hunger and fatigue lined their faces, but neither spoke of the grueling torture of the ride. Floundering through drifts, sliding down ridges into uncharted blackness, their only thought was to keep their guns dry.

Midnight came and the two men halted on the long, bare ridge that led down to the river bottoms where the Rafter T cabins were hidden in the darkness. Loosening their saddle girths, they rolled cigarettes and let their horses rest for half an hour.

Suddenly, from that opaque blackness of the river bottom far below, came the flat, menacing crack of a rifle.

"God!" breathed McClean, and jerked tight his saddle cinch.

"Jackpot's done opened," grunted Ike, swinging into his saddle.

Indifferent now to the slippery footing, they spurred their horses down the long adobe ridge.

Like popcorn held over a hot blaze, the gunshots cut the night. Streaks of crimson flame. The booming crash of .45s. The flat, echoing crack of .30-30s. Shouts, curses, the thudding of stampeding hoofs as horses ran in the dark. A mêlée of sounds and movement, half cloaked in the blotched moonlight beneath the tall cottonwoods.

In the open, men on foot took shelter behind trees and corrals. In the cabin, Pete Carver and his men, half clothed and bewildered by the unexpected suddenness of the night attack, worked the levers of their Winchesters and took snap shots at the shadowy forms that crossed the moonlit spaces. Hot lead spattered against the log walls and shattered the windowpanes. Inside the cabin, men groaned from the pain of wounds. Pete Carver swore indifferently at a ragged gash in his thigh and dragged himself to a window.

"Take 'er easy, boys," he cautioned. "We got 'em whupped."

He spoke with conviction that gave courage to his men. Spoke without reckoning the odds against them. Odds, to Pete Carver, counted less than nothing. He had fought Indians years before when numbers mattered not at all.

"When one of them varmints looms black again' your gun sights, pull the trigger!" he called. "Save your lead. We ain't got more'n we need. Watch clost there by the door. They're tryin' fer to close in and rush the cabin."

Stealthily, as Indians attack, Bartlet's men dodged from tree to tree, edging closer to the cabin. Now and then a rifle cracked in the cabin and a dodging form spun about, then sank limply, a huddled, shapeless blot on the moonlit ground.

In the shelter of the low-roofed cow shed where frightened steers milled and bawled, Jim Bartlet turned to several men who crouched in the shadows, reloading their guns.

"Only fer some fool shootin' his gun accidental, we'd 'a' snuck up plumb easy on that cabin," he growled, shoving cartridges into the magazine of his carbine.

"What's the odds, Bartlet?" asked one of the group, one of the two who had spent the past weeks with Jim Bartlet at Rocky Point. "We got them gents anyhow, ain't we? Makes 'er more interestin' thisaway. If you're rearin' to know who let his shootin' iron go off as we was sneakin' up, I kin tell you. It was my gun. I had 'er cocked and kinda pulled 'er off sudden, when I trips in the dark. What's the odds, anyhow, if —"

Jim Bartlet's gun roared. The man, without a sound, dropped in his tracks, shot through the head.

"Damn him fer a drunken, keerless idiot," snarled the murderer, shoving a fresh shell into his gun. "That'll learn 'im."

Bartlet's ugly face twitched with rage and his voice was coarse and harsh as a rasp. The other men, aghast at the cold-bloodedness of their leader, drew back into the shadow.

"He's got money on 'im," leered Bartlet. "Frisk 'im and split it between you. Who's got a bottle? I need a drink. And don't go gettin' squeamish, boys. That dead 'un was no good no how. Cow thief and ex-con from Texas. Knew him down south. Ain't none of you gents got a bottle?"

One of them produced a pint of whiskey and they all drank. The dead man was searched and his money divided.

"Time we charged that cabin," growled Bartlet, moving away. "Foller me, fellers."

They obeyed half-heartedly, fearful of this killer's wrath, yet nauseated at the cold-blooded cruelty. Cattle stealing, to them, was but a way of making a living. Wanton killing of men was distasteful and dangerous.

"We got the law behind us!" called Bartlet. "C'mon. You hired fer tough hands. Play your string out."

Shifting, blurred shadows, they slipped toward the cabin.

The firing seemed to have increased in volume now. Orange streaks from the rifle barrels cut the dark. Ricocheting bullets droned like hornets.

Into this hail of hot lead rode Ike Rutherford and Bob McClean. Not until the sheriff's horse was shot from under him did the two check their pace. Ike's long arm swung downward, gathered in the stunned sheriff, and the horse sped back to the brush with its double burden.

"Told you we was fools to rush the cabin, Ike," panted Bob. "Like as not it was one of Pete's men shot that hoss, thinkin' he was bringin' down a Bartlet man."

"Well," growled Ike, wiping blood from his cheek where a bullet had cut the flesh like a knife, "what'll we do? Set here like two long-tailed birds?"

"None whatsomever, you bonehead. Gimme time to think a minute. We ain't doin' nobody no good by chargin' across that clearin', gittin' shot by our friends. Situated as we are, we're as harmful as two prairie dogs. Lemme think, Ike."

"Think! Goshamighty, you danged old horny owl, how kin a man think while seventeen million bad shots is a-throwin' lead into our midst? Rid your manly bosom of one half-growed, half-reasonable idee fer pullin' us outta this mess and I votes fer you next term. Otherwise, I does my best to elect a sheriff that *sabes* Injun warfare."

"You struck it, Ike," hissed the old sheriff. "We play Sioux with these jaspers."

"How?" Ike shifted a long-barreled Colt to his left hand and brought forth a plug of tobacco. Filling his cheek with a generous bite, he returned the plug to his pocket, spun the cylinder of his gun, and spat into the dark.

"We split here, savvy? One by one, we puts these here bushwhackin' snakes outta commission. Spot 'em by their gun flashes, slip up behind 'em, and bend your cannon between their horns. If you got ary hoggin' strings, tie 'em, then step on to the next party. In due time, we has the enemy worked down to our size and under complete and entire control, as the war general says. Kin you find ary blemish on that idee?"

"Nary, Bob. We starts from here?"

"We does. You might kinda keep tally on them that you put to sleep."

"Bet a new hat I downs more'n you does."

"Takes the bet. *Adiós*."

"So long."

With the stealth of Indians, they slipped through the brush. Ike, jaw bulging with tobacco, gun swinging loosely in his big hand, crouched low and made his way toward a tree from whence he had seen a streak of rifle flame. A moment later, he shared the tree with one of Bartlet's followers. The man, thinking him one of the posse, gave him a cursory glance in the half light and lined his sights on the cabin.

Ike grinned, spat, and his gun barrel swung in a short arc.

"Good night, cowboy," he murmured. "May your dreams be sweet as sorghum."

The gun barrel thudded against the man's skull and he went limp in Ike's arms. The big cowman tied him with his neck scarf and moved on to the next tree.

38

Suddenly Jim Bartlet's voice roared above the din of firing.

"All ready, boys! Charge!"

With a wild cheer, the attacking party crossed the clearing at a run. Ike, interrupted in the business of tying his second victim, grabbed up his gun.

Squatting, he fired methodically at the swift moving forms that swarmed across the clearing. His gun empty, he grabbed up the carbine that had fallen from his victim's hands. The tobacco-bulged cheek lay along the gunstock and his long fingers pressed the trigger. *Spat! Crash!* His gun belched flame until the steel barrel felt warm to his touch.

"Wisht I was among 'em yonder, dang it," he muttered. "But I better stay put. Pete's a-holdin' 'em, looks like. Yeah. They're comin' back now, what of 'em kin make it. Look at 'em come. Wisht I'd known which was Bartlet, I'd split his brisket with a . . . comin' my way, feller?"

A man was running toward the tree where Ike squatted. The big cattleman got to his feet and leaned against the tree trunk. As the runner slipped behind the shelter of the cottonwood trunk, Ike felled him with a blow on the head.

"That" — he grinned — "is what a man might call real accommodationment. Come a-lopin' up, purty as hell, fer his nightcap. Tally three."

He paused to tie three knots in his handkerchief, then moved on.

In the cabin, Pete Carver took toll of his men. One lay dead by the window. Four more were suffering from wounds. Half sick from the wound in his thigh, the cowman called in a cheering tone to the men who crouched in the dark.

"How's the cartridges holdin' out, boys?"

"Not so good," replied a Rafter T man.

"My gun's done gone dry," announced the foreman.

Others made similar replies. Quick calculation disclosed that but a dozen cartridges remained among them.

"Hold 'em fer the next charge, boys," said Pete grimly. "When they hits the cabin, swing open the door and let 'em in. We'll whup 'em at clost quarters. I done recognized Bartlet's voice, fellers. Dunno what kind of game he's playin', but I'm thinkin' we'd be in a bad way if we was to git captured."

Bartlet's men were keeping up an intermittent fire. He moved from one man to the next, giving orders.

"They done quit shootin', yonder in the cabin." He chuckled. "Done run low on shells, I bet. We got a tail holt on the Rafter T now, gents."

He dodged a clear space, slipped into a brush patch, then leaped behind a wide-trunked cottonwood where a man's shadowy outline showed.

"We got the damned Ts on the run, feller," he panted. "All we gotta do is . . . McClean!"

The sheriff, grinning wickedly, had stepped into the light that Bartlet might recognize him.

"Stick 'em up, Bartlet," he said quietly. "I want you."

The sheriff's .45 was covering the big murderer. Bartlet's hands lifted skyward. McClean took a step forward, gun held in careless readiness.

With a swiftness that was surprising in so big a man, Bartlet leaped sideways. McClean's bullet clipped his ribs. Then the cow thief was on top of the old sheriff, a clubbed gun swinging viciously. A sickening *thud* as the weapon crashed across McClean's eyes. Again and again it crashed into the old officer's face, across his head, and Bartlet, holding the unconscious man in a vise-like grip, mouthed curses as he swung the blood-spattered weapon. Then, when his frenzy had worn itself out, he flung the limp form from him and kicked it savagely where it lay on the ground.

Standing over the huddled form that lay still as death, he cocked his gun and pointed the muzzle downward.

"I'll pump so damn' much lead in you that it'll take a work hoss to pack your carcass . . ."

A terrific crash came from the cow shed behind him. Like a thunderclap it made puny the sound of gunfire. Then the earth trembled as if shaken by an earthquake. The next instant the clearing was choked by a sea of fear-maddened, stampeding cattle. Wild-eyed with fright, packed so densely that some of the weaker animals were tossed above the seething mass of hair and horns, they crashed across the shattered corrals, mowing down all that lay in their path. Tossing, clashing horns, thundering, sharp cleft hoofs, a swift-moving, stampeding death to anything that lay in its path.

A man, caught in its sweep, screamed as the herd caught him. Then the echo of his cry was drowned in the clash of horns. Bartlet, frightened from his

41

murderous intent, gave an inarticulate cry and ran. Beyond stood a cluster of three giant trees that afforded better shelter than the one behind which he stood. Dropping his gun in momentary panic, he ran toward the largest of the trees. Fifty feet behind him raced the herd. He glanced over his shoulder. A quick fearful glance. His spur caught in a bush, and with an agonized cry he fell headlong. With a scream of terror, he struggled to free himself, only to fall again as the spur still held him. Then, shrieking, he threw his arms around his face, half standing, half kneeling. White moonlight fell about him, making of him a grotesque mockery of a man kneeling in prayer. Scarcely fifteen feet away stood the giant cottonwood that meant escape from a terrible death.

Something moved in the shadow of the big tree. A rope shot out, its noose settling about Bartlet's shoulders. A terrific jerk and Bartlet was jerked free and yanked behind the tree. The next instant the stampede crashed past.

Pasty-faced, shaking as if stricken by a chill, Bartlet lay sobbing at the feet of the man who had saved his life. He started to rise. A boot heel clipped him under the jaw.

"Lay down, you damn' skunk," growled Ike Rutherford, flattening himself against the tree that shook with the impact of the stampeding herd. "Dang me fer a chicken-hearted sheepherder. I'd orter've let you git ketched. I take after my mammy thataway. How come this here jasper, layin' alongside you there, was packin' this rope? Speak up, you white-livered, yaller-hided varmint afore I 'rassels down this here weakenin' heart of mine and pitches you into them runnin' steers. What's the idee of this here rope I took offen that gent I knocked between the horns? Is this here a lynchin' party?"

"Yes," came the croaking reply.

"Aimed to hang Pete Carver?"

"Yes." Bartlet's voice was hoarse with fright. His narrow escape had completely unnerved him.

"Thought so. Well, take good keer of that rope, you skunk. We'll be needin' it, quick as these cows quit a-runnin' past. I'm aimin' to hang you, personal. Brings my tally up to five."

Ike shifted his tobacco to the other cheek and flipped several hitches about the body of his prisoner, binding him securely.

"I'll have to hang you by myself, Bartlet. Don't dast wait fer Bob. He'd like as not raise a kick again' stringin' you up. Kick number four in the belly, will you, and see if he's dead or playin' 'possum. Them danged cattle give me a bad scare, jest as I swung, and I'm afeered I hit 'im a mite harder'n I figgered."

There was a hysterical, unnatural pitch to Rutherford's voice that escaped Bartlet. In gaining the tree where he had felled the man with the rope and later rescued his enemy, two bullets had torn through Ike's body, leaving wounds that, while not serious, were bleeding profusely. Blood soaked the leg of his overalls and filled his left boot. The other shot had caught the doughty old cattleman in the muscle of his shoulder leaving a neat hole, thanks to the steel-jacket bullet. Now he stood above Bartlet, grinning twistedly and swaying slightly, like a man who sleeps on his feet.

The main force of the stampede had passed, leaving the drag end of weak cows that straggled along, wild-eyed and bawling with fright. Ike saw them but dimly, for the pain and loss of blood was telling on his vitality. He wrapped and tied the rope about Bartlet, then sat down weakly. He felt weak and sick and dizzy like a man stupefied by too much bad liquor. A buzzing, humming sensation came in his ears and he lost consciousness.

CHAPTER
FIVE

It was sunrise. Pete Carver and his men, heavy-eyed from loss of sleep and pain of bandaged wounds, talked in low tones. The odor of frying bacon and strong coffee filled the cabin.

In a corner of the cabin Jim Bartlet and ten of his men sat on the floor, arms bound behind them. Sullen-eyed, they maintained a stoic silence. Warrants for the arrest of Pete Carver and Rafter T men lay on the table where Pete had tossed them after reading them.

Ike Rutherford, lying on a cowpuncher's bed, groaned and opened his eyes. He blinked curiously as he looked into Pete Carver's face.

"Howdy, you old sheep thief." He grinned. "Glad to . . ."

He broke off in his greeting, scowling. Pete had deliberately turned his back, ignoring the peaceful overture of his old friend. Ike made as if to rise, then lay back, puzzled and angry. His hands and feet were tied.

Pete, his broad back turned on his friend, hobbled across the room on a crude crutch, and spoke to his foreman who was bending over a man who lay on Pete's bunk.

"Bob McClean still alive?" he asked listlessly.

"Plumb, Pete. He's bad beat up, but breathin' strong. Whoever beat him up, done a good job. Seems like he's movin' a mite, Pete. He'll come alive directly."

"Call me when he wakes up," said Pete. "I'll be outside. Air's bad spoiled in here by so many skunks."

When Pete had gone outside, the Rafter T foreman walked to Ike's bunk, staring down into the big cattleman's bloodshot eyes. There was no light of friendliness in the foreman's eyes. Ike's lips parted to frame a question, then snapped shut.

"Pete's sent fer a doctor, Rutherford, to patch you and your outfit up. It's a damn' sight more'n you and McClean has got comin'. We're short-handed, bein' you and your men has crippled and killed half our boys. Them as kin sit a hoss is gatherin' the cattle you stampeded on us last night."

"You mean you think me 'n' Bob was . . . ?" Ike broke off with a harsh laugh that held the tone of a sob. Realization that Pete thought them party to such a dastardly attack flushed Ike's lean cheeks with hot anger and humiliation. "Lucky fer you and your mule-brained boss that I'm tied, young feller," he growled. "Otherwise, I'd whup you both till you couldn't stand. Git away from me, damn you! Clean away!"

"Directly, Rutherford, when I've said my say. Pete's too dang' flabbergasted to talk, but I ain't. We did kill some Bar L stuff, Rutherford, along with our own and a few head belongin' to them dirty calf-stealin' snakes settin' yonder. But fer every head of your stuff that was shot, fifty was saved by feedin' 'em Rafter T hay. If we done broke the law, we'll stand trial, mister. Pete Carver ain't the kind that runs. Neither is he the kind that sneaks up on folks in the dark. When you're able to serve 'em, Rutherford, you and McClean'll find your bloody warrants layin' right there on the table."

There was no mistaking the contempt in the foreman's voice. It made Ike sick at heart to be so suspected. The full portent of the Rafter T man's words left the old cattleman speechless with dumb misery. With dulled eyes, he watched the man cut his fetters, then contemptuously turn his back and stalk out of the cabin.

For some time Ike lay staring at the log ceiling, sick with pain and misery. Finally he sat up, swung his legs over the edge of the bunk, and stared across at the bunk where Bob McClean stirred feebly. Then he rose and limped to the stove to pour himself a cup of coffee. Bacon and biscuits stood in their pans on a table but Ike was too sick at heart to eat.

"Well, Rutherford," sneered Jim Bartlet, "how d'you like it out West as far as you bin? How does it feel to be classed with us boys, eh? You're in dang' good company, fer onct."

Ike turned on him, scowling from under bristling brows. "You was nigh the Big Divide last night when I saved your hide, Bartlet, but not half so clost to sudden death as you are right now. Another word outta you and I'll choke you to death."

"My boys is witness, Rutherford. You'd hang fer it. Best bet you kin make is to throw in with us. You should've tied us tighter last night. We was all loose when the Carver outfit grabbed us, afore we could bunch up to fight 'em off. Our stories make you and McClean as deep in this as we are. Evidence backs us. We kinda let Carver think you was sorter leader, savvy. Our stock inspector deputized us all. Afore he died, yonder by the cow shed, I hears him tell you to carry out the raid. He gives you his badge that you pins on your vest. You're still wearin' it, Rutherford!"

A leering grin on his lips, Bartlet nodded his head toward the star pinned to Ike's vest. In a moment of quick-witted desperation, just as Carver's men swooped down on him in the gray light of dawn, Bartlet had fastened the metal badge to Ike, and shoved the warrants in Ike's pockets as he lay, unconscious, by the tree.

Ike fingered the bit of shining metal, then ripped it loose and tossed it on the table beside the warrants. Then he gulped down his coffee and made his way to the sheriff's bunk.

Bob stirred feebly and his eyes blinked open.

"Take 'er easy, Bob," said Ike. "Don't make no talk yet till you feel better."

"Where's Bartlet, Ike? How come we're here? Where's old Pete?"

Briefly, in sentences tinged with bitterness, Ike told Bob of their predicament. Bob's lips pursed in a soundless whistle of blank astonishment.

"My God, Ike. You must be loco. Pete'd never believe . . ."

"But the old fool does, Bob. These low-down calf-thievin' coyotes a-settin' yonder has lied us into the deal, bad, too. Jest the same, a man orter whup that Pete Carver till he can't stand up for classin' us with them yaller-hided varmints. How you feelin', Bob?"

"Like a yearlin'," lied the sheriff, sitting up and feeling gingerly of the crude bandages about his head, put there by Pete. "Let's have a jolt of coffee and some grub. Then we'll plan out a scheme. Dunno as we orter be too hard on Pete. He got treated rough last night. Circumstantial evidence says me 'n' you had throwed in with the Bartlet spread. We'll figger a way to win out, Ike."

At a nearby cabin that Pete had converted into a hospital for his men, the Rafter T foreman and his employer conversed in earnest tones, eyes fixed on the river a scant 100 yards away.

"Water's riz three feet in the past half hour, Pete. She's nigh over the banks. A six-foot rise'll wipe us out. Glad I had the boys shove the cattle up on the ridges this mornin'. They'd orter have 'em purty well gathered by now."

"Git four hosses hitched to the mess wagon," said Pete. "We gotta start movin' these wounded boys out to high ground. The cook's out there now, loadin' in what grub we'll need."

The hot Chinook wind, melting the snow on the ridges, had made raging torrents of the cañons. Foot by foot the water rose in the river. The boom of cracking ice crashed like distant cannon. Trees, dead stock, débris of every description were borne along with the swirling muddy current. A few hours more and the Missouri River would be out of its banks, roaring, churning, carrying with its icy rush all that lay in its path.

"Yonder comes a haystack, floatin' along," said the foreman.

"Looks like a hen house behind it. That'll be the Long X Ranch on its way to Saint Louis," added Pete. "The X boss was braggin' about them sorrel hens of his. Wisht we had time to foller that there hen house and ketch 'er when she floats on a bar. Ain't seen a aig since August. Well, son, better get the team hooked up. Spring movin' come sudden this year. The alfalfa is shore gonna git irrigation."

Half an hour later, four stout horses dragged the mess wagon, loaded with wounded men, up the long adobe ridge. Rutherford and the sheriff watched it leave. The Rafter T foreman led around horses, saddled and bridled.

"All you law enforcers step out," he growled through the open door. "You kin untie your men's legs, McClean, but leave their hands hobbled. Me 'n' Pete ain't got time to fool around a-fightin' 'em. Onct we gits the outfit moved to the ridges, we'll go along to town. Not afore then. We got every damn' gun on the ranch so you ain't in no shape to argy. I'm escortin' you personal. Rutherford, you and McClean stays here till the wagon makes the next trip. We're short of saddle horses. Bartlet'll stay, too. We aims to keep you three where Pete kin ride herd on you. Move fast, there. Rattle your dewclaws, polecats." He backed the command with a .45.

The foreman rode away with his prisoners. Pete Carver, squatted on a stump just outside the door, smoked in silence, a sawed-off shotgun across his knees. He seemed ill at ease as were Ike and Bob.

Jim Bartlet took advantage of the situation to indulge in sarcastic pleasantry.

"We didn't figger on this when we left town, eh, McClean?" he said in a loud enough tone to carry outside to Pete.

The sheriff fixed him with a cold stare and said nothing. The pain in his head and across his blackened eyes was almost blinding.

"Too bad that Helena stock inspector got killed," Bartlet went on. "It'll go hard with Carver."

"You ain't got no witnesses now, Bartlet," said Ike quietly. "I'm still rearin' to carry out that chokin' idee of mine. Better quit jawin'."

This silenced Bartlet who now devoted his attention to stealthy attempts to slip his hands free of the ropes that bound him. Bit by bit, he was loosening the hastily tied knots. Ike and Bob had turned their backs on him as if the sight of such a human sickened them. Bartlet grinned mirthlessly and slipped a hand free. A few moments and his feet were free of the rope.

Above Bartlet was a window, its glass smashed by the night's bombardment. Ten feet beyond, grazing with dropped bridle reins, was Pete Carver's horse.

Inch by inch, Bartlet edged closer to the window. A sudden leap and he was on the ground outside, running toward the horse. The house shut the fugitive from Pete Carver who rose to his feet at McClean's startled cry.

"Bartlet!" bawled Ike. "Jumped the window. Ketch him, Pete!"

The *thud* of running hoofs as Bartlet vaulted into the saddle and, bending low on the horse's neck, jabbed the spurs in the sides of the startled animal. Pete's gun flipped up. His finger pressed the trigger, then eased off.

"I can't," he muttered, lowering the gun, "without shootin' my pet hoss!"

Bartlet swung the horse toward the ridge road, the only passable trail out of the Rafter T Ranch. The three men at the cabin watched him go.

"He's turned," grunted Bob. "He's comin' back!"

Then they saw the reason for the abrupt change of course. The Rafter T foreman and two cowpunchers were coming down the trail from the ridge. They were armed. Bartlet had no gun.

"God!" gasped Pete. "He's headin' fer the river! He'll drown hisself and the hoss. Hold on there, Ike Rutherford! Where the hell you goin'?" he shouted as Ike, forgetting the stiffness of his wounded leg, leaped through the open doorway and ran toward the corral where a team of work horses stood, harnessed and haltered to the feed rack.

"I'm goin' after Bartlet!" called Ike without looking back. "Shoot and be damned you danged old settin' hen!"

52

With a wild leap, Ike was on the back of the horse that he had untied with a jerk of the rope end. Trace chains clanking, he headed for Bartlet who was racing for the sea of muddy water in front of him.

Back in Bartlet's scheming brain was the conviction that his fabricated tale of law enforcing was too weak to stand the acid test of a jury trial. His own men might weaken; McClean and Rutherford would tell too straight a story. The district attorney was a weakling, too inexperienced to put up a crafty fight in court. Bartlet's safest course lay in flight, and, as he headed his horse for the river, he set his heavy jaws and trusted his life to the gameness of his horse. A cold-blooded, calculating killer was Jim Bartlet, but he was no cringing coward. Death lay in that muddy current, but he faced it unhesitatingly.

Below, Ike Rutherford watched for a moment, then urged his horse into the water, heading the animal at an upstream angle toward Bartlet and his mount who were being swept toward him by the current.

"Drop that fool gun, Pete Carver, and git ropes," snapped Bob. "It's time you come outta your loco drunk. Move, dammit! Ike needs us!"

Pete, an agonizing groan bursting from his lips as he saw the treacherous undercurrent pull Ike and his horse under, leaped to his feet and ran toward the river. Then his leg gave way, and he fell.

The sheriff, grabbing up a lariat that lay by the door, followed at his heels, not giving the fallen cowman so much as a passing glance. With Pete hobbling and crawling behind him, Bob reached the riverbank.

Ike's work horse, tangled in the harness, fought wildly. Ike slipped from his back and struck out against the current. An indifferent swimmer, burdened by soggy clothes, he was hard put to keep afloat. Yet he made no effort to regain the shore. Eyes glued on Bartlet and his horse, he fought the current and waited for his enemy to float downstream to him. Twenty feet, ten feet separated them. Then Bartlet and the horse were on him.

Bartlet, twisting sideways, aimed a vicious blow at Ike's white face. It grazed the cowman's cheek. With a grunt, Ike threw an arm up and, with his knees braced against the side of the swimming horse, jerked quickly. Bartlet was pulled from the saddle. Locked in tight embrace, the two men went under. The frightened horse, now completely bewildered, pawed at the two struggling men. Shod hoofs lashed the water about the heads of the fighting men, as they came to the surface.

A sickening *thud* as a steel-shod hoof struck Bartlet on the head. Ike, panting and half blinded by water, felt Bartlet go limp in his arms. Dizzily, one hand gripping Bartlet's collar, he struck out.

A swift side current swung the struggling horse free. Ike, breath coming in sobbing, choking gasps, fought to keep his face above the muddy surface. A whirlpool sucked him under.

Dazed, exhausted, he rose again to the surface. He did not hear the shouts of the sheriff on the bank or see the flung rope that came within easy reach, then was carried down by the current. His one conscious thought was to hold to Bartlet, regardless of all else.

Something solid struck him in the face. Something swept harshly across his face, tearing the skin. A tree, half submerged, had caught him. Ike, with a gasp, grabbed a branch and clung to it. In his other hand, clutched in a steel grip, floated Bartlet, blood sluggishly flowing from his gashed head.

Like a man awakened from a bad dream, Ike heard McClean's shouts now. The flying rope struck him fully in the face where he lay in the tangle of branches.

"Slip 'er over your head, Ike!" bawled Bob.

Ike obeyed. A jerk and he was pulled free from the floating tree. As the rope pulled him under the surface, Ike shut his eyes and fastened both hands on Bartlet's hair.

To Ike it seemed the passing of hours. In reality it was but a few seconds before he was jerked ashore.

"Ike! Ike! Ike!"

Insistent, like the beating of a drum, the name dinned into Rutherford's pounding, aching ears. With a sigh, he opened his eyes wearily to look into the face of Pete Carver.

Tears dimmed Pete's eyes and his voice was choked with dry sobs.

"Thank God, Bob," he called brokenly. "He's alive!"

"Bartlet?" Ike asked.

"Dyin', Ike," came the sheriff's voice from nearby. "He's conscious and talkin'. Unburdenin' his black soul afore he goes to meet the devil. He's tellin' it all, Ike."

"Ike," groaned Pete, holding the other's head in his lap. "I done wrong. I bin a damn' fool."

"Two of us, Pete." Ike grinned weakly. "Old fools, the both of us."

He sat up, Pete's arm about him. The mess wagon drove up and the Rafter T foreman and his two men gazed with astonishment at the men on the ground.

"There's about enough cattle left in the two brands to make one fair to middlin' herd, Ike," said Pete. "I bin waitin' all winter to proposition you regardin' a pardnership."

The look in Ike Rutherford's eyes spoke louder than any words that could have come from his sob-choked throat.

"When you gents gits through settin' there in the water which has riz till it's got you dang' nigh swimmin'," suggested the foreman, "we'll load you all in the mess wagon and pull out fer high ground. You act fer all the world like schoolmarms at a sewin' bee, augerin' to and fro regardless of hell, high water, or the elements. Will you ride your waterlogged hoss which is grazin' yonder, Pete, or does you set in the wagon with these two gents, which you admitted an hour ago was worse'n skunks?"

The foreman was grinning widely, anticipating the fun he would have telling the Bar L foreman of the reconciliation. Just how it had come about, he could only guess.

56

"I rides with these two old rannihans, son." Pete chuckled.

Ike fished a soggy, sodden mass of brown substance from his hip pocket, wiped it on his wet overalls, and held it toward Pete.

"Chaw, *pardner?*" he invited.

South of the Law Line

"South of the Law Line" first appeared in *Action Stories* (8/24). Jack Kelly, who was in charge of editing the Fiction House magazines, died in 1932 and Fiction House went into a period of reorganization. For a time in 1933 all publication ceased. Walt Coburn was released by Fiction House and he had to expand his markets elsewhere. He wrote again for *Adventure* and *Western Story Magazine*, and became a regular contributor to Popular Publications pulps such as *Dime Western* and *Star Western*. Fiction House resumed publication only slowly. *Action Stories* became bi-monthly, then quarterly. *Lariat Story Magazine* became bi-monthly. *Frontier Stories*, which had the longest hiatus from September, 1934 until Spring, 1937, returned as a quarterly. All the Coburn stories appearing in these magazines henceforth for their duration consisted of reprints of stories he had written from 1924 to 1932, usually with new titles. "South of the Law Line" was reprinted even before that time. It appeared under the title "Ranger Code" in *Action Novels* (4/31).

CHAPTER
ONE

The Mexican bartender was nervous. The smile on the thick lips beneath his neatly pointed moustache was fixed and mirthless and his pudgy hand shook as he set forth bottles of tequila and mescal for the half-dozen heavily armed and villainous looking Mexicans that lined the bar.

"*Uno peso*," he ventured politely when the men had drank. "*Uno peso, señores.*" A dollar, Mexican money, was a small enough sum for the liquor consumed, considering the fact that each of the unwelcome customers had imbibed freely of the stuff, yet the bartender's tone was apologetic as he asked payment.

The big Mexican at the end of the bar, evidently leader of the sextet, grinned leeringly as he poked the corpulent dispenser of drinks with his .45.

"Pancho Cordero and his men pay for nothing," he announced with a display of white teeth. "You have heard of Pancho Cordero, no?"

"*Sí,*" was the hasty reply. "*Sí! ¡Viva Cordero!*" He shoved another bottle across the bar and Cordero sheathed his gun with a flourish, joining heartily in the ribald laughter of his followers. "Who is the *gringo* yonder?" he asked, indicating with a nod of his huge sombrero an American who sat at a table in a far corner of the room. Seemingly unaware of the presence of Cordero and his men, the white man slumped in his chair, a half filled glass of white liquor in his hand. Immaculate in his white flannels and panama, the man made an odd figure in such squalid surroundings. His averted face kept him from noticing the sharp scrutiny that was being bestowed upon him.

The bartender tapped his forehead and winked broadly. "The *gringo* is loco, *muy* loco," he whispered. "Each day he sits there, drinking one bottle after another of mescal until he goes to sleep and is carried off to bed. Sometimes he takes something from his pocket and looks at it, then puts it back. Could you guess what it is the loco *gringo* looks at? No? The picture of a *señorita* of his country! I saw it once. Why should a man waste his time on the picture of a woman when there are a dozen live *señoritas* here in town, pretty ones, too, much fatter than this one whose picture he makes love to? Is that not proof that the *gringo* is loco?"

"He has money, this loco one?" asked Cordero, a wicked gleam in his dark eyes.

"Money? *Sí, mucho*. More money than twenty men could spend."

"Ah!" The leader and the man next to him exchanged a meaning look. "'Sta bueno. Good! Is it not right that one with so much money should give some to poor Pancho Cordero who has great need of new boots and a sombrero with much silver on it, and perhaps new boots for his men? Soon I will talk to this loco one who makes silly love to a picture."

He poured himself a drink and handed the bottle to the next man.

"Stick 'em up, gents!" called a voice from the narrow doorway. The speaker repeated the command in Spanish, emphasizing his words with a slight motion of the six-shooter he held carelessly in his right hand.

Six pairs of dirty hands raised ceilingward. The *gringo* in the white flannels downed his drink and leisurely turned his head, a smile spreading over his thin face as he took in the little drama.

"I'm Bill Douglas of the Rangers," announced the newcomer, a bronzed, big-shouldered youth in worn chaps and jumper. "I've done rode a long ways to take you in, Cordero. You're wanted plumb bad up in my country fer murder. All hands face the bar and keep them dirty paws high lifted while I collect the artillery."

All obeyed except Cordero who eyed the Ranger with an air of bravado.

"You are in Mexico, my frien'," he spoke in English. "Your arrest paper, she ees not work down here."

"Mebby not, Pancho, but this here shootin' iron works on a hair-trigger and works plumb purty. Face the bar, you murderin' polecat afore I cut loose. The warrant reads dead or alive in good American Texas English, and you're a heap less trouble dead. *¡Pronto!*"

Cordero turned with a shrug. As the Ranger advanced, the outlaw leader whispered something to his men.

Douglas advanced, his high-heeled boots clicking on the hard-packed adobe floor, the rowels of his spurs tinkling an accompaniment. The man in the flannels nodded approvingly and poured himself a drink.

"A clever bit of work, hang me if it isn't," he muttered softly.

Suddenly a keen knife blade flashed! A gun roared! Douglas was the center of a group of shouting, cursing men, each holding a knife or a clubbed gun.

A streak of white! A *thud* as a shining liquor bottle left the loco *gringo's* hand and knocked Cordero senseless. Swinging a heavy chair like a flail, the white man in flannels literally mowed the bandits down. Douglas, again on his feet though bleeding from several knife wounds, swung his .45 with uncanny accuracy, grinning cheerfully as he floored two men. He looked around in time to see the other white man leap at a knife-wielding Mexican, dodge a thrust of the shining weapon, and close in. A sharp, sickening *crack* and he stepped away. The Mexican's knife dropped to the floor and its owner looked down dazedly at his arm that hung uselessly at his side, broken between elbow and wrist.

"Sufferin' horny toads," gasped the Ranger. "How did you do it?"

"Togo taught me that one. Togo's my Jap valet," said the other, readjusting his lavender tie. He produced a silver cigarette case, snapped it open, and held it toward the Ranger.

"The battle being over, suppose we smoke, comrade? I have these made in Virginia. Good weeds." He

64

suddenly bent double with a fit of coughing; the silver case dropped with a clatter. At last he straightened and pressed a white silk handkerchief to his lips. It came away stained with crimson.

"First coughing spell I've had today," he explained with a ghost of a smile. "Let's have a drink before your friend Pancho comes alive and renews the carnage."

Admiration and pity mingled in the Ranger's eyes as the two Americans walked to the bar from behind which the fat bartender was slowly emerging, pasty yellow with fear.

"Here for your health?" he asked embarrassedly.

"Came here to die. Van Duzen gives me size months this side of the Great Divide. Outspoken chap for a doctor, Van is." The man in the panama smiled whimsically.

"And who," asked Douglas, "is this Van Duzen gent?"

"Runs a sanitarium across on the Arizona side of the border. Milk diet and pills. I threw the milk away and gave the pills to Togo. He's saving them."

"Did this doctor come down here with you?" asked Douglas.

The other man chuckled. "I slipped him and Togo in El Paso. Here's lookin' at you, Mister . . . ?"

"Douglas. Ain't used to the 'mister' handle. Call me Bill."

"Slats goes for me, Bill. I got that title when I enlisted."

"Army?" inquired Douglas.

"Leathernecks. First Marines. What outfit were you in, Bill?"

"Ninety-First, machine-gun company.

"Did you get the bum lung across the pond, Slats?" asked the Ranger as he turned to handcuff Cordero, who was showing signs of returning consciousness.

"Yeah. Touch of gas. Figured I had a chance until Van told me I was . . . what's the matter, Bill?"

For answer the Ranger held out something he had picked up near Cordero. "Where do you reckon this *paisano* got this picture of an American girl?" he asked, holding the picture toward Slats.

"Mine," said the invalid, the spots in his cheeks redder than usual. "Dropped it during the ruckus. It's the picture of the girl I'd have married except for this." He tapped his chest.

The Ranger looked away to keep from seeing the bitter twist on the sick man's lips.

"It's . . . it's hard times, Slats," he muttered as he laid an awkward hand on the thin shoulder of his companion.

"Yes, it's a bit tough, Bill," said Slats in a low tone, a mist dimming his fever-bright eyes as he looked into his half filled glass of mescal. "But a man must face a thing like that without whining. It's playing the game, *comprende?* That's why I came here to go out alone. No use staying in New York or some silly sanitarium where she and the guv'nor would be around. Let's have another drink, Bill. I was on my first quart when the ruckus started."

"I reckon I gotta be goin', Slats. Gotta get Pancho on American soil afore they locate me and take him away. I'm breaking the law by grabbing him this side of the line without extradition papers. Hoped I'd be able to dab my rope on The Hawk, too, but he ain't here." The Ranger had jerked the now conscious Pancho to his feet.

"The Hawk? I don't quite make you, Bill?"

"Pancho's sidekick. White man outside but black as a crow where his heart is. As low-down a renegade as ever plugged a man in the back. His range is south of here on the Cinder Cone Mesa. His name is Jack Mapes, but they call him The Hawk down here. A bad *hombre*. Look out for him. And so, Slats, afore I drag it, I wanna thank you a heap for savin' this worthless hide of mine. I . . ."

"Lay off, Bill. Forget it." Slats smiled. Their hands met in a grip that caused the sick man inwardly to wince.

"Any word I kin take to your folks or anything like that?"

"Not a thing, Bill. I have a letter ready to send them when I get ready to go west. So long, buddy."

He watched the Ranger and his prisoner as they rode away. After they were lost to sight along the trail that dissolved into the mesquite, he turned to the bartender.

"Stake yourself to a bung-starter or whatever it is that a Sonora bartender uses for a weapon, and we'll give these jovial lads the bum's rush." He grinned, as he propelled one of the half-conscious desperadoes to the door and lifted him outside with a well-placed kick.

The bartender, understanding but little of the American's speech but grasping the idea, sprang into action. When the saloon had been emptied and the outlaws had ridden swiftly away, he turned to the man from across the border.

"*Muchas gracias, señor.*" He beamed. "Much thanks to you. You 'ave broke your bottle. The 'ouse ees pay for the next one. W'at you 'ave?"

"A little more of the same, Pete. *Vive* . . . what, old trapper?"

"*¡Viva el americano!*" responded the fat Pedro enthusiastically. "Mebbyso you may be loco, but *Madre*, how you fight! Ten devils!"

But the American did not hear. Once more he had slumped in his chair, a glass of mescal in his hand, his fevered gaze caressing the picture of a girl in an oval frame of silver.

CHAPTER
TWO

Bill Douglas, back in El Paso, whistled softly as he read the note from his captain.

Good work, Bill,

Have another job for you. Jack Mapes is smuggling dope to a Dr. Van Duzen who runs a joint under the guise of a sanitarium. V.D. is staying at the Paseo Hotel. You are to go back to Gonzales and stay until you get Mapes. Government man here watching V.D.

Good luck, boy

Bill consulted his watch, then strolled down the street. He had an hour to kill before train time.

Van Duzen, eh? mused Bill. Bet a spotted pony it's the same gent Slats told me about. Reckon I'll stroll down to the Paseo and see if this doctor is hangin' around. Me go back to Gonzales and land Jack Mapes, eh? A man's size job. I'll see Slats, too. While I'm waitin' for Mapes to move, I'll separate Slats from his licker, feed him up on frijoles and fresh air, and send him home to his girl. That

69

hop-peddlin' doctor has bin lyin' to the kid, that's all.

Elated at the thought of salvaging the human derelict, Bill swung into the hotel and dropped into the cavernous depths of a huge leather chair. His gaze fell on a man seated a few feet away. Bill immediately recognized him as a government official. Their eyes met for the fraction of a second.

Harry Trask, mused the Ranger. And he don't want to be talked to. Bet he's the gent that's shadowin' Van Duzen.

Some sixth sense told Bill that someone was watching him. Schooling his features, he glanced toward the desk and found himself gazing squarely into a pair of piercing gray eyes. The owner of the eyes was a heavy-built man above medium height, clean-shaven, and carefully groomed. He was dressed in well-tailored riding clothes.

Bill returned the man's gaze with disarming frankness and the big man turned his piercing eyes toward Trask, who had hidden behind a newspaper. Bill saw a slight narrowing of the gray eyes as they dwelt on Trask. Then the big man picked up a traveling bag at his feet and, waving aside the uniformed bellhop, crossed the lobby and disappeared into the darkness outside.

Trask rose, shot the Ranger a meaningful glance, and, tossing aside his paper, followed the big man into the street.

You're too late, Trask, mused Bill. That gent had you spotted.

70

He was about to turn to the desk when a dapper-looking little Jap, carrying a small suitcase, slipped past him and out the door.

Dog-gone, thought the Ranger, *now where did he come from? He wasn't in the lobby a second ago. Ah! That room where the bellhops change clothes.* He stepped to the desk.

"Is Doctor Van Duzen staying here?" he asked the clerk.

"Van Duzen? He just left. Big chap in riding clothes. He's checked out."

"Know where he's headin' for?"

"The doctor was inquiring about the train for Gonzales. Perhaps he's going there. The train leaves in ten minutes."

The Ranger grinned his thanks and with swift strides crossed the lobby and stepped outside.

He was about to hail a taxi at the curb when it suddenly shot away with a jerk. For a second the street light illuminated the interior of the cab and he caught a glimpse of the little Jap and a woman. The Jap reached to pull down the curtain, but in that fleeting instant Bill caught a glimpse of the woman's face. It was the girl whose picture Slats had shown him!

Bill jumped into a waiting cab and shoved a banknote into the driver's hand.

"Make that Gonzales train, pardner!" he called. "Step on 'er."

"Can't exceed the speed limit, boss. It's against —" The driver gasped as a long-barreled .45 jabbed him in the back.

71

"Step on 'er!"

"Yes, sir!" The cab left the curb with a jerk.

A traffic jam held them for what seemed hours to the impatient Ranger. Bill swung aboard the rear platform of the last car just as the train pulled out.

"Whew!" he grunted as he climbed over the rail and stood on the platform. "I like to've missed 'er."

"So it would seem, friend," replied a voice behind him.

Bill turned to gaze directly into the suspicious gray eyes of Dr. Van Duzen.

The doctor's big bulk seemed to fill the narrow platform. Otherwise Bill might have seen the huddled form of Harry Trask lying bruised and unconscious on the far side of the railway track.

CHAPTER
THREE

A silver case, filled with monogrammed cigarettes, an unopened quart of tequila, a .45 Army automatic, and the picture of a girl. Odd equipment for a man desert-bound. Perhaps the oddity of it appealed to Slats for he smiled as he distributed the articles about his person. A final glance in the cracked mirror told him his fresh flannels were immaculate, the white silk shirt spotless, the gay-colored tie faultlessly knotted. The heavy automatic bulged a bit in its armpit scabbard and the tequila made an awkward bundle. Slats spent a full minute in mental debate whether they should be left.

A bit inconvenient but both necessary, he decided with a shrug. He adjusted his Panama to a jaunty angle and stepped from his adobe house into the street.

Although it was yet early morning, the heat was noticeable. Slats stepped into the shadowy interior of the saloon.

"A last drink with you, Pete." He smiled.

Pedro set out a bottle and two glasses. "You are go away, *señor?*" he inquired without surprise. He had long ago ceased to be surprised at anything the loco *gringo* might do.

"I'm going on a journey, Pete. A long journey. I don't expect to return."

"*Sí, sí, señor.*"

"I've left one or two details for you to attend to, Pete. My luggage is tagged and ready for shipment. It goes to New York. You will see that it goes out?"

"*Sí,*" came the ready reply.

"There are two letters on my desk. One is addressed to James Hadley, the other to Josephine Craig. Mail them. You'll find a roll of bills on my table, a thousand dollars or so. It's yours. That's all. Here's to your very good health, Pete." Slats downed his drink and walked toward the door.

"Which way are you go, *señor?*" called the bartender, shaken from his indifference.

Slats paused in the doorway, a faint smile playing about his lips.

"West," he replied, then turned on his heel and started down the street.

Pedro, shaking his head, waddled from behind the bar and from the doorway watched the American until the white flannels and the Panama were lost to sight in the mesquite brush.

"Loco," said Pedro sadly. "*Muy* loco. He say he ees go west and yet he take thees trail that go south? *Muy* loco." Still shaking his head, he walked back to the bar and poured himself a drink.

Without a backward glance toward the squalid little village that he was leaving, Slats walked along the trail that led across a seemingly endless sea of sand dotted with mesquite, yucca trees, and cactus. Far to the southward, against the cloudless sky, the peaks of the distant hills danced in the heat waves.

Not a sound broke the quiet of the desert morning. No living thing moved. Slats might have been the only living being within a thousand-mile radius. As he walked on, he started to whistle. The sound of his own making grated on his nerves, and he ceased abruptly. The heat was increasing as the sun mounted. It grew uncomfortably hot and he paused long enough to shed his coat. He removed his tie and tossed it aside, then loosened the collar of his shirt. Tiny streams of perspiration trickled from beneath his hat, splashed in the loose sand at his feet, and were sucked up by the sand. The man watched the bits of moisture evaporate, picked up his coat, shrugged, and trudged on.

Picked a warm day for the going-out party, he mused. *Might as well have gone out back yonder in my room. Messy, though. Mexicans crowding around, staring and pawing me over. I prefer being pawed over by coyotes and buzzards.* There was a hard look in his eyes as he looked toward the distant skyline and his jaws clamped until the muscles quivered. *A bit hard on the guv'nor, but he'll forget soon. Funny how Wall Street can devour a man's heart like quicklime. Joe will think I've been unfair. Game little buddy, Joe is. Gamest ever. She'd marry me in a minute, bum pump and all. But I mustn't let her, that's all.* Slats reached for the bottle. Extracting the cork, he tipped the bottle upward, gulping down a drink of the fiery stuff.

"*Ugh,*" he coughed. Then he slowly poured the liquor out and watched it disappear in the sand. When the bottle was empty, he tossed it aside.

"There goes my Dutch courage," he muttered as he picked up his coat and went on. "I'll no doubt regret that rash act this evening when the sun goes down. I figured on being full of hooch when I pulled the trigger. But I'll be sober, cold sober, and, when old Sol drops behind the hills, I'll go with it. And that's that."

Tired, thirsty, his clothes sweat-soaked and dusty, late afternoon found Slats far out on the desert. He seated himself in the shade of a Joshua tree and lit a cigarette. Every line of his figure drooped with fatigue.

The cigarette smoke burned his parched throat and he threw it away. Stretching out, he pillowed his head in his arms and closed his eyes. In no time he was asleep.

CHAPTER
FOUR

The chill of night roused him and he sat up, blinking with surprise. The night air penetrated his thin clothing and he shivered as he slipped on his coat.

"Overslept, by Jove," he muttered aloud. He started to button his coat and his fingers touched the automatic. Slowly he drew the weapon out and examined it. Even in the faint moonlight he could tell that the mechanism of the gun was choked with sand.

Gathering some dry brush, he kindled a fire and, seating himself beside it, disassembled the weapon to clean it. So engrossed was he in his labor that he did not heed the stealthy approach of three men who crept through the brush toward the fire.

"Grab a couple of handfuls of sky, mister!" called a voice from the brush.

Slats started with surprise. His hands raised a trifle in obedience to the command, then lowered.

"I'm not in the habit of grabbing sky," he replied, and again lowered his head over his task.

"Throw your paws up or I'll shoot," growled the voice.

"Shoot 'way, friend. I hope you're a good shot," replied Slats evenly. He looked toward the spot in the dark from whence the voice had come. He thought he could catch the sound of men whispering.

The attack came with sudden ferocity, surprising the man by the fire. Three husky bodies seemed to fall from the sky on his shoulders. Too surprised to resist, he was easily conquered. Deft hands searched him for weapons even before the ropes about his hands and legs were twisted into secure knots.

"I reckon you won't cause much trouble now, pardner," came a sneering voice and Slats looked into the face of his captor. A face covered with black whiskers, sharp beady eyes, and white teeth that gleamed in the firelight.

The man gave a command in Spanish and the fire blazed up as two ragged, heavily armed Mexicans fed brush to the flames in obedience to the gruff order.

"Is this the gent?" growled the white man.

"*Sí, sí*," came the hurried reply.

The white man jerked Slats to a sitting posture and seated himself opposite. The Mexicans squatted on the other side of the fire.

"We rode into Gonzales after you, but you'd gone," growled the leader.

"So?" inquired Slats, mildly curious.

"Yeah. The boys tell me you helped that Ranger capture Cordero. I aim to make you pay aplenty for hornin' in, Mister Short Horn."

"How interesting. I suppose you are Jack Mapes, otherwise known as The Hawk. Why call you Hawk? Why not Meadowlark or Hummingbird, or perhaps Buzzard? I presume these two unwashed but doubtless lovable companions of yours are The Bluebird and The Robin." Slats grinned amiably.

The grin was short-lived. The outlaw's arm swung upward viciously and a fist crashed into the prisoner's face, knocking him backward. Then a rough hand jerked Slats to a sitting posture once more.

"I reckon that'll keep you from makin' any more bright cracks, mister," leered the bearded man. "Jack Mapes ain't a gent to fool with, savvy?"

"I hope I get a chance to pay you with interest for that little love tap," muttered Slats grimly, blood trickling from his bruised lips.

Mapes laughed harshly. "I wouldn't give two bits, Mex, fer your chances, *hombre*. You'll be about as dangerous as a hog-tied calf fer some time. After I collect ransom on you, I'll have one of the boys knock you on the head."

"Pleasant thought, Mapes. From whom do you expect to extract this ransom, may I ask?"

"From your father in New York. Your friend Pedro had a couple of letters of yourn. He kicked through with 'em when I worked him over with a six-gun."

"I see," replied Slats through set teeth. He was thinking of the letter he had written to Josephine Craig. "You got both letters?"

"I got the one to your old man. That sneakin' Pedro burned the other afore I could grab it."

"Good old Pete," muttered Slats. "Have you started negotiations with my father?"

"Not yet. Plenty of time. May be a week afore I git to it. These two boys will take you to Cinder Cone. I got some important business that will separate you from my pleasant company fer a day or two. The boys will know how to treat you, though." Mapes rose to his feet, a cigarette drooping from the corner of his thin-lipped mouth. As he stood over the prisoner, he took a final drag at the cigarette and dropped the lighted butt down the open neck of Slats's shirt.

Slats winced but did not cry out as the hot ash seared his breast. Raising his bound hands, he crushed out the sparks and looked with narrowed eyes into the leering face of his captor.

"What a low-down cowardly dog you are, Mapes," he said quietly.

The outlaw darkened with rage. His booted foot crashed into the prisoner's face, the sharp-roweled spur leaving a bloody trail across the bound man's cheek. "A sample of what you'll get from my men," he sneered as he mounted his horse.

The horse and rider faded into the shadow and the prisoner was left to the mercy of the two Mexicans.

Lying on his side, he watched the two bandits as they sat by the fire. Villainous-looking brutes, unkempt and ragged, they squatted on their bare heels, smoking husk cigarettes. Presently one of them produced a bottle of liquor and it passed back and forth between the two with much talking and subdued laughter. Now and then they eyed the prisoner with sneering looks.

Slats was more thirsty than he had ever been in his life. He asked for water, receiving nothing but ribald laughter in return. He rolled over on his other side, his back to the Mexicans who seemed in no hurry to start.

80

The bandits had finished their bottle of tequila and produced a second bottle. One of them hurled the empty bottle at the prisoner's head, missing his target by a scant two inches. Slats ground his teeth in silent rage as the bottle shattered against a rock a foot from his face.

Suddenly a look of cunning crept into Slats's eyes. With a covert glance at his captors, he edged cautiously toward the pieces of broken glass. The base of the bottle offered a jagged edge. With one eye on the two Mexicans, Slats sawed the rope that bound his wrists against the sharp edge of glass. Slowly, strand by strand, the rope parted. His hands were free!

The Mexicans were heatedly arguing over something now, paying no attention to their prisoner. Slats doubled up until he could reach the rope that bound his ankles. A couple of minutes of desperate work and his legs were loose from the rope. At that instant a shot crashed! Slats, thinking his ruse had been discovered and that he was being shot at, sprang to his feet. Astounded, he saw one of the Mexicans fall face forward into the fire.

The smoking gun in the second bandit's hand told its story. Slats sprang like a tiger, putting all his weight behind the right swing that crashed against the Mexican's unprotected jaw. The outlaw sank limply to the ground.

Disarming the unconscious man, Slats turned his attention to the bandit whose clothes were beginning to catch fire. He dragged the bandit from the hot coals and made a hasty examination. He was dead. The bullet of his companion had found the mark. Slats picked up a partly filled canteen of water and drank thirstily.

"I wouldn't swap a swallow of this water for all the booze in the world," he reflected as he lowered the canteen. "From now on, I'm boosting for good old water, believe me." He turned to the bandit who was beginning to show signs of returning consciousness. Picking up a rope, he bound the Mexican securely.

The bandit groaned and opened his eyes, scowling at the white man who sat near him.

"Where was Mapes headed for when he left here, *hombre?*" asked Slats.

"*No sabe,*" growled the bandit.

"*No sabe,* eh?" said the American. "I think that you'll *sabe* in a short time, my friend." Reaching forward, he pulled a rifle toward him. He thrust the barrel into the fire. When he withdrew the rifle barrel, it was red hot. "I'll give you a dose of your own medicine," Slats said with a pleasant smile. "You *sabe* branding, I take it? Well, I'm about to brand you, *amigo*. Start talking." He brought the hot gun barrel close to the bandit's face.

"I tell! I tell!" pleaded the Mexican. "Hawk ees gone toward Gonzales. Many men weel hold up train thees night near Gonzales."

"The Hawk's men?"

"*Sí.*"

"They'll head this way after the hold-up?"

"*Sí.* They go to Cinder Cone Mesa, the beeg camp. Mebbyso Hawk come back weeth them. Mebbyso not.

¿*Quién sabe? El hombre* Hawk ees not say much to hees men about where he go."

"Huh. Don't know as I blame him. If the rest of his gang are as easily persuaded into talking as you are . . ." Slats grinned. "I'm going to leave you tied here. You'll no doubt get loose before morning. But you'll be afoot, *sabe?* I'm taking the horses . . . and the guns. I'll shoot you if you get in my way any more. I'm going after Jack Mapes, The Hawk, and I aim to treat him rough when I find him. Good night, *amigo!*"

CHAPTER
FIVE

No two ways about it, mused Slats, *I'm lost*. He pulled his horse to a halt and lit a cigarette.

Tired and hungry, his clothes soiled and torn, he bore little resemblance to the carefully groomed young man who had left Gonzales that morning on his mission of death. There were other marked changes, also, had there been anyone there to note. His once pallid cheeks were sunburned but beneath that sunburn was the barest glow of swift-running blood. His eyes had lost their look of despair, his mouth no longer twisted in that bitter smile that had touched the heart of Bill Douglas.

Jove! He grinned to himself in the darkness. *I haven't coughed once since I left Gonzales. That's odd. Slats, old top, I wonder if we haven't been acting a bit of the fool? Because Van Duzen said I'd six months to live, I loaded up on Mex hooch and cigarettes. Then got morbid and decided to put an end to the game. Bright lad, Slats, and so brave, too. Friend Hawk proved an angel in disguise.* The boy's head tilted back and he laughed for the first time in months. Then he sobered and a dangerous glint crept into his eyes.

"I owe Mapes a sound thrashing and I'll find him if I have to spend a year in this desert," he muttered grimly. "I will — "

He broke off abruptly, his hand on his gun. Somewhere in the maze of brush thickets ahead of him a horse had nickered!

Slats slipped from his saddle and led his two horses into the brush. Gun ready, he crouched close to the ground.

Presently the faint sound of scraping brush and creaking saddle leather could be heard. Another instant and two horsemen were silhouetted against the skyline.

"Reckon that fool pack horse must've smelled something or he wouldn't 'a' nickered, Harve," said one of the riders.

"Smelled water, mebby," growled the other rider sleepily. "We must be clost to the water hole at the foot of the mesa. Mapes said to wait there for orders. Now what . . . ?" The man in the lead quit talking as his horse jumped sideways, snorting with fear.

The hammers of two .45s clicked as one. The men sat tensely in their saddles.

Suddenly one of Slats's horses nickered softly. *I'm in for it now*, decided Slats, crouching lower. *That calls for a showdown.*

"Hands up, gentlemen!" he called aloud. "Make it quick!"

A muttered curse and a shot was the answer. Slats heard the whine of a bullet past his head. The gun in his hand roared and one of the riders cried out in pain, dropping his gun.

The second outlaw spurred his horse toward Slats, shooting as he came.

The ex-Marine dodged to one side, his gun spitting fire. Horse and rider piled up in a heap.

"First horse I ever killed, hang it," muttered Slats as he warily approached the fallen animal. The rider, pinned beneath the dying horse, was groaning and cursing profusely as he shot at random.

With a cat-like leap, Slats was on top of the outlaw. His clubbed gun swung downward across the man's wrist, sending the outlaw's gun spinning.

A dry twig snapped behind him and Slats whirled just in time to dodge the descending rifle barrel of the other outlaw. Before the man could recover his balance, Slats fired. The man crumpled in a heap, shot through the heart.

"I quit!" called the other man frantically. "Don't shoot me, pardner!"

"I wish I'd plugged you instead of the horse," growled Slats as he extricated the man from beneath the dead horse. "Stand up and see if you can walk." He prodded the outlaw with his gun barrel.

"My leg's busted, pardner," groaned the outlaw. "She's shore busted. Pains somethin' fierce."

"Stand up! Huh, thought you could," snorted Slats as the man got to his feet and took a couple of limping steps. "Take a look at your partner and see if he's dead. I think he is. Good riddance, no doubt, but I'm not fond of shooting people. Figured that first shot would stop him, but he came back for more . . . and got it."

86

"Joe's dead, all right," grumbled the outlaw. "You'll pay aplenty for killin' him, too. Don't fergit you're a long ways from home, Mister Customs Officer. A danged long ways from home. Say, you ain't got a chance of gettin' home, feller. You done for Joe and you done captured me and the load of dope, but what's your next move, eh?"

"My next move will be in your direction if you don't can that silly chatter," said Slats grimly. "Any water near here?"

"About a quarter mile east of here."

"Any grub in that pack?"

"Grub aplenty."

"Then hit the trail. We'll pitch camp at the water hole. I'm waiting for an ill-mannered bird named Mapes, your boss, I believe."

CHAPTER
SIX

Bill Douglas recovered quickly from his surprise at seeing Van Duzen. In the flash of a second he caught himself wondering where Harry Trask was and what had become of the Jap and the girl. Van Duzen's grating voice brought him up with a jerk.

"You seem to have torn your coat climbing aboard, my friend." Van Duzen, a faint sneer on his face, indicated the torn lapel of the Ranger's coat.

Bill grinned to cover his chagrin as he looked at the torn lapel. There, in plain view, was his Ranger badge and Van Duzen was looking directly at it.

The doctor turned abruptly and entered the car, carrying his black leather bag.

"Smart guy, ain't you?" muttered Bill as he watched the doctor's broad back squeeze through the narrow door. *Darn the luck, anyhow. Looks like we play all cards face up from now on, mister. I know you. You got me spotted for an officer. This is goin' to be some game.* His features relaxed into that carefree, easy grin as he shoved open the door and followed Van Duzen into the car.

The doctor was already at the front door and without a backward glance opened it and passed through. Bill saw him enter the next car. He was about to follow when he caught sight of a girl seated at the forward end of the coach.

Slats's girl, mused the Ranger. *Trask must be watching this Van Duzen. I'm goin' to powwow some with the lady.* He slid into the vacant seat behind her and removed his coat.

"Beggin' your pardon, ma'am, but would you mind fixin' this here coat for me? I done fergot to bring my sewin' tools." The girl started nervously, then smiled faintly as she looked into the clear eyes of the Ranger. No trace of the insulting boldness of the male flirt there, only the frank friendliness so characteristic of the open range where convention is a thing unknown. Then her glance lit on the shining badge.

"You are a policeman?" she asked as she took the coat.

"No, ma'am. Texas Ranger."

Bill's glance flitted to a figure across the aisle. A red serape, a huge sombrero, and the blue barrel of an automatic pointed directly at him. The Ranger grew tense, then laughed softly.

"If that's Togo that's hidin' under that ten-gallon hat, call him off afore he lets that cannon go off," he told the girl in a low tone.

"Togo? You know who . . . ?" The girl paled.

"Yes'm. I know who you are. Slats told me. Don't get scared, ma'am. Slats is my pardner, savvy? His friends are mine. I got news of him that I reckon you'd like to hear."

The girl signaled the serape-clad figure, and the automatic disappeared. For some minutes Bill talked earnestly while the girl listened.

"He's down in Gonzales, tryin' to drink all the hooch in Mexico, thinkin' he kin forget. That hound of a doctor has him thinkin' he's about at the end of the trail. We'll save him, ma'am, don't worry."

The girl nodded. "Togo told me Slats had run away. It was he that wired me to come to El Paso. Thinking that this scoundrel of a doctor might know where Gerald was, we have been following him."

"Gerald?"

"Slats, then. He hates the name Gerald. We call him Gerry, but he likes to be called Slats."

"I kin see where he's right. Gerald is shore an awful name fer a gent to be burdened with. So you followed Van, eh?"

"Togo trailed him like a shadow. Did you know that this Van Duzen gives his patients drugs?"

"I'd heard somethin' like that, Miss . . . ?"

"Craig. Josephine Craig." The girl smiled.

"Proud to make your acquaintance, ma'am. I'm Bill Douglas."

Togo had slid to the edge of his seat and had lost not a word. The little Jap was grinning like a schoolboy, his little eyes snapping with excitement.

"Ever see this here doctor peddle any dope, Togo?" asked Bill.

"Yes-s-s. Many time."

"Ready to swear to it in court?"

"Yes-s-s. You betcha. Can prove."

"Good. I'll hunt Trask and he kin grab this gent right now and take him back. Take it easy, ma'am. I'll be back directly."

Josephine delayed him for a moment while she deftly mended the coat.

The Ranger thanked her half embarrassedly and lurched down the aisle of the swaying car. He had reached the door when the train slowed to a stop.

Stepping into the dark vestibule of the car, he glanced out the window. As he did so, a crowd of Mexicans swarmed aboard the train.

Flattening himself into the shadow of the poorly lit vestibule, he watched the men enter the car ahead and drop into seats.

Unless I'm loco, those gents are some of Jack Mapes's gang. This town must be Los Gatos. We're ten miles on the Mex side. Uhn-huh. And there'll be a car ahead loaded with supplies for the rurale police station at Gonzales. Two and two makes four. The Hawk is plannin' on stickin' up this train and grabbin' those supplies. They'll wait until we're about twenty miles this side of Gonzales, then pull the trick. Here's the girl on the train. And here's Van Duzen. Those wolves will spot her sure. Van will be among friends. Half a dozen of them paisanos that just got aboard know me by sight. Bill, old-timer, we gotta use our head careful, that's all. Hell's gonna pop pronto.

The train started with a jerk. Bill slipped to the door of the forward car and peered through the glass. His keen gaze swept the length of the car. Van Duzen sat smoking a cigar, his face toward the door through which Bill was looking. But not a trace of Harry Trask.

Shifting his gun to a convenient position, Bill pushed open the door and walked boldly down the aisle toward Van Duzen. A dozen pairs of dark eyes followed him and a dozen brown hands shifted toward concealed guns.

Apparently unconscious of the stir he had caused, the Ranger slid into the seat beside Van Duzen.

"Don't pull that gun you got your hand on, Doc," said Bill in a low tone. "One bad move and I'll kill you like I'd tromp out a rattler."

Van Duzen paled as he read the message in the Ranger's steel-gray eyes.

"Where's Trask?" asked Bill abruptly.

"I don't know. I — "

The barrel of the Ranger's .45 jammed against the doctor's ribs. "Where's Harry Trask?"

"I . . . I had to knock him out," stammered Van Duzen, his face a mottled, pasty color.

"Thought so. You're under arrest, Doc."

"But we're on Mexican soil," blustered Van Duzen. "Your authority ceased when you crossed the border."

"This old Forty-Five is my law, pardner," Bill assured. "Border lines don't count for much when a Texas Ranger goes after a man. I'd a heap rather take you back dead than alive, savvy? You're a snake. A low-down poison snake. Shootin's too clean a death for skunks of your breed. I got respect fer a gun-totin' hard-ridin' outlaw that plays his game like a gent and takes his medicine like it was good licker. But I ain't got any time fer dope peddlers and that breed of polecats. I'm rearin' to pull the trigger on this smoke-pole, so kinda bear that in mind if you feel a hankerin' to start somethin', mister."

"I . . . I . . ."

"Dry up! What's in that bag?"

"Clothes. I am . . ."

"Come clean! What's in that bag?"

"Money." Van Duzen's voice was scarcely audible.

"You mean to say you let Mapes coax you over on this side of the border with a bag full of money? You're a fool as well as a snake, Van Duzen. Mapes is the best double-crosser in the business. You signed your death warrant when you crossed the line with that dough."

"What do you mean, man?"

"See that gang that just got aboard? Ary one of them would kill you in a second fer five bucks, Mex money. They'll have your hide on the fence afore you're a day older."

Van Duzen was cowed. His eyes shifted with the look of a hunted animal. Bill eyed the big man with frank contempt.

"I'm goin' to give you a chance to save that worthless hide of yourn, Van Duzen. A fightin' chance. Will you take it or shall I pull this trigger?" Bill punctuated his question with a sharp jab of the .45.

"I'll take it," gasped the big man.

"Good. We'd orter be about thirty miles from Gonzales now. No time to lose. You are to get up and stroll into the rear car. You'll see a girl sittin' there. Tell her that Bill Douglas says to get ready to quit this train, savvy? When you've told her that and she's ready, pull the air cord three times. That's the stop signal, savvy? As soon as the train slows to a stop, you and the girl and the little Jap that's with her are to slip off on the right side of the rear platform and take to the brush. I'll join you. Got that straight?"

"Yes," came the husky answer.

"All right. Gimme that gun of yours."

"But I . . ."

The Ranger's .45 jabbed him remindingly. The doctor handed over a pearl-handled automatic.

"I'll take care of the bag, Doc. Get goin'!"

Van Duzen rose reluctantly and made his way to the rear door. Bill watched him until he passed through the door. Then he rolled and lit a cigarette. A faint smile played about his straight lips, but his eyes were cold and hard as frozen steel.

Minutes passed draggingly. Then the stop signal sounded and the train began to slow up. The Mexicans exchanged surprised glances and low-spoken questions passed to and fro among them.

The train halted with a bumping jerk and simultaneously the Ranger's gun flashed into sight.

"Hands up!" he called loudly.

A Mexican near the door jumped into the aisle, his gun spitting fire at the Ranger. A bullet whistled past Bill's left ear.

Still smiling, Bill fired and the Mexican sank to the floor, a lead slug in his shoulder. Stepping into the aisle, he picked up the bag and walked deliberately toward the door of the car, herding the Mexicans before him. His gun seemed to cover every man present as he came toward them.

"Pile into that corner!" he called in Spanish.

A round face appeared at the door. It was Togo and the little Jap was grinning widely as he smashed the glass with his automatic.

"Missy send me to help," he explained. "Me one time soldier. Shoot straight. You want help?"

"Shoot any of 'em that makes any funny move, Togo. Miss Craig safe?"

"You tell them all the world," said the Jap. "She wait like you say. All safe."

"Good enough." Bill had gained the door now. Shouting a last warning to the cowering outlaws, the Ranger and Togo jumped from the car and were lost to sight in the darkness.

Togo guided him to a brush patch, where Josephine and Van Duzen were hidden. Bill grinned his approval as he saw that the girl was outwardly calm and her slim fingers gripped a little automatic.

"Are you wounded . . . Bill?" she asked.

"Nary a scratch, ma'am. I hope you're a good walker. We're goin' to hike to Gonzales."

The Ranger's tone was as light-hearted as he could make it. The darkness hid the worried frown that puckered his brows. He was thinking of the march that lay before them. A long hike without food or water, in a country infested by outlaws who called Jack Mapes their leader.

CHAPTER
SEVEN

Jack Mapes was in an ugly mood. Proof of it lay beside the torn-up railway track in the tangible form of four lifeless, rag-clad bodies. The four leaders of the outlaws who had failed to stop Bill Douglas and Van Duzen had paid the extreme penalty.

The Hawk, a smoking .45 in each hand, turned to a dapper-looking young Mexican in faded khaki.

"That'll learn the rest of these yaller-hided coyotes that my orders is to be carried out without bunglin'. I wanted them two men. Reckon that'll teach the rest of these paddle-footed *peónes* a lesson, eh, Chávez?"

"Per'aps," shrugged the one in khaki. "*¿Quién sabe?*"

"What do you mean, kin savvy? What's to prevent it?"

"Those *hombres*." Chávez waved a cigarette toward the dead men. "They 'ave frien's, *sabe*? It ees well that you sleep weeth your back against the wall, *señor*. See the *hombres* who are load the pack mules? They smile at you weeth the lips, but the eyes do not smile. It ees like the trainer weeth a pack of animals. He ees safe so long as he does not turn hees back, onderstan'? Someday he grow careless, a knife flash. *Pouff! Señor*

97

Hawk ees dead the same as the *peónes* yonder." Chávez smiled, his white teeth gleaming.

Mapes laughed harshly. "Let 'em try it," he growled. "I'll go through that gang like a wolf through a bunch of rabbits." He looked keenly at his lieutenant, a gleam of suspicion in his narrowed eyes.

"Are you ribbin' these *paisanos* to kill me, Chávez?" he asked, his voice husky with anger. "If I thought you was, I'd shoot you down in your tracks."

Chávez shrugged. "And you would die before the sound of your shot die away, *señor*. All those men are my frien's. Three, four, five years some of them have follow me. Sometimes we 'ave fight weeth the rebel army, sometimes weeth the federal soldiers, whichever side ees stronges', onderstan'? That ees why we 'ave live' so long. We are like the rats on the ship. We leave before the ship sink. Be careful that *your* ship does not get een the rough water, *señor*. When I and my men come to you, you 'ave promise much. Money from the smuggleeng, plenty of mescal and fine clothes. Look! No money, no shoes on the feet of the men, no clothes, notheeng. That ees not so good, *señor*. And now, because those four men do not keel two *gringos*, one a Ranger, the other a stranger who you say you do not know, you 'ave thees four men shot. Go careful, *Señor* Hawk, thees ship which I speak of, she ees begin to leak." Again Chávez smiled.

The Mexicans, sensing that something unusual was taking place between Mapes and Chávez, had stopped their work and were crowding closer, their eyes on the dapper man in the faded uniform.

"It ees best that you do not keep your hands on the gons, señor," warned Chávez.

"Call 'em off, Chávez," growled Mapes in an undertone, realizing that a move meant death. "Call 'em off and you and me will talk turkey."

The lieutenant turned to the men, giving them an order to go back to their work. When they were again busy loading pack mules with supplies from the rifled car, he turned to Mapes.

"Now, Señor Mapes, you and I will 'ave this turkey talk, eh?"

Inwardly cursing this smiling, debonair soldier of fortune, Mapes puffed thoughtfully on his cigarette.

"I never give you credit fer bein' so slick," he admitted. "You're a smart 'un, ain't you? Perhaps, seein' you're so wise, you can guess what kind of a proposition I'm goin' to put you?"

"Per'aps," admitted Chávez. "It ees about thees gringo stranger who ees get away weeth the Ranger, no? You know who he ees, maybe, and what he carry een the bag?"

"What makes you think that?"

"For a Ranger you would not keel four good men. But for a gringo who ees carry moch money, that ees different. No? Señor Hawk, who ees the gringo who 'ave the bag full of money?"

"His name is Van Duzen. He was comin' to Gonzales to buy . . ."

"The drugs which you are to deliver to heem," finished Chávez.

"What do you know about the hop?" growled Mapes.

"You fool Cordero, *Señor* Hawk, because Cordero ees uneducate and a fool. Those two cowpunchers, Harve and Joe, which sometimes come to Cinder Cone, they say they are gathering cattle, yet they do not carry a running iron and their riatas are not used and there are no rope marks on the saddle horns. Always they ride fast horses and their pack horse ees fast like the racehorse. Also the pack is light. That ees why I begin to suspect and send one of my men to follow thees Harve and Joe. I'm find out plenty 'bout them. Now, señor, w'at ees thees turkey?"

"Van Duzen has fifty thousand dollars in that bag. Harve and Joe should be camped at the water hole at the foot of Cinder Cone unless something has delayed 'em. They have a shipment of hop to run across the border as quick as I kin locate a market fer it. I aimed to take Van's money, put him outta the way, and find a new market, savvy?"

"*Sí.* That ees w'at the *gringo* calls the double-cross, no?"

"I reckon that's it," was the outlaw's unblushing answer. "Now here's the idee. Fifty thousand bucks, split up among all the gang, won't buy cigarette papers fer none of us. But divided two ways, say, between me and you, it's a nice stake. Get me?"

"I am get you, *señor.* You weesh me to, w'at you call, double-cross my men, eh?" Chávez smiled.

"Why not?"

"Exactly, *señor.* Why not? There ees notheeng to stop us, eh?"

"Not a thing, Chávez. I figgered you'd get the idee. Harve and Joe will expect a cut of the money. That would cut your and my profit. I reckon we won't need them two gents no longer. Simple enough to put them outta the way."

"The double-cross, eh, *amigo*?" queried the Mexican.

"You ketch on quick, Chávez." Mapes winked broadly.

Chávez blew a cloud of cigarette smoke skyward. "You 'ave stop that leak in your ship, *señor*. We start after the Van Duzen *hombre pronto*, eh?"

"As quick as the pack train starts. Pick ten of the best men and mount 'em on good horses. We'll need ten if that Ranger has ammunition. Bill Douglas is a tough *hombre* in a scrap."

"Beel Douglas? That's the Ranger?"

"Know him?"

"I 'ave known one Beel Douglas. He was a soldier. Sergeant of a machine-gun company. Per'aps it ees the same one as thees Ranger. Sergeant Beel Douglas was w'at you call heem, a fighteeng fool."

"What do you know about machine-gun companies and sergeants in the American Army?"

Chávez pointed to a faded emblem on the khaki blouse.

"You see? Ees faded now. Once it ees green pine tree, which mean the Ninety-First Division, American Army." The slim shoulders straightened. A wild light came into his dark eyes. "Powder River! A mile wide and a foot deep! Let 'er buck," he called softly, a touch of reverence in his voice. "Ah, there was an army,

101

señor. That was fighting. Thees!" Chávez waved toward the derailed train. "Thees is notheeng! The pack train ees loaded, *Señor* Hawk." He turned on his heel and walked toward the waiting men.

I'll have to go easy with that greaser, mused Mapes. *He ain't nobody's fool.* He watched Chávez pick ten men and, riding at the head of his little troop, approach.

Fifty thousand dollars, he mused. *Am I goin' to split it with that greaser? Not if Jack Mapes knows it!* He was grinning amiably as the lieutenant brought his men to a halt.

"I was jest thinkin', Chávez," he began, "Harve and Joe is liable to pull out with that stuff. Supposin' I take these men and go after Douglas and Van Duzen? You take four or five men and head for the water hole. Get the stuff that's in the pack and take it to Cinder Cone camp. I don't trust Harve and Joe."

Chávez seemed buried in thought for a minute. At last he looked up with a smile of assent.

"*Bueno*. There ees one theeng I 'ave just learn from some passenger who are on the train. They say there was a girl and a Jap who went weeth Van Duzen and the Ranger. Who are thees *señorita* and thees Jap?"

"You kin search me," admitted Mapes. "It's the first I heerd of any women or Japs."

"What you do weeth thees woman and Jap, *señor*?"

"Kill the Jap and hold the girl fer ransom if she looks rich."

"*Bueno*," agreed Chávez. "That ees good. It ees bad to harm American women. She may 'ave husban' or

102

father who ees general or senator or sometheeng. He would send soldiers down here and I 'ave no desire to fight weeth the American soldier."

"Don't worry, we'll see the woman ain't hurt. Speakin' of ransom, you'll find a skinny-lookin' gent at camp. A *gringo*. He'll bring a fat ransom and your men kin have the dough that's left after me and you git our cut." Mapes gave his lieutenant a meaningful look.

"Not the loco *gringo* that was at Gonzales?"

"The same. He helped capture Cordero. We'll begin on him when we've got Van Duzen and this Ranger outta the way."

"*Bueno*. I will meet you at Cinder Cone day after tomorrow. And *Señor* Hawk . . ."

"Yeah?" Mapes, just starting away, turned in his saddle.

"When you get the bag weeth the money, don't try to run away. I 'ave told my men about thees double-cross game which you are play so well!"

CHAPTER
EIGHT

Slats Hadley, camped with his prisoner at the water hole, was as light-hearted as a schoolboy. Ragged, unshaven, the dead outlaw's hat and jumper replacing his own, he was fully as desperate-looking as the sullen Harve when they pitched camp.

Securely tying his prisoner to a mesquite tree, he set about hobbling the saddle horses and unpacking the slender-legged pack animal.

"A mighty fine animal you have here, Harve," he said as he admiringly viewed the bay horse. "Too good to be used as a pack horse. What's wrong with him?"

"Nothing," growled the outlaw. "You don't reckon we use stove-up stock to run the line with, do you?"

"I don't get you, Harve. Run the line? What line? Ah!" Slats had been delving into a rawhide-covered kyack, or pack box, that had been slung to the pack saddle. He now brought forth a package wrapped in oiled silk. Slitting the covering with his pocket knife, he looked frowningly at its contents. A smile of enlightenment lit up his sunburned features. "I get your drift now, Harve. Hop, eh? And you and your erstwhile partner are smugglers. Quite so. More profitable than even bootlegging, I take it?"

"Cut out the funny cracks," growled the outlaw. "You gover'ment gents give me a pain. You got the evidence and you got me, but you are still a long ways from your home range. Wait till Mapes shows up."

"Just what I intend doing, buddy. You still persist in calling me a government official. Have it your own way, old chap. Mapes, so I understand, went to hold up a train. Versatile chap, that Hawk person. Smuggler, hold-up man, holds folks for ransom, and murder as a sideline. It must keep him busy. Where do you keep the bacon? The other box? Here it is. Now for a grand old breakfast. Never so hungry in my life. And that confounded cough has left me entirely. I'd like to meet Van Duzen. I'd tell him . . ."

"You'll meet Van Duzen on the far side of the Big Divide, Uncle Sam."

"So?"

"Yeah." The outlaw chuckled. "The Hawk is goin' to cold deck him with this shipment."

"Meaning just what?"

"The Hawk figgered Van was about done for as a market. The gover'ment was gettin' wise to that sanitarium gag. So he's coaxin' him over on this side of the fence. Them hop-head *patients* of Doc's will wait a long time for their medicine."

Slats was smiling oddly. "Is Van Duzen in the habit of telling his patients that they have about six months or so to live?" he asked as he cut strips of bacon from the slab.

"Shore thing. Part of the game. Makes 'em fall fer the dope all the quicker, savvy?"

105

"I savvy," replied Slats thoughtfully. "Togo was right, bless his brown hide. I'd like to have about five uninterrupted minutes with friend Van." Slats paused in his labor to swing viciously at the air. "One of those, then an uppercut, and I'd make a convert out of that big bird." Then, grinning widely, he resumed the business of preparing breakfast.

He ate heartily, fed his prisoner, then turned to the pack. Gathering all the packages of drugs, he tossed them into the fire. The outlaw groaned as he watched the stuff sizzle and catch fire.

"Fifty thousand dollars gone up in smoke," he moaned.

"I wish Van Duzen was here to watch it burn," replied Slats grimly.

"You'll pay fer this," growled the prisoner. "The Hawk will skin you alive."

"I've always wondered how it felt to be skinned alive," said Slats. "Better do all the talking you can while the going's good. You won't be able to talk after a while."

"What do you mean?"

"I'm going to gag you, Harvey, my lad. You make too much noise with your mouth. It gets on my nerves, so to speak. Then I'll tie you up and let you think beautiful thoughts while I look around a bit."

Humming gaily, Slats put his threat into execution. The sun was two hours high when he saddled up the pack horse and rode away.

A few miles farther on, Cinder Cone Mesa rose abruptly from the flat desert. Its perpendicular walls rose vertically upward, impassable as the wall of a fortress. Humming softly, thoroughly enjoying the ride, Slats gave the horse free rein.

If there's a trail leading to the top of the mesa, you'll know it, pony, mused the rider. *Doubtless there's water and grass up there where Mapes has his main camp. Unless I'm doping this thing out all wrong, the camp will be deserted save for a guard, perhaps.* "Atta boy, pony. Thought you'd locate the trail." Slats smiled grimly as he hitched his gun forward.

Glancing down at the purloined boots, chaps, and jumper he was wearing, Slats chuckled. *With a reasonable amount of luck, I'll pass the inspection of the Mex guard. I'd scarcely recognize myself beneath the whiskers, dirt, and sunburn that I've accumulated since leaving Gonzales. A careful imitation of Harvey's idiomatic and picturesque lingo, coupled with the few Mex words I've picked up, and I'll pass for a member of The Hawk's gallant band of cut-throats. Ah, the guard!*

At the foot of a steep trail that led up the side of the mesa, a heavily armed Mexican stepped from behind a boulder, gun leveled at the approaching rider.

Slats advanced carelessly, the horse, head up, ears forward, shying playfully as he eyed the guard.

"*Buenos días, señor,*" called Slats, as he let his horse stop. Paying no heed to the Mexican's threatening carbine, he reached for tobacco and papers. Slouching sideways in the saddle, he looked down at the scowling guard. "Put up the gun, pardner," he drawled. "The thing might be loaded and go off accidental. Where's Mapes?"

"Who you are?" growled the guard suspiciously.

"One of the outfit, *amigo*. I come up with Harve and Joe, savvy?"

"Where they are, thees Harve and Joe?" The carbine did not lower an inch.

"Camped at the water hole. Harve is snake bit. Got any medicine up at camp?" Slats nodded toward the top of the mesa.

"*Sí.*" The gun was slowly lowering. "Planty medicine. Mescal and tequila." The guard grinned meaningfully. "That w'at you want, eh?"

"You guessed it." Slats nodded. "'*Sta bueno* for snake bite, eh, *amigo?*"

The trick of fooling the guard was proving simpler than he had dared hope. Slats gathered his slack reins and was about to urge his horse along the trail, when a ragged figure emerged from the brush behind him. Slats turned quickly at the sound of breaking brush, his heart skipping a beat.

The guard, attracted by the newcomer, turned his attention from Slats. The next instant the white man was out of the saddle, a .45 in his hand. The heavy gun crashed against the guard's head and the man crumpled with a groan. The .45 now swung to cover the approaching *peón*.

"Come on, *hombre!*" called Slats sharply. "And make it snappy. *Pronto,* savvy?"

"Don't shoot, *señor!*" begged the ragged outlaw, advancing fearfully.

108

"Then hurry up," ordered the white man. "Take the rope off my saddle and tie this bird up."

Five minutes later Slats again mounted and started up the trail. Hidden in the brush below, bound and gagged, were the two Mexicans.

A hard climb up a narrow, winding trail brought him to the top of the mesa. Slats slipped from the saddle and loosened the cinch to let his horse breathe. A quarter of a mile away was a cluster of tents pitched on the shore of a lake that shimmered in the heat waves. Not a soul was in sight. Slats grinned and reached for tobacco.

"Good morning, *señor!*" called a soft-toned voice so close behind him that Slats jumped. He whirled to look into the black muzzle of a carbine.

A small, slender Mexican in a thin khaki uniform was holding the gun. Clean-shaven save for a slim moustache waxed to needle points, neat in appearance, the man was a decided contrast to the ragged *peónes* Slats had met heretofore. The man was smiling but his dark eyes blazed dangerously and the carbine was cocked.

"Hanged if I don't believe you're the most dangerous one I've met yet," growled Slats as he raised his hands. "I bet you'd shoot in a second."

"With pleasure." The Mexican smiled. "I don't quite place you. You must be a new member of the gang."

"What gang?" frowned the white man.

"The Hawk's gang? What else?"

"The Hawk's gang? Say, who are you, anyhow?"

"I am captain of the *rurales*. That was one of my men you killed at the foot of the trail."

"You win, Cap. You win all bets. The man was not killed, however. He was coming to as I left. What do you intend doing with me, may I ask?"

"Shoot you, *señor*. What else? I have no time to spare with taking prisoners. Throw your gun away, *señor*, then you may lower your hands. Let me warn you not to try anything rash. I shoot straight, for a Mexican." The *rurale* captain smiled at his own subtle humor.

"Supposing I convince you I'm not an outlaw, Cap?"

"That, *señor*, would be one hard job. Appearances are against you."

"So they are, *amigo*. But if you'll send a man or two back to the water hole, you'll find a member of The Hawk's gang tied up. He'll tell you I'm not an outlaw."

"You mean the man coming up the trail?"

Slats, following the captain's gesture, was astounded to see Harve, under guard, riding toward them up the steep trail.

"I spotted the smoke of your campfire and sent two men to investigate. You will hold out the hands for the handcuffs, please?"

Slats shrugged resignedly and held out his hands. The handcuffs clicked shut just as Harve and his guards topped the mesa.

The outlaw frowned in a puzzled manner as he saw that Slats was a prisoner. Then he laughed sneeringly.

"Tell the captain here who I am, Harve," asked Slats. "He thinks I'm one of your gang."

"Yeah? And he's goin' to shoot you?" The outlaw grinned.

"Unless I convince him that I'm not an outlaw."

"Now ain't that nice," leered Harve. He turned to the captain. "This here gent is The Hawk's right-hand man, Cap. Him and me had a fallin' out last evenin'. He . . ." Harve paused, listening intently. From below had come the sound of a shot.

One of the guards said something in his own tongue to the captain. The captain nodded.

"Go on with your story," ordered the captain, turning to the outlaw.

"He tied me up because I throwed the hop in the fire." Harve's coarse lips widened in a sneering grin. "Better kill him quick, Cap. He's a snaky *hombre*."

"Well, I'll be dog-goned! My hat's off to you, Harvey, old top. You're the smoothest single-handed liar I ever listened to." Slats suddenly recalled the Mexican outlaw who he had tied up with the guard below.

"There's a Mexican tied up in the brush at the foot of the mesa, Captain. He'll explain who I am," said Slats, his hopes rising.

"I'm afraid not, *amigo*." The captain smiled. "You heard that shot? The guard has killed him. It is as I told you. We cannot waste time with prisoners."

CHAPTER
NINE

Daybreak found Bill Douglas and his party in the rough hills. The Ranger called a halt, and, leaving Togo in charge, he laboriously climbed to the summit of an adjacent peak.

For some time he swept the surrounding country with a pair of small, but powerful binoculars. At last, with a grunt, he focused them on a group of horsemen who were spreading into the hills.

Eleven riders, he mused. Ten besides the leader, who looks a heap like Mister Mapes himself. I could make it alone, but, with the girl to take care of, we ain't got a chance of makin' it. Van Duzen's as much of a burden as the girl, hang his big hide. Grumblin' about blisters on his feet and how dry he is. And not a whimper outta the girl. She's game, but, gosh, you can't expect a woman to go chargin' around over these hills without grub or water. If I kin locate water, we'll make a stand. Lemme see. Yonder's Diablo Peak with Granite Wash to the left. Granite Wash is dry as a bone. Seems to me like there orter be a spring in that cañon just across the ridge. Camped there onct huntin' horses. Yeah, we shore did find water there. Plenty of shelter, too, if I recollect right. Worth tryin'.

Slipping his glasses back in the case, Bill slid, rather than walked, down the steep slope.

"Come on, folks, we're a-movin'!" he called cheerfully. "Think you kin make it, ma'am?"

"You bet," said Josephine gaily, although she ached from head to foot and her mouth was parched.

"Prod that big elephant to his feet, Togo."

"I tell you my feet are rubbed raw," whined Van Duzen.

"Then shoot him between the horns, Togo," was the Ranger's unsmiling order. "Come on, ma'am, so's you won't have to watch him kick." Bill picked up the bag and with the girl at his side started off.

Togo, grinning widely, drew his gun. "It iss pleasure to get rid of such bad nuisance," he said softly.

"Put it up! Put that gun up, you murdering little hound!" protested the doctor, springing to his feet. "I'll walk, confound you!" He started limpingly along in the wake of the girl and Bill.

A tortuous climb to the top of the ridge, then an abrupt descent into the cañon below. There, among the huge granite boulders, shaded from the sun by the branches of a giant hackberry tree, a tiny spring trickled.

Van Duzen, pushing aside the girl, was the first to gain the water. Bill, leaping forward, swung with all his might at the doctor's jaw. The big man dropped in his tracks.

"Some gents jest ain't nacherally got no manners, ma'am," said Bill, dragging the doctor's big frame to one side. "Drink hearty, Miss Craig."

113

When Van Duzen awoke, the rest of the party was stretched out in the shade, munching on something that looked like dried string beans. He eyed them with a dark scowl as he gingerly felt of his jaw. Then, without a word, he lay prone and drank.

"Don't I get any food?" he whined. "You wouldn't let me starve, would you?"

"Starving's too easy an end fer such snakes as you," replied Bill. "We're eatin' mesquite beans. Cow food. You'd orter thrive on it. Help yourself, Doc."

"They aren't so bad, are they, Mister Douglas?" commented Josephine bravely as she washed down a mouthful of powdery beans with a swallow of water.

"I wisht you wouldn't go callin' me 'mister' all the time, ma'am. I ain't no ways used to it. Has me feelin' like my collar was tight or somethin'. Suppose you make it jest plain Bill. No'm, mesquite beans ain't so bad as some things, cactus with the spines on, fer instance. Injuns pound 'em into meal and make bread of 'em. Never et none myself, but I knowed boys that has. They claimed it was good. They was both purty fair liars, though, as I recollect. Most cowhands is bothered thataway at times. They like to tell it scary when they git holt of some gent that they kin lick if the said gent questions the truth of what they're sayin'. I'm troubled some myself along them lines. Better lay down and see if you kin grab some shut-eye. I'll mount that pinnacle yonder and stand guard. Togo, keep an eye on Doc and the bag."

Bill sauntered away. Once out of sight, he quickened his pace. The amiable grin was gone from his face.

114

I might've bin mistook, but I thought I heerd a hoss down the cañon, he mused. *No use gettin' the girl het up till I'm plumb sure.*

He climbed part way up the ridge and sat down behind a boulder. Again the binoculars came into use. Suddenly he lowered the glasses and drew his .45. Below, creeping through the brush toward the camp, was a man. His horse was behind, partially hidden by the brush.

Bill drew careful aim, then lowered the gun. *If I move fast, I'll beat him to it,* he thought. *He's follerin' our sign. If I kin git him without shootin', so much the better. A shot will bring the rest of 'em on the run.*

With the stealth of a panther, the Ranger slipped from his hiding place toward a point between the camp and the approaching outlaw. A bit out of breath, he gained his vantage point just as the man emerged from a brush thicket. Half crawling, the man crept along the trail. Bill gathered himself for a spring.

The outlaw, seeming somehow to sense the Ranger's presence, whirled quickly at the instant Bill sprang. A gun roared and the Ranger felt the powder burn his face as his own gun crashed down on the Mexican's skull.

"The stuff's off now," groaned Bill as he rose to his feet. "You're done for, *amigo*, but there's ten more of your friends that'll be quirtin' and spurrin' to git here." He stripped the dead man of weapons and ammunition.

"The outlaw iss come?" Togo, his gun ready, stood beside the Ranger.

"They'll be here mighty quick, Togo. Git the girl and Doc. I'm goin' to hide this gent's horse in case we need it. The big show is on. Huh? No, I ain't hurt."

A few minutes and the horse was hidden in the brush. Bill grinned cheerfully as he met the girl, white but fighting against her fear.

"We'll make a stand here in the rocks, ma'am. We ain't whipped yet. As long as we have water and mesquite beans, we kin hold them gents off. Doc, what'll you do if I stake you to a gun?"

"I'll . . . I'll do my best, Douglas," faltered Van Duzen.

"Here's a gun and some shells. Git behind that boulder. Make every shot count, savvy? Togo, me and you will take these other two boulders." He turned to the girl. "You lay in between them two big rocks. Don't come out till I tell you. I put you off to one side so's you won't git hit by no stray bullets. Everybody take your places. Don't be scared, ma'am. We'll win out yet."

Far down the cañon three shots in quick succession shattered the quiet.

"The signal to bunch up, I reckon!" called Bill. "They'll be comin' in a few minutes. Grab your rocks, folks."

"Aren't you going to hide?" asked the girl from her shelter.

"Later," replied Bill. "I'm goin' back to the ridge to halt 'em first."

Armed with the outlaw's carbine, the Ranger again climbed to the rock on the side of the slope. For a full minute he crouched, waiting. Then he raised the gun, aimed, and fired. Three times the Ranger's gun cracked. Then he slid from the rock and presently took his place near Togo.

"Got three of 'em afore they had sense enough to take to the brush," he called softly. "That leaves seven. I've bin in heaps worse tights than this and come out. Watch that brush patch, Togo. Doc, keep your eye on the ridge. Shoot at anything that moves and shoot straight!"

Minutes of tense silence followed Bill's command. Minutes that seemed hours to the frightened girl hidden between the boulders. Once she saw something move and was on the verge of crying out, when Togo's gun roared and a crash of brush told her the Jap's bullet had found its mark.

A return shot from another quarter threw bits of flying granite in Togo's face and the little Jap crouched lower, his teeth showing in a mirthless grin.

Bill aimed at the puff of white smoke in the brush and fired. The brush tops moved and he fired again. A cry of pain from the brush patch brought a flicker of triumph into his keen eyes.

"Winged that 'un," he muttered, then dropped lower as several bullets spattered against the rock close to his head.

Van Duzen, pasty-faced and inwardly quaking, was striving his utmost to hold his gun steady. A born coward of the bully type, the big doctor was screwing his courage to the sticking point. He emptied his gun, shooting at anything that moved.

117

"Steady, Doc!" called Bill. "You're wastin' good ammunition thataway. Save it." A shot from the brush silenced the Ranger. "Good shootin'," he muttered. "That was Mapes, mebbyso." He removed his hat, placed it on the end of his rifle barrel, and raised it slowly until the top of the crown showed above the edge of the boulder.

A rifle cracked and Bill lowered the hat. There was a neat hole through the soft felt crown. Bill again raised the hat, this time higher, so that the rifle barrel showed. He thought that he caught the sound of a muttered curse from the brush.

"Better luck next time, Mapes!" he called jeeringly. "Better put your marbles in your pocket and run home! I'm goin' after your taw!"

"You stand a fat chance of gettin' it, Douglas! I'm goin' to get — "

The Ranger's rifle cracked, cutting short the outlaw's reply. Bill chuckled to himself. "I reckon I come close to his ugly head that time."

The firing became less frequent as the day wore on. The Ranger, well schooled in this sort of warfare, knew that Mapes was waiting for the arrival of darkness before he came to close quarters. Then the outlaw would gather his men and attack the party. By concentrating the attack upon one point at a time, he could annihilate the little party, one by one, where they lay behind their rocks.

I'll have to bunch up our gang, Bill decided. *And do it as quick as dark comes. Scattered out like we are, ten, twenty feet apart, it'll be pickin's fer The Hawk to*

118

put us out. Lemme see. Those rocks where the girl is hid is the best place. If I kin only git word to Togo, he kin pass it on to Doc. If I call out, Mapes will git wise. I wonder if the little Tap savvys international code. I'll try him.

The Ranger picked up a rock and tapped the boulder. *Click! Click — click! Click!* Carefully he spelled out the name Togo in dots and dashes, repeated it twice, then waited.

Then from Togo's rock came an answering message. "What is it?"

Bill laid aside his rifle and with the zest of a schoolboy trying out a new toy sent his instructions to the Jap with orders to repeat it so that there would be no mistake. He grinned widely as the repetition of his order came back to him. Leaning back against a rock, he rolled and lit a cigarette.

Suddenly, from the rocks that hid Josephine Craig, came the *tap-tapping* of a code message! Bill straightened in startled surprise. Where had this girl learned the code? No time to question now. Bill bent his thoughts to the deciphering of her message.

"I get you, Bill. Learned it from Slats. Be glad to see you." She signed off in the approved manner.

Well, dog-gone! There's a real girl, that 'un. Don't blame Slats fer . . . He broke off in his musing to shoot at a noise in the brush that told him a man was shifting his position. A groan and the increased cracking of brush followed the shot. Bill fired again and the cracking ceased.

Six of 'em left if that last shot hit home. I reckon it didn't, though, he amended grimly as a bullet whistled close to his head.

The afternoon slowly passed and the first shadow of the short twilight began to darken the cañon. Throughout the long afternoon, the Ranger had cheered up the girl with code messages, marveling at the pluck that she was showing.

Togo, at Bill's suggestion, had penciled a note and tossed it to Van Duzen, informing that member of the party of the plan. Van Duzen seemed to have recovered from his panic and was doing his bit toward keeping off the bandits.

When the Ranger could no longer see the front sight of his carbine, he prepared for the perilous journey across the thirty feet of open space that lay between his hiding place and the boulders that hid the girl.

Lying flat on the ground, he wriggled from behind his rock. Five feet, ten feet, and then the Ranger's form stiffened to immobility. Not two feet from the man's face was a coiled rattler. The warning *whirr* of the snake's rattles sent a shiver down the spine of the Ranger. The slightest move on his part and the snake would strike! Tense, breathless, Bill waited. Then slowly the snake uncoiled and wriggled away toward his hole in the rocks. Breathing a silent prayer of relief, Bill crawled on.

The crash of a rifle and a bullet threw dirt in the crawling Ranger's eyes. Springing to his feet, crouching as he dodged in a zigzag series of leaps, he gained safety and threw himself flat.

"I've done made it, ma'am," he called softly, then sat up with a jerk. He was alone. Josephine Craig was gone!

CHAPTER
TEN

"Would you prefer being shot separately or together, *señor?*" asked the *rurale* captain.

"Separately, if you please, Captain," replied Slats. "Kind of you to be so considerate."

"Not at all. I recognize a gentleman when I see one. You, I believe, are one. A gentleman gone wrong, perhaps?"

"Perhaps. Perhaps not. Admitting that appearances are decidedly against me, I still claim no affiliation with the genial Hawk and his blackleg following. I die under protest, as it were. Speaking of gentlemen, you seem to be one yourself, Captain." Smiling, Slats proffered the *rurale* captain a cigarette from the silver case which he still retained.

"Thank you," bowed the Mexican with a display of white teeth. "For the compliment and the cigarette. It is the excitement that lured me to the *rurales*. My father is governor of the state. I was educated in your country. Harvard, you know." He turned to one of his men. "Take the other one away," he ordered curtly.

"So long, Harvey!" called Slats. "Remember you're an American when you face the firing squad."

"I'm as game as you are, pardner," growled the outlaw. "Come on, let's get it over with, you yaller-hided little coyotes." Harve fell in between the two guards. Ten feet away was the perpendicular wall of the mesa. With a quick leap, the white man was at its edge. Another instant and he had leaped into space!

One of the guards ran to the edge of the precipice and peered over the edge. Then he rose with a shrug.

"Dead?" inquired the captain.

"*Sí*. It is two hundred feet to the rocks below."

"Too bad. I wanted to ask him a few questions. Americans are very impatient, *señor*."

"Great guns, man! You value human life at a low rate!" gasped Slats, aghast at the Mexican's indifference.

"Why not? He was a bad man, an outlaw. He gambled his life against big stakes. He lost."

"But surely a lawbreaker has the right to be tried for his crimes?"

"Trials are expensive and tedious. He might escape. Come, *señor*. We'll go to my tent. You are not to die until sunrise, you know. We will spend the evening, each in good company. It is two years since I have seen the cities. I have many questions to ask. The operas, the gossip, the new movie stars, and so on. Over a bottle of good wine and with good cigars, you and I shall talk. See, it is noon. You are hungry?"

"Rather. Lead on, buddy," replied Slats, his smile hiding the heaviness of his heart, for Slats Hadley was beginning to love life as he had not loved it for many months. Convinced that he was far from being the invalid Van Duzen had claimed him to be, he had taken a new lease on life.

They had seated themselves on camp chairs in the captain's tent when the Mexican nodded toward the prisoner's manacled hands.

"If you will give me your word that you will not attempt to escape, señor, I will remove the handcuffs."

Slats shook his head. "Sorry, old chap, but I can't do it. I'll do my best to slip out of your hands if the opportunity offers. No doubt you grasp my viewpoint of the situation?"

"Thoroughly, señor. I would do the same. But the handcuffs are awkward. There is another alternative. Here in Mexico, we have a form of refined cruelty known as ley de fugo ... law of the fugitive. The prisoner is apparently free and is allowed his liberty to a certain extent. In an hour, a week, or perhaps a year, he is killed while attempting to escape! A nerve-racking ordeal for the prisoner, that waiting for death that lies just around the corner. You would care to try it, señor?"

"You mean that instead of having a certain hour set for my light being put out, I have the freedom of the camp, no handcuffs, no guard over me?"

"And the hour of your death will be any time from now on, do not forget that, señor."

"And the hour of my death any time from now on," repeated Slats. "It's a go, Captain." Smiling grimly, he held out his manacled hands.

The rurale captain unlocked the handcuffs and dropped the shining bits of clinking metal on the table. He called a guard stationed just outside the tent and gave him a rapidly spoken order. The guard saluted and retired.

"It is done, *señor*. Let us eat now."

A servant brought tortillas, beans, and beef. Slats ate heartily of the highly seasoned food, gulped down a cupful of strong black coffee, and accepted the cigar the captain offered him. For some minutes they smoked in silence. Then the Mexican turned to a compact portable desk in a corner of the tent.

"I have some business here that will occupy me for perhaps an hour, *señor*. You will make yourself at home while I work?"

"Sure. Believe I'll take a stroll around camp. That is permitted under the terms of our agreement, is it not?"

"Surely, *señor*. There is one annoying detail. I must ask you to let me search you. You may be carrying papers of value. In case you should follow the example set by the impatient Harvey fellow, those papers might be a bit soiled by the . . . ah . . . descent."

"I see." Slats raised his arms outward. "Search away, old chap. I'm afraid you'll be disappointed."

The captain, with an apology for the humiliation caused by the search, systematically went through the prisoner's pockets.

The cigarette case, matches, a penknife were brought forth and placed upon the table. Then came the picture in the silver frame. The captain gazed at the picture of Josephine Craig with unconcealed admiration. Then he handed it back to the prisoner.

"I beg your pardon, *señor*," he murmured. "Such a thing is sacred. I have overstepped the limit of a

125

gentleman by profaning it with my glance. A thousand pardons." The Mexican was sincere in his apology.

"That's all right, Captain. No hard feelings. The lady is . . . was my fiancée."

"The face of an angel, señor, if I may voice my opinion."

"And the heart of an angel, Captain. I wish . . . you will grant me a favor, Captain?"

"Surely. Anything you wish, señor . . . except your life."

"I'd like to send a message of farewell to this young lady."

The captain waved a hand toward the desk. "There are writing materials, señor. I will deliver the message in person if you so desire."

"Not a bad idea, Captain." Slats smiled whimsically. "Then, when it is too late, you'll learn that I did not lie when I said I was not one of The Hawk's men."

"The word lie is taboo between gentlemen, señor. Write the message. I will deliver it at the first opportunity."

Slats wrote a message of farewell, put it in an envelope, and laid the addressed envelope on the desk, together with the picture.

"Thank you, Captain," he said earnestly. "You have still a couple of pockets to search." Again the prisoner held out his arms.

Further search revealed nothing except a handful of small white tablets. They were from the first package of morphine that Slats had opened at the water hole.

Absent-mindedly Slats had shoved a handful of the tablets in his pocket.

The captain's eyes narrowed a trifle as he examined the drug. Without a word, he put them back in the prisoner's pocket.

"You are at liberty to go now," he said with a bow. He gave the American an odd, searching glance.

"Thanks, old man," replied the prisoner. With a careless salute, he left the tent. It was not until he had gone some distance that the significance of the captain's glance hit home. Slats halted abruptly.

Great guns, the man thinks I'm a drug addict! he gasped to himself. He was about to return and correct the impression when the humor of it struck him and he dismissed the idea with a shrug. *Can't blame the guy,* he mused. *Bandit and drug addict! Gosh!*

Shifting his sombrero to a jaunty angle, the American commenced his tour of the camp. Occasionally he encountered a *rurale*, who would invariably treat him with utmost courtesy. Had he been some honored guest of their commander, they could have shown him no more deference. Only when he started down the trail that led to the desert did the iron hand beneath the glove vent its power.

"Excuse, *señor*," was the almost apologetic request of the *rurale* guard. "You are not to go down the trail."

Slats's gaze dropped to the cocked carbine that covered him unwaveringly.

"I get you, buddy. I'll stroll elsewhere." He wandered along the edge of the cliff. Pausing, he looked over the edge to the jagged lava rocks below. The American's pulse quickened.

An easy way out of it. Easier than waiting for that shot in the back, he mused. Then his shoulders straightened. *Don't be a quitter, Slats, old man. You aren't a coward, are you?* He picked up a rock and tossed it to the rocks far below. Half a dozen buzzards rose from the rocks, frightened by the missile. A shapeless object lodged in the jagged rocks caught the man's gaze. His lips set grimly as he turned away.

The impatient Harvey, he thought. *Poor devil!*

As he wandered aimlessly on, his eyes searching always for some vulnerable spot in the sheer wall that would afford an avenue of escape, Slats became aware of the fact that he was being followed. True, he had not caught more than a fleeting glimpse of the lurking form behind him. Several times, when he wheeled in his tracks, he caught sight of a shadowy something that would vanish into some shelter. He began to feel a vague uneasiness. Suave and polished as the captain was, the American had also seen the cruel, merciless side of the *rurale* commander. A cat playing with a mouse, purring as it buffeted the smaller animal about, letting it almost get away, then unsheathing the claws that were hidden in the velvet-soft paws, that was the captain. The American's whistle of bravado died a tuneless death on his pursed lips.

A great life if you don't weaken, not exactly an original thought but never more apt, mused Slats. *Maybe this human shadow of mine is a bum shot. Maybe I'll find a way down this cliff. Maybe I can . . .*

128

aw, shucks, I'm going back to the tent. I'll wear this chap out and he'll lose patience and shoot. I'll meander back to the tent of my host and . . . gosh! Gosh all hemlock and then some! I've hit it! A chance in a thousand but worth trying. He quickened his step as he headed toward camp.

If this shadowing fellow don't pot me before dark, I'll try it! He entered the tent in an almost gay humor.

CHAPTER
ELEVEN

The captain looked up with a smile. "I was hoping you would return, señor. I have missed your delightful company. Did you find any weak spot in the trap that holds you?"

"Not a one, Captain. The only weak spot I discovered is a spot between my shoulder blades. I've been expecting a hunk of lead in that spot for some minutes. Dashed uncomfortable feeling, I assure you, Captain." Slats made a wry face as he reached for a cigar.

A noise outside the tent caused both men to turn that way. The guard ushered in a man, then withdrew.

Ragged, his face and clothes spattered with dried blood, the man swayed unsteadily as he stood at attention. The newcomer was a Mexican, a *rurale*, no doubt, the American decided.

The captain waved the man to a seat. For several minutes the man talked rapidly. The captain nodded often, sometimes smiling, again frowning. Finally the man finished speaking. The captain shoved him a plate of food and a bottle of tequila, then turned to Slats.

"I have news that may be of interest, *señor*. I tell you because you have not long to live and it will give you an idea of the method I am using to wipe out The Hawk and his band. You care to listen?"

"Fire away, Captain," the American said, nodding.

"It is like this. The *Señor* Hawk depends on what he steals in the way of supplies. Good. I wait until I think he is badly in need. Then I let the news escape that a car of provisions is to be shipped under heavy guard on a certain date. *Bueno* again. The *Señor* Hawk gathers all but a few of his men, gets a pack train ready, and leaves his stronghold practically unguarded while he holds up this train. I move in while he is gone. Again, *muy bueno*." The captain lit his cigar, then continued. "The *Señor* Hawk holds up the train, kills the guards, who are locked in the car so that they will fight to the end instead of running away, loads his pack mules, and returns to camp. When they arrive, tomorrow or next day, I will get them as they get to the top of the trail. You grasp the idea?"

Slats nodded. "Kinda hard on the *rurales* in the car, is it not?"

The captain smiled broadly. "The ones locked in the car were members of The Hawk's band. I took them prisoner a month ago and saved them for that purpose. This man here, who rode in the coach as a passenger, was the only *rurale* on the train."

The diabolical cleverness of the *rurale* captain staggered Slats. "All you have to do now is wait here

131

and pot 'em as they come up the trail, one by one. Is that it?"

"Unfortunately there are complications that force me to alter my plans somewhat. Mapes, as you know, is as wily as a fox. He can scent a trap with uncanny shrewdness. Three times he has slipped through my fingers when I was about to close my hand on him." The Mexican closed his outstretched hand in illustration and again Slats mentally compared him to a cat. "Tonight I myself will lead a detachment into the hills after this Hawk."

"He's discovered the trap?" asked the American.

"Not yet. He and ten of his men are chasing a party of your fellow countrymen. A Ranger named Douglas, a Doctor Van Duzen, an American woman, and a Jap."

"Douglas! Van Duzen! You're positive?"

"Beyond a doubt. You know the men?"

"Rather. I helped Bill Douglas capture Cordero. I have an account to settle with Van Duzen, the hound!"

The captain's brows lifted incredulously. Then he smiled, that same odd smile that he had bestowed upon Slats when he handed back the morphine.

"I think I understand, señor. This Van Duzen is a receiver of smuggled drugs, so it is rumored. Your partner in crime, perhaps. The Cordero incident is an hallucination that is excusable in a man who is addicted to drugs."

Slats sprang to his feet, white with rage. "Why, confound your impudence, I . . ." He composed himself

132

with an effort and sank back into his chair, smiling grimly as he saw the guard in the doorway sheath the automatic in his hand.

"You were as close to death as you ever have been in your life, señor," the captain smiled frigidly. "The guard is a crack shot."

"Bad form on my part to lose my temper, Captain. Sorry. Pray go on with the yarn."

A grunting noise from the ragged courier caused Slats and the captain to look that way. Slats grit his teeth in silent rage as he saw the grimy hand of the man holding the picture in the silver frame. He was jabbering excitedly. The captain listened, frowning in a puzzled manner. At last the man quit talking.

"What's he saying?" asked Slats, his voice trembling with anger. "If he doesn't take his filthy paws off that picture, I'll live long enough to throttle him, guard or no guard!"

The captain uttered a curt command. The man dropped the picture with a muttered apology.

"He says" — the captain smiled as he measured his words slowly — "that this is the image of the lady who is with Van Duzen, Douglas, and the Jap."

"Joe here in Mexico? Impossible! What sort of devilish ruse is this? Answer me truthfully or I'll choke the life out of you! Kill me if you wish! Do any damned thing you like! But tell me the truth or I'll kill you." His eyes blazing, his hands clenched into knots, the American faced the *rurale* captain.

The guard in the doorway slipped the safety catch on the automatic, waiting the nod from his commander.

"Calm yourself, señor," said the captain. "The man told the truth. There is something very queer about it that I don't understand. Beyond a doubt this lady is with Douglas and Van Duzen. I will be sorry to miss the pleasant evening we were to spend together. However, the pleasure of delivering your message soon will, to some extent, make up for it." The captain picked up the letter and picture and thrust them into the pocket of his blouse.

"You mean to leave me here while you go?"

"A prisoner would be a white elephant on my hands. You are still a prisoner, you know, under the sentence of *ley de fugo*. Perhaps you will be here when I return, perhaps not, *quién sabe?*" The captain shrugged, twisting his tiny moustache.

"*¡Capitán!*" called the guard from the doorway.

"What is it?" snapped the commander.

"A prisoner!" came the reply in Spanish.

"Bring him in."

There followed a moment of silence, then a man was pushed through the doorway.

Slats, watching curiously, saw a trim figure in faded khaki, erect at attention. The man was smiling defiantly and his dark eyes blazed with a fire unquenched by fear.

"Ah," sneered the captain, "this is indeed a pleasure." He went on in English: "Eduardo Martínez Chávez, the soldier of fortune, or is it misfortune?"

"The fortune for you, *Señor Capitán*. The misfortune ees belong to me."

"I will enjoy shooting you, *Señor* Chávez. You have caused me much annoyance. I go now to clip the wings of The Hawk. When I return, I myself will shoot you."

"Ees very stupid of me to get capture. It weel give me much pleasure to show you, *Señor Capitán*, that thees soldier of fortune can die like a man!" Chávez, his arms tied behind his back, bowed stiffly.

The little gamecock, mused Slats admiringly.

The captain buckled on his saber, surveyed himself in the mirror, and faced his prisoners.

"You, *Señor* Chávez, I will see again soon. To you, *au revoir! Señor Americano*, for you and me, it is goodbye. I salute you!" The *rurale* commander's boot heels clicked as he raised his hand in a formal salute.

Slats, inwardly amused at the pomp, carelessly returned the compliment. The ragged, unshaven American made a ludicrous figure as he slumped back into his seat.

The tent flap dropped into place and the two prisoners were left alone.

Chávez eyed the American, a flicker of amusement in his dark eyes. Slats, meeting his glance, laughed softly.

"Ees fonny, thees *Señor Capitán*, eh, *amigo?*"

"Yeah, funny as a funeral, that guy. A firing squad is his idea of a joke." Slats was eyeing the faded emblem on the khaki blouse.

Chávez, following his glance, straightened proudly. "You *sabe* thees pine tree, eh? In the pocket you will find the cross which one French general pin on me."

135

"The Croix de Guerre?" gasped Slats.

"*Sí*. Ees hard name to remember, that one."

The American's voice dropped to a whisper. "Listen, buddy, come over closer. I've got a plan. If it works, we'll turn the tables on friend captain."

"Ah! Ees w'at the *Señor* Hawk call the double-cross!" Chávez grinned. "*'Sta bueno*."

CHAPTER
TWELVE

For some minutes the American talked in a low tone, Chávez listening raptly, his dark eyes glowing.

"'*Sta bueno*, w'at you call excellence, thees plan. The *caballos*, the horses, you know where they keep them? Yes? *Bueno*. We 'ave two guard here. From them we weel get the guns. It weel be dark. You and I wear the sombreros and serapes which we 'ave take from the guard. Let me do the talk when we ride up to thees guard at the trail. It ees good theeng for us eef he make no troble, bad, *muy* bad for thees guard eef he do make troble, eh, my frien'? Then down the trail into the hills. Ah!" Chávez shook his head, frowning.

"What's wrong now, buddy?"

"I am afraid I weel 'ave to work thees double-cross on *Señor* Hawk. You are my frien', my *amigo*, *sabe*? *Señor* Hawk, when we find heem, weel 'ave fifty thousand dollars. Half belongs to me, half to heem. For you, who are my frien', I weel keel the *Señor* Hawk, and you shall 'ave hees half. Then you can buy the fine clothes, the tequila, the saddle weeth moch silver. You can steal the horse. Yes, I am afraid I mus' again try thees double-cross."

"You mean you'll kill Mapes and take this money so that you can give it to me?"

"¡Sí! Sure Michael! You 'ave call me your boddy. I am very proud for that. To the *Señor* Hawk I am Chávez, the greaser. He weesh me to lie to my men, who are sometimes hongry and 'ave no shoes. To them I do not lie, *señor*. I tell them w'at the *Señor* Hawk say een thees proposition he put to me, thees double-cross, onderstan'? I tell them that, when we get thees money, they shall 'ave planty shoes and grob and mescal. I do not know then that the *rurales* 'ave call keno and we are all caught een trap. The *rurales* weel not leave many of them, *señor*." From outside came the sound of a bugle. Chávez shrugged. "I was afraid of that," he mused aloud.

"Afraid of what? What does the bugle call mean?"

"Ees mean that all the *rurales* except the guard are leave camp. Ees like thees. When I come back here to Cinder Cone, I breeng three men. Two are keel, the other I send back *pronto* to warn the pack train. *Señor Capitán* 'ave question the *rurales* who stop us. They 'ave tell heem about thees man I send back. There weel be beeg fight, per'aps. My men weel scatter and get away onless the *rurales* ride good horses. However, ees all the better for you and me. While they are fight, we go to the heels where the *Señor* Hawk ees to catch the Van Duzen *gringo*."

"You know about Van Duzen? Is Bill Douglas with him? Is there an American girl and a Jap in Van Duzen's party?" Slats asked excitedly.

138

"*Shh*. The guard, *señor*. Not so loud. *Sí. Sí.* Ees all those people."

"Then we've got to ride like the devil was after us. The girl is my fiancée, the girl I'm going to marry."

"*¡Santa María!* Who are you, señor?"

"My name is Hadley. That *rurale* captain thinks I'm a member of The Hawk's outfit."

"Hadley? *Señor* Hadley! El Loco! You are the *Americano* who'ave help capture Cordero? Ees fonny!" He laughed softly. "Always he was stupid, thees one who ees *rurale capitán. Shh!*"

The guard entered and asked a question in his own language. Chávez turned to the American.

"The guard weesh to know eef we want supper now."

"Tell him, yes."

Chávez interpreted the request and the guard withdrew, returning in a moment with a huge platter of food and a pot of steaming coffee. Plates and cups followed. The guard released the Mexican prisoner's bonds, then slouched back to the doorway, his carbine covering the two men at the table.

Chávez, his mouth full of food, raised his head and addressed the guard, using their own language.

"The *gringo* prisoner who is soon to die asks a favor," he said with a shrug. "He wants you to bring two more cups, that you and the other guard may drink with him."

"The other guard is on watch at his post outside. Why does the *gringo* ask such a thing?"

"*¿Quién sabe?* He is, perhaps, a little loco. It is the request of a man who is about to die. It would be bad luck to refuse."

"*Sí.* It is a small thing to ask, after all. Besides the night is cold. I will get the cup." He slipped out the door.

Slats and Chávez exchanged a quick look. Chávez nodded. The American pushed his cup full of steaming coffee to the edge of the table. The guard entered with a tin cup and set it down beside the pot.

Slats filled the cup and held it up as if he were holding a glass of wine.

"A toast to your captain." The American smiled.

The guard, understanding the word "captain" and catching the significance of the lifted cup, picked up the cup of coffee at the edge of the table. With the coffee in his left hand, an automatic in his right, he grinned widely.

Chávez raised his cup and all three drank. Slats made a wry face.

"Coffee's bitter. Tastes like it had boiled for a week."

Chávez translated the American's speech. "Strong coffee for strong men, eh, *amigo?*" he added.

The guard nodded, then as if to prove the assertion, downed his coffee in great gulps, set down the empty cup, and wiped the back of a grimy hand across his lips.

"That is all, *señores?*" he asked.

"That is all." Chávez nodded.

When the guard had taken his place outside the tent, the two prisoners exchanged a significant look.

140

"His coffee must have been bitter as gall, Chávez. Hope I didn't put enough morphine in his cup to kill him," whispered Slats.

"Ees born to be shot, not poison', that one." Chávez grinned. "Ten minutes and he weel be 'sleep. Some more of the beans, if you please, *señor*. Ees well to 'ave planty grob put away inside us. We ride far thees night, eh, *amigo?*"

Slats, following the Mexican's example, ate heartily.

Then Chávez lit a cigarette, and rose leisurely. He cocked his head to one side, listening intently. He chuckled softly.

"The guard, he ees snore like sawmill." He stepped to the tent door. There followed a soft scraping sound and he returned, dragging the unconscious guard.

"Which you 'ave, *señor*, carbine or Luger?"

"The Luger, if you please." He took the pistol and belt that Chávez held out.

"Sombrero and serape now, *señor*. Ah! Now you look like *rurale* for sure."

Slats grinned his approval as he surveyed himself in the mirror. In the huge sombrero and the gay-colored serape, he looked the part he was about to play.

Throwing a blanket over the unconscious guard, who lay huddled in a corner, Chávez picked up the carbine.

"Come, *señor*," he called softly as he stepped outside. Slats pulled his sombrero lower over his eyes and followed.

It was almost dark now. The two escaping prisoners, keeping well in the shadow of the brush, stealthily approached the horse corral.

A dark figure loomed up in front of them as if by magic.

"*¡Alto!*" came the curt command in Spanish. "*Q¿uién es?*"

Slats gripped his Luger as he caught the *click* of the *rurale's* carbine coming to full cock.

"Friends," replied Chávez boldly. "*El capitán* has ordered us to follow him. We want horses."

"You lie!" growled the guard. "You are Chávez, the bandit! I am one of those who helped capture — "

The carbine in Chávez's hand roared. The guard lurched forward on his face.

"*¡Pronto!* Queeck, *señor!* Get your horse. I'll be weeth you *pronto!*"

Slats saw Chávez bend over the *rurale*, stripping off serape and sombrero. A group of saddled horses stood tied to a rope corral. The American mounted. Chávez swung into the saddle of another horse.

"One more guard to pass, *señor*. I ride ahead," whispered the Mexican.

Spurring his mount to a trot, Chávez led the way. Presently they came to the guard at the top of the trail.

"*¡Buenas tardes!*" called Chávez. "The *gringo* prisoner is dead. You heard the shot? *Bueno*. I am Ramón, come to relieve you. You will take the horse back?" Chávez swung to the ground.

"*Sí. Gracias, señor*. I have had no supper," replied the guard as he stepped toward the horse.

The instant the *rurale* gripped the saddle horn and placed his foot in the stirrup, Chávez sprang like a tiger. His slender fingers gripped the *rurale's* throat, cutting

142

off the warning cry that rose to the guard's lips. A minute of futile struggling and the guard was bound and gagged.

"'*Sta bueno, Señor* Boddy!" called Chávez gaily. "Come!" He urged his horse down the steep trail, Slats at his heels. The Mexican hummed softly as he dropped his reins over the saddle horn and rolled a husk cigarette.

The enchantment of the desert night crept into the American's blood. The low-hung canopy of stars, the black chasm beneath, the soft tenor of a Mexican love song with the click of shod hoofs for accompaniment conjured up the vision of the girl he loved. Slats breathed a prayer as he rode down the trail.

"It ees fine thing to be alive, *señor*," said Chávez over his shoulder. "To be alive and to be in love ees more better. That ees w'at the song say. Do not be sad. Soon you weel see thees *señorita* that you love."

"I hope so, buddy," was the American's fervent answer.

"Ees fine to love, eh, *amigo?*"

"You have loved, too?"

"Many times. The las' time almos' cure me. Dolores was *muy chiquita*, very beautiful, *señor*. I was then lieutenant een federal army. Thees one who ees now *rurale capitán*, he ees general. Per'aps it ees the gol' braid of the general which catch the eye of Dolores. Per'aps ees because he 'as more money. *¿Quién sabe?* Any'ow, Dolores ees marry the general."

"Tough luck, buddy," consoled Slats. "You must have felt mighty cut up about it."

"*Sí, señor*. I get very dronk. *Santa María*, but I get dronk! Then I go away to the war een France. Two years I am gone. Then, when the Germans do not keel me as I 'ave hope they would, I come back. One day, een the plaza, I meet Dolores. *Santa María*, she 'ave two children and ees fat, so fat I 'ardly know 'er. Per'aps that ees why the *Señor Capitán* weesh to shoot me himself, eh?" He laughed softly.

Again came the lilting refrain of the love song, the tinkle of spur rowels, and the creak of saddle leather. From far away sounded the patter of rifle fire.

"The *rurales* 'ave attack the pack train." Chávez shrugged. "May the saints protect my men in their flight. Ees fine night for a battle . . . or love-making, eh, *señor?*"

CHAPTER
THIRTEEN

Bill Douglas, hoping against hope that the girl lay hidden somewhere close, felt cautiously about in the dark. A scuffling, scraping sound and Togo stood beside him.

"Miss Craig's done disappeared, Togo," whispered the Ranger.

The little Jap groaned aloud.

"That you, Doc?" whispered Bill as a second dark shape took form in front of him.

"What's left of me," whined the doctor. "I was never so thirsty or miserable in my . . ."

"Shut up," growled Bill. "You'll be a heap worse off afore long, if you don't quit whinin'. I'll shoot you in the laigs and leave you."

"Listen," whispered Togo.

Bill paused, listening.

"Hey, Ranger!" called The Hawk's triumphant voice from the dark. "I reckon me and you is due fer a powwow, eh?"

"What makes you think so, Mapes?"

"I done played the joker, *amigo!* The lady is my prisoner!"

Bill cursed softly beneath his breath. He tried to keep the chagrin and disappointment from his voice as he answered. "Mebbyso you're lyin', Mapes."

"Reckon not, Ranger. Tell him about it, ma'am."

"He's speaking the truth, Bill," came the girl's voice from the brush. "I'm captured. But don't let that interfere with your plans. Carry on. Never mind me." She laughed aloud, but the keen ears of the Ranger caught the terror in that laugh.

"Cheer up, ma'am. We ain't whipped yet!" he called. "I call your bet, Mapes. Put your proposition."

"That proposition is fer me and you alone, Ranger. Where will you meet me?"

"Wherever you say, Mapes. Behind the boulder next to the hackberry tree suits me. Come alone."

"It's a go. Me and you fer it, Ranger. If you try ary trick, my men will kill the girl, savvy?"

"I savvy, Mapes. Get a-goin'." Bill shook off the detaining hand of the protesting Van Duzen and crept toward the boulder. Rounding its smooth side, he came face to face with The Hawk. Both men tensed, their hands on their guns.

"Here we are, Mapes." Bill grinned. "Do we set down and talk or do our jawin' standin'?"

"Let's set, Douglas. How about a smoke? I shore feel the need of one."

The two men relaxed, rolled cigarettes, then waited, the same thought preventing each of them from lighting a match. The light of that match would throw into relief the head of the man who held it. Neither man trusted the other. That brief instant when the match holder

146

would be blinded by the sudden light might mean instant death.

"Never was a heavy smoker," said Bill as he regretfully tossed aside his unlit cigarette. "Hard on you, Mapes."

"You're a cheerful liar, ain't you?" growled the outlaw as he followed suit. "I bet you'd give twenty bucks fer a smoke."

"There's a heap of difference between twenty bucks and a man's life. Put your proposition, Mapes."

"I got the girl, ain't I?" sneered Mapes.

"Yeah."

"All right. You and Van Duzen give yourselves up and I turn the girl loose. Simple enough."

"It shore is. Too simple, you might say. You must think I'm loco, Mapes. Me and Doc surrender, you shoot us both, and keep the girl to boot. I reckon I still got some sense, pardner. Nuthin' doin'."

"You'll never git away alive no how, Ranger," growled the outlaw.

"No? I reckon you're wrong, Mapes. You know you're wrong. You know danged well that I kin be plumb outta this country afore mornin' if I've a mind to try it."

"But you won't try it, Douglas. You'll not leave as long as this here girl is my prisoner."

"Don't bank too strong on that, Mapes. She ain't no kinfolk to me. I reckon I'm the one to make terms here."

"She ain't kinfolk to you, Douglas, but she's a woman and you're a Texas Ranger. No Ranger ever run from trouble, so *they* claim. Put *your* proposition, mister."

"Here it is, Mapes. If I give myself up, you kill me, don't you?"

"With pleasure, Mister Ranger."

"You'll like as not kill Van Duzen, too. You want that money he's packin' in the bag."

"You don't have to be 'specially bright to guess that."

"Here's the idee, Mapes. Me and Van Duzen will give ourselves up when I see Miss Craig and Togo top that ridge yonder on the two best horses in your outfit."

"Who is Togo?"

"The little Jap feller that come with her. We wait till daylight, savvy. You and your men will stay in camp. Me and Van will stay in our place. The girl and Togo will ride away, both armed. The ridge puts them close enough to Gonzales to make it easy. They light a smoke signal when they reach the ridge. When I see the smoke, me and Van Duzen will surrender. Not till then."

"I call the bet, Ranger. We take it easy till mornin', eh?"

"A truce till mornin'," agreed Bill. "You needn't tell Miss Craig the truth, Mapes. She'd balk. Tell her I'm payin' you fifty thousand of Doc's money to turn us all loose. Tell her I've done pulled out fer Gonzales and her and Togo follers me. It's the only way she'd agree to pull out. She's game, that lady."

"I'll fix that, Ranger. I'm going back in the brush now and have a smoke. See you in the mornin', Douglas. Send the Togo gent over at daylight. Then

148

watch fer the smoke signal that Togo will light. So long!"

"So long, Mapes. See you later." Bill slipped into the shadow. When he had safely gained the shelter of the rocks, he explained the proposition to Togo and Van Duzen.

"When you top that big ridge, make a smoke signal, Togo," the Ranger finished. "Then me and Doc will give ourselves up."

"*You* may, but don't count on me, Douglas," snarled Van Duzen. "Why should I sacrifice my life for this girl?"

"You'll do it because I'll make you do it, you low-down coyote," said Bill calmly. "I don't reckon you ever did nobody a favor in your life, Van Duzen. You've sent many a poor devil to a living hell with your dope. Mebbeso, if you give yourself up like a man to save the life and honor of this girl, the big boss on the upper range won't be quite so hard on you when you come up for trial. You'll do as I say, mister, bet on that. Whether you do it of your own free will or at the point of a gun, depends on how wide that yaller streak is that runs down your back."

The three men behind the rocks settled themselves and waited for the coming of dawn.

Van Duzen, panic-stricken at the thought of surrender to the cold-blooded outlaw, grew desperate. Covertly watching Togo and the Ranger, he waited his chance. If he could only get hold of that bag that Togo was so carefully guarding! But that would be futile. Always the little Jap held the bag and its precious contents between his legs. Van Duzen edged toward the opening between the rocks. Bill and Togo were talking in low tones. Van Duzen slipped through the opening and stood erect. A spurt of flame, followed by the echoing crack of a rifle! Van Duzen crumbled, shot through the heart.

Bill and Togo, startled into action, grabbed their guns. The doctor's huddled form told its story. Bill dragged the lifeless form to one side.

"Good shootin', Mapes!" he called.

"I was hopin' it was you, Ranger," replied Mapes.

"No such luck, Mapes. You potted Van Duzen."

"A damned good riddance. He'd done played his string out at the game he was playin'. A good riddance."

"Don't know but what you're right," agreed Bill.

"Remember that fifty thousand belongs to me, Ranger. Guard it keerful."

"Shore thing. Gettin' daylight, Mapes. All set?"

"All set, Ranger. Horses saddled. I'm turnin' all of you loose for that fifty thousand *as we agreed!*"

"Can you hear me, Miss Craig?" called Bill.

"Yes, Bill," replied the girl's voice.

"Do as Mapes says. It's all right. I'm goin' to leave here by another route. A shorter one," he added, smiling grimly.

"All right, Bill. Goodbye until we meet again."

"Goodbye, ma'am . . . and good luck. If I don't see you again, remember me to Slats."

"That I will, Bill. But you'll surely stop at Gonzales, won't you?"

"Don't know as I'll get to stop anywhere until I get to the end of my trail, ma'am. Gonzales is kinda outta my way. Tell Slats howdy. So long!"

"Goodbye, Bill."

The Ranger turned to Togo. "Remember the smoke signal," he cautioned in a low tone.

"I remember. You are brave man to do this." Togo held out his hand. "I like to shake your hand, Mistah Bill, please."

Their hands clasped. "Ride like the devil, Togo. Guard her with your life. Good luck. Goodbye."

The little Jap, still wearing the huge sombrero and the red serape, slipped through the opening between the rocks. Bill saw him walk boldly toward the brush.

Presently there came the sound of horses' hoofs and Bill caught a fleeting glimpse of two riders as they rode down the cañon, disappeared in the thicket, then in a few minutes climbed the trail that led in a winding S shape up the long ridge.

The girl rode in the lead. Behind her Bill could make out the red serape and big sombrero of Togo.

It seemed hours before they gained the top of the ridge. Two tiny dots against the distant barren slope. Then a thin column of smoke rose skyward and the Ranger rose to his feet.

"All right, Mapes!" he called. "I'll show you that a Texas Ranger keeps his word."

"I'm waitin', Douglas," came the triumphant reply.

Bill stepped boldly into the open and, unbuckling his belt, let his gun drop. Then with raised hands, a smile on his lips, he walked forward. Rough hands grasped

151

him and in a second his arms were bound. Then he was led into a little clearing.

A human form, bound and gagged, threshed about on the ground. Bill gasped.

"Togo!" he cried. "What does this mean, Mapes?"

The outlaw grinned derisively. "One of my men took his place. Him and the girl will be back directly. Her and the Jap kin bury what's left of you."

"What a fool I was to think you'd play square," groaned Bill. "I hope you die slow and hard when your time comes, Mapes. I never wished that about a man before . . . and I've run ag'in' many a bad 'un. You lyin' yaller coyote!"

"Aw, quit runnin' off at the head, Ranger." Mapes accompanied the words with a slap that brought blood to the Ranger's lips. "Where's that money?"

"Where Van Duzen left it when he died, you buzzard."

Mapes turned on his heel. A moment and he was back, the leather bag in his hand. He tried to open it, but the lock held. Impatiently he drew his knife and slit it from end to end, thrusting an eager hand inside.

Suddenly the outlaw spat out a curse. Bill's jaw dropped. The gaping slit in the side showed the contents of the bag. It was filled with dry leaves!

Bill was the first to recover. "It looks like Van Duzen kinda slipped one over on you, Mapes." He laughed.

Mapes, his features working with rage, tore about like a madman. The dead body of Van Duzen was stripped, but not a trace of the money could be found. Togo and Bill were roughly searched, but to no avail.

"Mebbyso Doc hid that dough in the smokin' car," volunteered the grinning Ranger. "I throwed a bad scare into him afore we quit the train."

"And we burned the car," groaned Mapes. He turned to two of his Mexican followers. "Take this Ranger outta sight and kill him," he growled curtly.

The Mexicans grabbed Bill and, roughly shoving him, hastened to obey the command. They led him for some distance, then halted him against a big boulder. One of them grasped the open collar of the prisoner's shirt and tore it open.

"Where you get that?" whispered one of the bandits, pointing to an ugly scar on the Ranger's right shoulder.

"In France, blast you!" replied Bill defiantly. "Now quit pawing me! Stand me up against this rock and shoot me. I'll show you how a Ranger dies."

The two Mexicans exchanged a quick look. Both nodded. The one nearest Bill whispered something in Bill's ear that caused the Ranger to look at him as if he thought the Mexican had gone suddenly mad.

"You weel do that? You promise?" whispered the bandit.

Bill nodded dazedly.

"'*Sta bueno*," whispered the Mexican. Then the two bandits led the Ranger to one side and backed away, cocking their guns. Bill's back was against a thicket of brush.

The rifles of the Mexicans raised slowly. Bill looked unwaveringly into the muzzles.

Mapes, a cigarette drooping from his sneering lips, sauntered into the clearing and took his place beside the two Mexicans.

"Wanted to see how you'd die, Ranger," he sneered. "Let him have it, boys."

The two rifles raised slowly, aimed, then roared with one report! Bill Douglas swayed, then fell forward on his face, and lay still.

"Reckon I'll give him one fer luck," said Mapes, drawing his .45 as he walked toward the motionless form of the Ranger.

"*Buenos días, Señor* Hawk!" called a voice.

Mapes whirled in his tracks to see the khaki-clad Chávez step from the other side of the brush. Behind the smiling bandit came Slats, but so changed, a Slats that Mapes had to look at twice to recognize him. The Ranger was momentarily forgotten.

"What are you doin' here, Chávez?" he growled suspiciously. "And what is that Hadley *hombre* taggin' you fer? He's a prisoner?"

"*Señor* Hadley *was* prisoner," corrected Chávez, smiling pleasantly. "Not now. Ees my very good frien' now, my *amigo*, my boddy, *sabe*? Because of that, I am come to play thees double-cross game weeth the *Señor* Hawk. I 'ave decide to geeve my *amigo*, the *Señor* Hadley, the part of the fifty thousan' dollars that belong to you. I 'ope you do not objec', *Señor* Hawk. Because, eef you objec', I mus' shoot you."

"So that's it, eh?" snarled Mapes. "Well, you'll have to find the dough first. Van Duzen slipped it over on us. The bag was full of dead leaves."

154

"So?" Chávez shrugged. "Ees too bad. I 'ope you are not lie to me, *Señor* Hawk. Ees not 'ealthy to lie to me."

"Ask the Mexicans," insisted Mapes. "They'll tell you I'm not lying."

The Mexicans vouched for the truth of the leader's statement. Chávez frowned, then shrugged away his disappointment easily.

"*Señor* Hadley," he said, turning to Slats, "I'm through weeth heem. Ask your questions."

"Where is Josephine Craig?" Slats hoarsely broke his silence.

"Far enough away so's you can't find her," Mapes sneered. "Look here, mister, what call have you got to horn in and ask questions? I'm holdin' that lady fer ransom, savvy? And I'm holdin' you fer the same reason. Chávez must be drunk or loco or both. I'm boss here. I run this spread and I run it with a six-gun. Chávez, you yaller-hided little polecat, you're my meat."

The Hawk's .45 exploded at his hip, its slug ripping open the cheek of the nimble Chávez who had side-stepped like a streak of light. The carbine in the Mexican's hands spurted flame and Mapes fell, a crimson stain covering the small black hole between his eyes.

Blowing the smoke from his gun barrel, Chávez turned to one of the Mexicans.

"You 'ave carry out my order about thees Beel Douglas?" he asked. "Thees Ranger have thees scar on the shoulder?"

"*Sí, señor*," came the quick reply.

He nodded toward the huddled form of the Ranger. "You tell heem to drop when you shoot? You tell heem that your bullets weel not hit heem?"

"*Sí.*"

"Then why ees he lay so still?"

"He bomp hees head on the rock when he fall, señor," explained the guard. "The bomp put heem to sleep. See, the *Señor* Ranger ees begin to wake up."

CHAPTER
FOURTEEN

"Powder River! A mile wide and a foot deep!" called Chávez, his dark eyes moist and his voice choking with emotion. "Sergeant Beel Douglas! Cut the ropes on Beel's arms, *pronto! Santa María*, it ees good to see you!"

"Chávez! You danged little banty rooster! Where did you come from? You fire-eatin' lil' ole son-of-a-gun! And gosh a'mighty if it ain't Slats! What's the idee?" The Ranger, his arms free again, held out a hand of welcome, his face alight with pleasure.

For a time all was a confusion of laughter and hearty, if somewhat profane greeting. Then the Ranger sobered.

"Reckon we'd better be hittin' the trail, boys," he advised. "Miss Craig's somewhere in these hills with one of The Hawk's *paisanos*. Togo's in the brush yonder, Slats. Better untie the little beggar afore he strangles tryin' to git loose."

The Ranger and Slats released the Jap, and after several seconds of explosive and picturesque Japanese profanity Togo was able to give a lucid account of his capture. He had been seized, bound, and gagged, and a

Mexican substituted for him. The girl, too, had been gagged and her feet lashed to the stirrups.

Chávez, during Togo's recital, had gathered his men and given them brief orders to scatter into the hills. News of the *rurales'* approach hastened their departure. Scarcely had the men departed when the keen eyes of Chávez picked up the little group of riders that was swiftly descending the steep trail. Calling to the Americans, Chávez pointed out the approaching riders.

"They're bringin' back Miss Craig, too," said Bill. "Thank God, she's safe!"

"Amen to that," chimed in Slats fervently. He turned to Chávez. "What's your program, buddy?"

The khaki-clad shoulders lifted in a shrug. "*¿Quién sabe?* First, I weesh to see the face of thees *rurale* captain w'en he see you an' me here. Then I weel play game weeth thees stupid captain. Do not geeve me away, *señores*. Remember, I weel talk to heem een English that you weel onderstan'. He 'ave 'ow many men weeth heem? Five? *Bueno*."

Chávez seated himself on a boulder and rolled a cigarette, humming softly. The two Americans and the Jap waited impatiently for the arrival of the *rurales*.

"Bill," said Slats in an undertone, "they'll shoot Chávez down like a dog. We can't allow that, you know."

"I reckon not," agreed the Ranger. "I got an ace up my sleeve. I'll play it if I have to. The danged little wildcat, he shore is nervy."

Came a sudden crackling of brush and the *rurales*, headed by the dapper captain, burst into the clearing, their carbines ready for action. They stopped short as they saw the little group. The captain frowned in a puzzled manner. He started as he saw Chávez and Slats, then, quickly recovering his composure, smiled silkily. His speech was directed to the Ranger.

"Perhaps you can explain the meaning of this odd assemblage, Ranger Douglas? I expected to find The Hawk here."

"And yonder he is, Captain," said Bill. "Where's Miss Craig?"

"Here I am, Bill!" called a voice, and Josephine Craig jerked free from the *rurale* who held her, half laughing, half crying as she sped across the clearing toward the Ranger.

"Jo," croaked Slats. "Don't you know me?"

Josephine halted abruptly. For an instant she gazed horror-stricken at the disreputable-looking figure under the sombrero. Then with a cry she was in his arms.

"'*Sta bueno*," said Chávez, rising and tossing away his half-smoked cigarette. He turned to the captain of *rurales*. "*Señor Capitán*, eet ees gran' pleasure to meet again, no? You 'ave five men. *Bueno*. Behin' thees rocks and een the brosh are ten of my *hombres*. All good shots. All brave. At thees minute, *señor*, ten guns are cover you, waiting for the order to shoot. Raise the han's, *Señor Capitán! ¡Pronto!*" Chávez barked out the command. The captain raised his hands. His men followed suit.

159

Chávez turned to Slats. "Collect the guns, *Señor* Boddy, eef you please!"

"Hope to tell you I will," said Slats. "Just a minute, Jo. Have to lend my comrade-in-arms a hand."

When a neat stack of carbines and side arms decorated the ground, Slats again took his place beside Josephine.

Bill Douglas looked uneasy as he built a smoke. Togo, grinning like an ape, never took his eyes from his beloved mistress.

"Dismount, *Señor Capitán*," directed Chávez. "That ees better. Now tell the men to dismount and face the brosh."

"You mean to shoot us?" asked the captain, showing no trace of fear or excitement.

"My men weel shoot the *hombres* yonder. I 'ave the pleasure and honor of shooting you myself. There ees one way to save your life."

"What is that way?" snapped the captain.

"Join my band. I make you lieutenant."

"I prefer to die like a gentleman rather than live like an outlaw. Shoot!" The captain stood stiffly at attention.

"Gad, these chaps are game, Jo," whispered Slats. "When Greek meets Greek, eh?"

"Before you die, I weesh to tell you that you 'ave made one bad mistake about the *Señor* Hadley. Per'aps you know that by now, eh?"

The captain nodded. "My apologies, *Señor* Hadley." He smiled.

"Thanks," replied Slats dryly.

"*Señor Capitán*, you are brave man. Ver' brave man. Ees pleasure to meet one who ees so brave like that. There ees only one theeng which ees finer. That ees brave man who know how to show mercy. I am teach you that lesson now. Take your men and ride to Gonzales without stop. We weel not meet again, *señor*. Tonight I leave Mexico. I go far away. Just where, I do not know. I am tire of being outlaw. Ees not for a brave man to be hunted like wild animal. Do not forget the lesson which I 'ave teach you, *señor*. Go!"

"No! Shoot me! I will not be disgraced by you. I . . ."

"You would rather be stubborn like the mule, eh?" snapped Chávez. "You would rather sacrifice the life of five brave men who 'ave follow you faithfully! So? Excuse, but you are peeg-head fool, *Señor Capitán*. Always, from a boy, you are stupid. I, who 'ave play weeth you then, remember you are stupid. Bah! Get on your 'orse and go 'ome!"

"Turn my men loose. Then shoot me," protested the captain stubbornly.

"No! All go or all die! W'ich you choose, *señor?*" Chávez was toying with his gun.

The captain, reading the look of appeal in five pairs of dark eyes, shrugged his shoulders. "I accept, *Señor* Chávez. I and my men thank you for your generosity. You are brave . . . and merciful." With a stiff salute the captain swung into his saddle.

"Always he 'as been that way," murmured Chávez softly, not without admiration for the pompous little captain with his waxed moustache and polished sword. "My love to the *señora* an' the small ones, *Capitán*."

The captain grunted as if struck a hard blow. Then he smiled. "Always, you were the lucky one, Eduardo," he returned.

There came the clatter of shod hoofs, the crash of brush, and a group of *rurales* burst into view, halting as they perceived their commander.

"The bandits have taken to the hills, *Capitán*," announced the man in charge, speaking in his own language. "We have searched the cañon on the way here. Not a one is left!"

With an exclamation of surprise, the captain turned to Chávez. That gentleman was smiling ruefully. Turning to Slats, he made a grimace.

"Jus' when I 'ave things going my way, thees 'appen. Well, ees something to've bloff thees stupid captain, eh, *amigo?*"

"Where are your men, Chávez?" whispered Slats.

"Long ago they 'ave gone to the 'ills. That was beeg lie that I tell about the ten men. Bloff, that ees all. And now the bloff ees call." He raised his hands in the air in token of surrender.

With a superior smile playing about his lips, the *rurale* captain gave an order to bind the prisoner.

"Hold on, pardner!" It was Bill Douglas who spoke. The Ranger stepped in front of Chávez. The *rurales* halted in their tracks.

"The Chávez gent is my prisoner, Captain." Bill's right hand caressed the butt of a .45. "I aim to take him back to the States. I hope we don't have to argue the question."

Slats had gently pushed Josephine behind a boulder. Then, thrusting an extra gun into Togo's hand, he and the Jap stepped alongside the Ranger.

"This is very unusual, *señores*," announced the captain.

"Kinda," admitted the Ranger. "Nevertheless, what I said, goes. Chávez is my prisoner and I aim to keep him."

An odd light came into the *rurale* captain's eyes. "'*Sta bueno, señor*. But a moment ago you saw me taught a lesson in mercy. I wish to prove that I have learned that lesson well, stupid as my friend of boyhood days claims I am. I turn Eduardo Martínez Chávez over to you." It was the girl, strangely enough, toward whom the captain turned his eyes, awaiting approval.

Josephine, clapping her hands, laughed her appreciation. "Bravo, Captain! Never have I seen such bravery and courtesy! When you come to New York, you will hunt us up, promise?"

"It is with the greatest pleasure that I promise, *señorita*." A quick salute, a curt command, and the captain at the head of his troop rode into the brush.

"I played the ace and it worked, Slats," said Bill, heaving a sigh of relief. "When do you want to escape, Chávez, old-timer?"

"When the *rurales* are 'cross the ridge, then I weel get the 'orse een the brosh and go. Tonight I weel cross the border into Arizona. There ees *hacienda* there. The old *paisano* who ees own the ranch 'ave many cattle. I myself help heem steal them. To heem I weel go and say . . . 'I 'ave finish fighting.' I weel marry the daughter and, w'at you call heem, settle up. "

"Settle down," corrected Slats. "But I thought Dolores cured you?"

"Almos'." Chávez smiled. "I weel go find the horse now." With a bow, he left.

Slats and Josephine were too busy talking to notice the departure of the still grinning Togo. So it seemed at least to Bill Douglas, who now shook his head as if deeply puzzled. He was wondering what that "deaf and dumb" message was that Togo and the girl had exchanged just before the Jap slipped out of sight. He had not long to wait for the solution.

"*Señorita, señores*, I thank you. Per'aps, when I 'ave settle *down*, you weel come to the *Hacienda* Chávez." The bundle in his hand he swung into the saddle. "*Adiós*, my frien's."

He whirled his horse and with a wave of his hand was gone.

"Wonder what he had in that bundle?" mused Bill aloud. "He acted like it was shore valuable."

"That was his wedding present from all of us," volunteered Josephine, a tantalizing brightness behind the tears that dimmed her gaze. "The fifty thousand dollars that belonged to Van Duzen. Togo had it hidden. He told me a moment ago, using the sign language I learned while nursing in France. I knew you'd all approve of the gift. None of us wanted the blood money. But the taint on it will not trouble Mister Chávez."

"I reckon not," agreed Bill. "Come on, Togo, let's rustle some grub. Them two folks might be able to git along without it fer a week or two yet, but I'm hungry."

From the distance came a sweet tenor voice, the voice of Chávez, soldier of fortune, as he rode away to his new life.

"What a sweet song," murmured Josephine. "I wonder what the words mean?"

"It is wonderful to be alive," answered Slats softly. "But it is more wonderful to be alive and in love. Those are the words, dear."

High Jack and Low

"High Jack and Low" first appeared in *Action Stories* (3/25). In it Coburn brought back for an encore the characters of Texas Ranger Bill Douglas and Eduardo Martínez Chávez who had figured so prominently in "South of the Law Line". "High Jack and Low" was later reprinted under the title "Hell on the Prod" in *Action Stories* (9/36).

CHAPTER
ONE

"Unlucky at love, lucky weeth cards! *Amigo*, thees man who 'ave say that ees dam' liar."

With a shrug of his well-shaped shoulders, Eduardo Martínez Chávez rose from the card table. In his slender brown hand was the deuce of spades. He tossed it across the table to the grinning American.

"Low," he grimaced.

"High jack, and game for me." Snowshoe Slade grinned. "Judging by the manner in which you play your cards, you must have learned the game of seven-up from an inmate of a state asylum."

Chávez smiled through the haze of blue cigarette smoke. There was a reminiscent gleam in his dark eyes as he looked down at his companion.

"Per'aps, *señor*. Per'aps that one who teach me thees seven-down game *ees* leetle bit loco. *¿Quién sabe?* Ees dead now, that one."

"Dead?" prompted the American when Chávez did not go on.

"*Sí*. And one should not speak bad of the dead, no? Loco? Per'aps, but ees brave man, that one. I salute heem!"

169

His spurred heels clicked together, the lithe form stiffened, and the right arm of Eduardo Martínez Chávez, soldier of fortune, raised in a perfect salute to one Corporal Mike Murphy, dead hero of the Argonne.

Snowshoe Slade, man of parts and many aliases, shifted uneasily in his chair and reached for a bottle of tequila. Not until he had gulped down a generous drink of the liquor did he speak.

"You're a queer one, Chávez. Who was this bird who was so brave and where did you learn that salute?" Slade's cold gray eyes surveyed Chávez suspiciously from beneath lowered lids. Things military annoyed Slade. They stirred up those dregs of a cup that had grown bitter as gall to his thin lips. For Templeton Slade was, and had been for several long, bitter years, a man without a country.

"Thees bird? That salute? We do not talk of that, señor." Chávez smiled.

"Why not?" Slade sneered, cold fury behind his mask-like face.

"Because of reasons personal, eef you please. And onless you are more foolish than I theenk, you weel let the gun stay where eet ees, Señor Slade."

The Mexican's white teeth flashed in a smile. As if by some magical power, a gun had appeared in his hand and its muzzle was carelessly covering the American.

Slade bit his lip. Slowly, under the watchful eye of Chávez, his right hand came away from the automatic.

170

"Ees ver' bad, thees gun play, eh, *amigo? Adiós.*"

With a smooth, unbroken movement, the gun was shoved back in its holster. The Mexican's left hand, holding a husk cigarette, waved a careless *adieu*, and with a tinkle of spurs and the *click-click* of high boot heels Chávez swaggered gracefully through the door of the *cantina*, out into the dusty street of Madrone.

Beneath his huge sombrero, his eyes smoldered with some inner burning flame. "Ees bad one, that *Señor* Slade," he muttered, then dismissed the offender with a shrug.

The sun had set and the long, purple shadows of the Southwest twilight were softening the harsh outlines of the squat adobe houses that lay scattered among the yucca trees. From somewhere in the distance came the strumming of a guitar and the voice of a girl singing a love song.

A soft smile playing about his lips, Chávez strolled in the direction from whence the music came. A moment later and he was standing in the entrance to a wide patio, hat in hand.

The haze of sunset still lingered in the patio, lending an air of enchantment to its humble adobe walls and red tiles worn uneven by countless bare and booted feet. In a corner of the patio, on a bench beneath a chinaberry tree, sat a girl. Head tilted, she gazed dreamily into space. Her slender fingers swept across the guitar strings.

Like the glorious bloom of the cactus flower in the midst of a drab desert, so grew María Nuñez, daughter

171

of old Julian Nuñez who spent his days plaiting rawhide ropes and quirts beneath the chinaberry tree. María, fairest by far of all the *señoritas* that one met in a week of riding in any direction. María, with the voice of a songbird and a rippling laugh that reminded one of the little silver bell that hung around the neck of *Padre* José's fat burro. María, whose tortillas were thin as paper and melted in one's mouth before they could be swallowed, whose chicken and chili had been praised by *el presidente* himself when that gentleman had stayed at Madrone to hide from the rebels.

Just whether it was the red lips and dusky eyes of *Señorita* María, or her laugh, or her singing, or her chili, that drew Eduardo Martínez Chávez as a magnet draws a needle, no one except Eduardo himself could have told. And Eduardo would have lied even then, lied like the *caballero* he was, gallantly. For, if the truth be known, it was the lean and wrinkled father of María who he came to see so often.

Did these two not spend hour upon hour beneath the chinaberry tree, smoking dozens of husk cigarettes, while they conversed in so low a tone that even María, her shapely ear pressed against the closed door ten feet away, could scarcely make out a word? Surely.

This was very annoying to María, for it piqued her vanity. Why not? Was she not beautiful? Had not every *vaquero* on the range paid court to her, braving the heat of the desert and the wrath of their *gringo* wagon boss when they lingered overlong? And now this Eduardo, this gamecock of whom much was whispered, chose to spend his hours in solemn talk with old Julian instead of basking in the sun of her radiant beauty! It was annoying.

She looked up with a petulant frown as she perceived him standing in the doorway.

"*Señorita*." Eduardo bowed low, sweeping the worn tiles with the brim of his huge sombrero. "Your music is as the music of angels," he told her. "Your eyes, the . . ."

"Shame on you, *Señor* Chávez," she checked him with a petulant stamp of her foot. "Is it not the teaching of *Padre* José that it is very wrong to lie? Think you that I am so stupid, then, as not to know that it is not I, but my father, who you come to see?"

Chávez laughed softly. "But he is not home this evening, that father you speak of. But half an hour ago I saw him ride forth on the south trail. A wise man is Julian Nuñez and one learns much by talking with him. But *pouff!* One cannot spend all his days and nights acquiring wisdom. There must be other hours when, instead of sitting quietly with the solemn face of the prairie owl, one dances and laughs, no?"

He crossed the patio to seat himself on the edge of the bench. María eyed him with mock disapproval, then laughed gaily.

"You speak after the manner of the *Americano*, the *Señor* Slade."

"He comes here?" Chávez frowned.

"Why not? And he is not so ill-mannered as some I know of. He does not spend all his hours whispering

173

and nodding. He has very nice manners . . . for a *gringo*."

"So?" He frowned thoughtfully at the toe of his polished boot.

María, vastly pleased at what she read to be jealous in the face of the man on the bench beside her, went gaily on. "Very nice manners. Did he not spend hours teaching me the words of a *gringo* love song? Listen, I will sing it for you."

Accompanying herself on the guitar, she sang:

I want a little bungalow
Where the red, red roses grow.
I want to make it nice and cozy,
Just big enough for me and Rosie.

"For Rosie, not María." Eduardo laughed. "These *gringos* make love so clumsily, no? But what does the *Señor* Slade have to talk about when he converses with your father, little one?"

María shrugged. "And how should I know? Think you that I have time to listen while they sit in the shade and talk and talk until one would think their tongues will surely wag themselves off and drop on the tiles? After all, the *gringo* is little better than you . . . you who come, so you say, to sing, but can find nothing to talk of but money and revolutions and *rurales* and smuggling!"

At the last word, she faced him, her dark eyes blazing.

"Smuggling?" Chávez eyed her sharply.

174

"That is what I said, stupid one. And some fine day the captain of *rurales* will find out and you and the *Señor Americano* will be stood against the adobe wall behind the fort and shot."

"So? And the *Señor* Julian Nuñez, your father? What of him?"

"Oh, he will come to me and say . . . 'Chiquita, make eyes at that *capitán* of *rurales*. Smile at him. Weep against his red coat. And save the hide of your poor old father, who is a good man and does no harm.' Save his hide that he may sit once more beneath the chinaberry tree and make riatas for the *vaqueros*. Have I not done it before? Did I not hide in the mesquite near that adobe wall and weep and pray for the souls of Pedro Navarro and Francisco Gonzales and cover my ears when the *rurales* fired their carbines? And does not *Padre* José tell me that the soul of my father will be surely lost if he does not mend his ways and confess his sins and do penance as he should?"

Behind the palm of his hand, Eduardo smiled. He was learning much — much that he suspected, to be sure, but it was gratifying to have one's suspicions verified. Slade, then, had lied. And in a like manner the wily father of María Nuñez had strayed far from the path of truth in some of his statements. Having learned all that he wished to know, Chávez turned with a shrug from business to the lighter amusement of lovemaking.

"Who is it now, who speaks of owlish things?" he chided her, careful not to remind her that not a word of money or revolutions or smuggling had passed his lips since he had entered the patio. Wise, far wise beyond his station in life, was Eduardo Martínez Chávez.

"Come." He smiled. "Let us not soil the beauty of such a night with such chatter. *Señor Diós* made these moons for lovemaking, and it would be no less than a sin to use such an evening otherwise."

Again came the strumming of the guitar. Now it was the man who played and it was his voice that sang Mexican love songs.

The twilight gave way to the star-dotted, moonlit night. In the deep shadow of the old tree the forms of man and girl moved closer on the bench. Eduardo's singing took on a softer note.

Beyond the wall of the patio, Snowshoe Slade, immaculate in white flannels, gave way to fervent American profanity. Heedless now of the yellow dust that was soiling his white canvas shoes, he made his way to the *cantina* to drown his disappointment in a bottle of tequila.

It took several drinks to put him in a better mood. He bent his thoughts on a plan to humble this cocksure Mexican who was so expert with gun and guitar. So engrossed was he in his plotting that he failed to notice the entrance of a tall, broad-shouldered American in worn cowpuncher garb.

The newcomer leaned idly against the bar, toying with his glass of mescal. Using the Spanish language with a fluency that spoke of years spent along the border, he was making inquiries regarding a place to stable his horse and was asking about the hotel

176

accommodations. The black-mustached bartender was giving the desired information.

The Mexican *vaqueros* in the place eyed the American a bit curiously. It was unusual for an American, even a cowpuncher, to be traveling alone in this rebel-infested part of the state. One or two of the Mexicans edged unobtrusively toward the rear door.

"Who is the *gringo?*" asked one of these. "Me, I don't like his looks. He wears his gun too low. And he holds his glass in the left hand. He looks for trouble, no?"

"*¿Quién sabe?*" returned another, loath to leave the place until he knew more of the strange *gringo*, yet burdened with the conscience of stolen cattle. True, he had confessed his sins to *Padre* José, but these *gringos* were a godless lot and knew not the meaning of a *vaquero*'s penance. They would laugh at one's atonement for past deeds, and turn you over to the *rurales*.

But the big American apparently came on a peaceful mission. He paid them no more heed than if they were so many goats.

Slade, sensing something unusual, looked up, his hand instinctively stealing to his automatic.

The big American at the bar had turned his back. Slade eyed the broad shoulders speculatively, frowning as he perceived the low-hung .45 and the tanned hand that rested idly near the weapon, thumb hooked in the heavy cartridge belt. There was something vaguely familiar about that broad back, something in the careless attitude of the cowpuncher that stirred the

177

renegade's memory. Then Slade stiffened. The man at the bar was watching him in the dusty mirror that adorned the backbar. Dim as the light was, he could make out the newcomer's tanned features.

For a moment Slade sat there, his jaw muscles tight. Then, with an air of bravado, he quit his seat and strolled to the bar, ranging himself alongside the cowpuncher.

"Drink up, Bill Douglas," invited Slade, a thin sneer on his lips. "Drink up and have one on me."

Bill Douglas, Texas Ranger and all-around cowhand, faced his fellow countryman coldly.

"I don't recollect your name, *hombre*," he said slowly. "But I mind where and when I seen you. You're one of that bunch that hung around Juárez, ain't you? Did I understand you to say you was askin' me to drink? I reckon not. I reckon it was my imagination. Yeah, reckon it must've bin. Don't trip over that dog yonder when you go back to your table."

"You're too damned good to drink with me, eh?" sneered Slade.

"You guessed it, mister," said Bill coldly. "I've knowed some gents that didn't never take a drink with a colored man. Others draws the line at Mexes. But I never could savvy their viewpoint. There's only one color line that I draw. It's the line that divides off them with a yaller streak down their backs. Get me?"

"I get you, Douglas. I get you more ways than one." Slade was white-lipped with fury. The fiery liquor had made him overbold and a dangerous foe. And the cold butt of the automatic added to his courage.

"Meanin'?" asked the Ranger, holding the gaze of Slade's bloodshot eyes.

"Meaning that your damned American law and your pretty tin star don't count here in Madrone. Down here, I'm as good as you are. Better, my friend, because the Mexicans hate a Ranger and I'm among friends."

"Yeah?" Douglas grinned. "But don't forget this. Down here, a man is as good as the speed he uses in limberin' up his gun. You might claim every *peón* in the place fer a pardner, but their friendship won't be much use to you if you can't beat me to the draw. Kinda mill that around in your skull, mister, afore you start into action with that popgun you got your hand on."

Douglas used the same tone that a tolerant parent might use in correcting a disobedient child. Grinning derisively, he made as if to turn his back on Slade.

White with rage, Slade whipped out his automatic, then dropped it with a yell of anguish as Douglas flipped the glass in his left hand so that the burning mescal shot squarely into the eyes of the slacker.

As if by magic, Bill's .45 had appeared in his hand. Still grinning, he faced the crowd of Mexicans. "The *gringo* yonder said he had friends here," he told them in their own language. "He lied, perhaps?"

Slade, half blinded by the stinging liquor, groped in his pockets for a handkerchief, cursing with rage.

Bill kicked Slade's automatic into a corner. Well he knew that there was more than one man present who hated the very words Texas Ranger — men who were as ready as Slade to burn gunpowder. He saw in half a dozen pairs of dark eyes that smoldering flame of undying hatred. Others, too, who would give their last *peso* to see this Ranger put away. Bill Douglas retreated, step by step, until his back touched the adobe wall. Still that smile hovered about his lips — a smile that gave lie to the steely light that flickered in his eyes.

Slade, his eyes still smarting with pain, took his place with the crowd that faced the lone Ranger.

"Shoot him, some of you with your guns already cocked! Don't let him bluff you! We're fifteen to one against him. He hasn't a friend in the place!"

"But one!" The voice came from the doorway. A deep-toned, sonorous voice. It belonged to a short, heavily built man clad in the dust-coated garb of a monk. Tanned a deep bronze, travel worn, yet jovial, was this man of God who stood in the doorway.

"*Padre* José!" gasped a *peón*, removing his hat.

"Who else?" replied the *padre*, overhearing the exclamation. "And it would seem that my arrival was well timed, no? Pedro, put away that knife. And you! And you!"

His pudgy forefinger singled out the very men who Bill had regarded as most dangerous. Ignoring Slade, he turned to the Ranger, his dark eyes twinkling humorously.

"You choose big odds, son. Either you have partaken too freely of Madrone's mescal, or else you are a Ranger."

180

"I wasted my only drink on yonder gent in the white pants, Father." Bill smiled. "I'd like to thank you fer savin' my hide. I *was* overmatched some." He sheathed his gun and grinned amiably at the *padre*, who nodded understandingly.

The *vaqueros*, uneasy under the frowning gaze of the corpulent *padre*, shifted about as if to hide behind one another. Then, as they saw the frown fade before his smile, they grinned sheepishly.

"Come, *Señor* Ranger," he said to Bill. "At the end of the street is my humble adobe. You will do me the honor of being my guest?"

Bill nodded in blank astonishment and, mumbling his thanks, followed the *padre* outside.

CHAPTER
TWO

"You have come to Madrone for a purpose, no?" *Padre* José smiled when he and the Ranger had partaken of a hearty supper.

"Why do you think so?" asked Bill.

"Texas Rangers usually travel for a purpose. It must be a grave mission that brings you to so dangerous a territory as this poor harassed state of Sonora. You men of the Rangers carry a sinister reputation, *señor*. Yet" — *Padre* José smiled reflectively, his eyes twinkling as he looked into the frank eyes of the American — "there are those among my people who say that there is much good to be said of you." He chuckled, wagging his short forefinger at the American. "I came by way of Caliente, *Señor* Ranger. Tell me, what became of your bed and provisions that your pack horse carried?"

Bill laughed embarrassedly. "You know, *Padre?*"

"I was in Caliente but two days ago. I halted on the trail to baptize the newborn child of a woodcutter. They told me of how a man who answers your description spent the night there. They told me how you had helped bring that child into the world. How you had sat up with them all night tending to the wants of the mother, feeding them from your stock of food. How the mother had no bed on which to lie and how you had given her your bed. The blessing of those poor *peónes* goes with you, *señor*. And with it goes the blessing of *Padre* José."

Tears stood in the *padre*'s eyes. Bill shifted uncomfortably.

"Shucks, sir, it wa'n't no more'n any man would've done. They was starvin'. You was askin' why I was here in Madrone. I've a mind to tell you, Father." Unconsciously Bill had lapsed into his own tongue.

"Perhaps I can help you," replied the *padre* in English. "It concerns the smuggling of opium?"

"You're a plumb good guesser, Father."

"We who carry the cross learn much, son. My vows do bind me to secrecy, as you know. Yet I can tell you this much, *señor*. Your mission is a dangerous one. Desperately dangerous. And hopeless, I fear. Six months ago I could have helped you stamp out these lawless ones who traffic in the sleeping death. But now . . . *quién sabe?*" He shook his head sadly.

"You speak strangely, sir," Bill replied in Spanish. "What change has come about in the past six months?"

"It is that countryman of yours that you met but a few hours since. The *Señor* Slade."

"He's no countryman of mine," Bill said.

"So be it, son. Yet here in Madrone, this man is not without a following. He has money and an oily tongue, that *hombre*. Well do I know that. The *pesos* that the *vaqueros* used to give the Church are now spent across the bar. Instead of spending their money for Masses for their dead, they lose it in gambling games. And, *Señor*

183

Ranger, they have ten times the number of *pesos* that they had six months ago. Where but a few *centavos* were wont to jingle in their pockets, now silver dollars of your rich country weight them down. Why? Because, my son, this man without a country has shown them how to smuggle this dream drug across the border. Do not underestimate the power of this Slade *hombre, señor.*"

Bill nodded gravely. "Slade, eh? *Hmm,* so this is the Snowshoe Slade gent, eh?"

"Snowshoe Slade?"

Bill laughed mirthlessly. "Cocaine is called snow across the border, Father. This Slade snake invented a hollow-soled, hollow-heeled shoe to carry the stuff across the line. That was in Juárez. I've seen a pair of these shoes that the boys at the customs office had taken off a dope peddler. He squealed on Slade, but Slade pulled out afore they grabbed him. I didn't connect the name with this bird till now. But these *hombres* must have a slick way of hiding the stuff. I've bin stopping every man that crossed the border between Black Mesa and Diablo Cañon, and I haven't found an ounce of hop. Knowin' that the stuff must be comin' by way of Madrone, I rode over to look around."

Padre José nodded. "There is one other trail that leads across the border, so the Indians say. The Pass of the White Buzzard. It is a treacherous trail, scarcely the width of a man's two hands in places. And sheer cliffs with sharp rocks hundreds of feet below. The Indians claim it is guarded by a white buzzard with a blood-red head that picks out the eyes of man or beast that travel it. All the money in Sonora would not be enough to hire an Indian to cross that pass."

"A white buzzard, eh? They must be dreamin'."

"I think not, son. There is such a bird. I know, for I have seen it. But as to the bird's war-like nature, I cannot say. No more than I can be sure just where the narrow trail leads. But I have it from the lips of one who I have never known to lie, that these things are true. And he, of all the men in the state of Sonora, should be the one to know of such a pass. He is an odd mixture of saint and Satan, that Chávez. A patriot to the last drop of his red blood. But, withal, a man who stands in dire need of spiritual guidance.

"It was to administer the last sacrament to one of his band that I negotiated the first part of that narrow trail. I shudder at the thought of it even now. Bad enough to travel such a path in the light of day, but at night! Picture a man of my bulk, señor, perched atop of a pony on such a trail! One believes in one's God at such times, señor. Thrice over did I say my rosary as that limber-legged animal scrambled on in the inky darkness. And ahead of me on the trail, this same devil-may-care Eduardo Chávez, singing love songs to the stars and talking of fiestas and revolutions and such nonsense with the same easy speech he might have used in traveling the King's Highway.

"And well did I scold him when we reached the camp. Yet, of all the men in Mexico, I love him best, that scatter-brained *caballero*. He has the heart of pure gold for all his pretending that he is wicked. Have I not confessed him? Do I not know?"

"Eduardo Martínez Chávez?" Bill smiled.

"You know him, then?"

"As well as a man can who has been under shrapnel fire in the same trench. A soldier, Father. A brave man and as true a friend as a man could ask for."

"Then you are Bill Douglas." The *padre* laughed. "Eduardo has spent hours in telling me of Sergeant Bill Douglas. It is a great pleasure to know such a hero."

Again Bill flushed with embarrassment. "I reckon that blamed little rooster has bin talkin' a lot of nonsense."

"I think not, son. For all his crowing, that rooster says much of the truth."

"Where is he now? I thought he had married and settled down."

Padre José laughed softly. "Married? Not he. No less than a dozen times has that rascal caused me a weary journey to perform his marriage ceremony. Each time it was a different *señorita*. And each time we were too late. The girl had married someone of more domestic temperament. Where is he now? In the hills, if the *rurales* are in town. If they are away, he is no doubt paying court to the daughter of Julian Nuñez, a stone's throw down the street. He is like your will-o'-the-wisp, that Eduardo." Again *Padre*

186

José chuckled until his paunch shook and tears streamed down his fat cheeks. It was plain that he loved this lawless rascal.

"He's bin bustin' the laws again?"

"Eduardo does not call it such. He is dreaming of freeing the state of Sonora. A futile dream, to be sure. The dream of an idealist. The mad hope of one whose love of freedom has blinded him to the overwhelming opposition that he faces. The federal government now in power has put a price on his head. The *rurales* have chased him until their horses gave out. Other rebel forces, mercenary and power-loving leaders, have sought to annihilate him and his men. But without success. It is like a pack of overfed hounds chasing the fox. Mexico would do well to enlist him as chief of their army, for he is a born leader and a wily tactician. Possibly they could persuade him to join them if they would put it to him in the right light. I have all but arranged a conference between one of Mexico's best statesmen and Chávez. It is my fondest hope that I may bring peace to Sonora through such a meeting. With Eduardo Chávez at the head of the Sonora army these rebel leaders would not dare to carry on their high-handed slaughter. They are without soul, these leaders. Even I am not safe among them. *Señor* Douglas, you have great influence with our Eduardo. Perhaps, if you could talk to him . . . ?"

"I'll do it, Father, if the chance comes up. Texas would give a heap to see a man like Chávez at the head of things down here. By Texas, I mean the United States, *sabe?*"

The hands of *padre* and Ranger met in a hearty handclasp.

"And now, my son, it is best that you leave Madrone. This Slade and his men are like snakes in the grass. They strike when least expected. Even the house of *Padre* José is not sanctuary to them. It is best that you ride out under cover of darkness. Head east toward the Black Mesa. At the *hacienda* near the foot of the mesa you will find shelter, if you tell them that I sent you and that you are friend to Eduardo Chávez. As for your mission, watch both the trail that winds across the lava bed on the mesa, and the Pass of the White Buzzard. *Adiós, amigo.* God be with you, for you are a brave man and fight on the side of humanity."

The *padre* let Bill out a rear entrance. The Ranger saddled his horse and was soon lost to sight along the brush-flanked trail that led eastward toward the jagged mountain peaks.

CHAPTER
THREE

The words of the Mexican love song, softly sung and vibrant with the pleading of an ardent wooer, sounded sweetly indeed to the ears of María Nuñez. Not altogether in vain was the plea of Eduardo Martínez Chávez as he sang his story of love after the manner of the true *caballero*.

Suddenly, swiftly approaching down the deserted street, came the *thud* of horses' hoofs.

"The *rurales*," whispered María. "May the saints protect you, Eduardo."

Chávez laid aside the guitar with a shrug of annoyance, his right hand falling to the butt of his gun.

"Always they are the grand nuisance, those *hombres*," he mused aloud. "You care then, María, what becomes of the Eduardo who has been so bold as to speak of love to one so beautiful."

"Yes, yes! But you are in danger! They will surely shoot you, Eduardo! Only but a few days ago did I hear *el capitán* vow that he would have you stood against the wall before the next new moon came. They have halted outside! The walls are too high for . . ."

Eduardo, his white teeth flashing in a smile, picked up a heavy cloak that lay on the bench. "What manner of gown is this, *chiquita*?" he whispered.

"It is the robe of the good *padre*, which I have been mending."

"*¡'Sta bueno!*" Chávez smiled, slipping into the brown garment and pulling the hooded cowl over his head. "Look you, beautiful one, do I not pass well in this dim light?"

"It is sacrilege! No good can come of such a thing!" protested the girl.

The abrupt entrance of half a dozen men stayed Eduardo's reply, but he winked at her as he pulled the cowl so as to throw his face into the shadow.

White moonlight bathed the patio, falling squarely on the robed figure that stepped from beneath the shadow of the chinaberry tree. The *rurale* captain, a trim, erect youth of military bearing, saluted stiffly, his boot heels clicking. A handsome and dashing enough man to quicken the pulse of any *señorita* was *el capitán* of the *rurales*. Straight-featured, olive-skinned, clean-shaven save for the tiny jet mustache waxed to needle points, he showed the Castilian strain of hot-blooded parentage. Gallant in love, brave in battle, a fit leader for these red-coated riders whose courage is a byword in the Southwest.

"*¡Buenas tardes, padre!*" he called. "We thought to find another here."

"It is my pleasure that you meet with disappointment, *Señor Capitán*," replied Chávez in a well-disguised voice. "For if that one you seek were here, I

190

should be elsewhere perhaps, and thus be deprived of the great honor of meeting so brave a soldier as this *muy bravo capitán* of *rurales*, of whom the whole of *Méjico* speaks praise."

"You flatter me, *Padre*." The captain smiled, not a little pleased at the compliment. "You are a stranger. You have come far, no?"

"Far, indeed, *Señor Capitán*, and the journey from Guadalajara is a weary one."

Chávez paused. As he perceived that the captain's glance dwelt on María, he smiled. The dark eyes twinkled in the shadow of the cowl.

"It is my great pleasure to bring you a message, *señor*," he went suavely on. "A message from your family. It is with great joy that I tell you that the *señora*, your wife, is in excellent health. A bit overweight, perhaps, but such things cannot be helped. The four children also are quite well."

The captain flushed crimson. Not without ample cause, for he had spent more than several evenings under that chinaberry tree with María Nuñez and not once had he so much as hinted of a fat wife and four children. Inwardly condemning this talkative *padre* to a warmer region, he bowed stiffly.

"You must be weary from your journey, *Padre*," he hinted. "The adobe of *Padre* José is but a few steps down the road. He will be pleased to share his lodgings. Stand aside, *hombres*, and let the good *padre* go his way." He added in English: "Odd, indeed, where that devil of a Chávez could have disappeared."

191

"Peace be to you, my children," chanted the grinning Eduardo in so perfect an imitation of *Padre* José that María caught herself bowing to the blessing.

Head bowed on his breast, hands hidden in the wide sleeves of his gown, Chávez stepped toward the doorway of the patio.

The *rurale* captain, still hot with the embarrassment of his recent exposure, stepped aside to allow the supposed *padre* to pass. Suddenly he frowned. There was a swagger in the gait of the cloaked figure that ill fitted the calling of a *padre*. Moreover, beneath that gown of coarse brown cloth showed a pair of extremely high-heeled boots to which were fastened silver-crusted, huge-roweled spurs that chimed like bells at each step.

"Stop him!" barked the captain. "Stop him, men!"

He leaped forward as he gave the command. His left hand tore away the gown, revealing the fancy garb of a *caballero*.

Like a flicker of flame from the gray ashes of a buried campfire, the scarlet-clad Chávez leaped from the folds of the somber-hued cloak. The *rurales*, more sluggish of wit than their leader, stood stupefied at the revelation. One of them, rather from instinct than otherwise, swung his carbine upward, thumb pulling back the hammer. A streak of white light as a keen-bladed knife left Eduardo's left hand. The *rurale*, with a startled cry, let go his gun, the weapon exploding harmlessly. That slender, keen-bladed knife was now hidden to the hilt in the forearm of the horrified *rurale*.

Chávez whirled to face the captain, who stood erect, the *padre*'s gown in his left hand, an army automatic in his right.

Eduardo's .45 and the army automatic were on a level. Like two gaily feathered gamecocks the two faced one another.

"*¡Madre de Diós!*" screamed María, suddenly roused from the paralysis of fear that held her. The next moment she stood squarely between the leveled guns.

The *rurales*, now galvanized into action, blocked the exit.

"*Diablo*," muttered Eduardo, then gracefully covering his chagrin with a smile, tossed his gun to the ground.

"We have forgotten the *señorita*, eh, *Señor Capitán*? It is not the way of a *caballero* to be killing *hombres* in the presence of one so beautiful. *Señor*, you have made me prisoner, no?"

"We crave your pardon, *señorita*." The captain smiled, not to be outdone by any strutting gamecock of an outlaw. "I would not stain the tiles of your patio with the blood of such carrion." He laughed musically. "Like the gay-colored butterfly coming from a dusty cocoon, the *hombre* yonder emerges from his sackcloth. Better to have stayed in the cocoon, gay-colored one. Your red wings will be scorched, I fear. Scorched by burning gunpowder."

Chávez smiled, then grimaced at María, who was sobbing softly.

"You were right, *chiquita*," he told her regretfully. "No good comes of profaning the garb of the Church. Still, if the cloak had been but a foot more in length . . . ?" He turned from María to the captain. "The adobe wall, sunrise, eh, *amigo*?"

The captain nodded briefly. "It will be my great pleasure to give the command to fire. You have caused me much worry, Eduardo."

Chávez shrugged. "But not once, *Señor Capitán*, have my men ever killed a *rurale*. More than once have I looked along my carbine sights to find you at the other end. Yet, always have I lowered my gun and let you ride along your foolish way, stiff in your saddle like a soldier on parade. Why have I done this? Because of that wife and children you have leave back at Guadalajara, *amigo*. With you dead, who would buy the sandals for those four small ones? Who would pay for those red slippers with the very high heels for the *señora*? A new pair every two weeks since she has grown heavier and runs the heels over like a bow-legged *gringo vaquero*? Have you told the *Señorita María* of her, *Señor Capitán*? How you and the poor Eduardo Martínez Chávez did sing beneath her window, night after night, each trying to sing the other into hoarseness? And how her old buzzard of a father would chase me away because, while my singing was better, just so was my pocketbook more flat than that of my rival? Tell me, *amigo*, do you support that old buzzard? If so I . . ."

194

"Off with the cackling parrot!" snapped the red-faced captain, scowling ferociously as he saw grins on the lips of more than one of his men.

"*Adiós, señorita.*" Chávez smiled, sweeping the tiles with his sombrero. "I have forgotten to tell you, *chiquita*. One of the guitar strings is almost worn in two. *Adiós*. And if your heart is kind, pray for the soul of your poor Eduardo." He stiffened with a snap, adjusted his sombrero, and plucked the cigarette from the lips of a grinning member of the *rurales*.

Humming softly, he strolled away with his guards, the captain following pompously.

In the shadow of the *cantina* an interested spectator watched the little procession that marched along the dusty street to vanish behind the high wall of the jail. The spectator was Snowshoe Slade. A sinister smile twitching the corners of his thin-lipped mouth, he waited until the *rurales* and their prisoner were hidden from view. Then he slipped along the shadow and entered the adobe house where he lived. Swiftly he shed his white flannels and donned rougher clothes. Riding breeches and boots, a dark flannel shirt, and a jumper replaced the finer garments. Lastly a well-filled cartridge belt and holster were strapped about his middle. A second automatic nestled in the holster, a mate to the gun that he had retrieved from the *cantina* floor and now wore in a shoulder holster under his left armpit. Plainly Slade wished to be well armed for what business lay ahead.

A scant ten minutes later he was in the saddle, riding along a dim trail that led across the desert.

"Neat work, tipping the *rurales* off to the Chávez bird." He chuckled. "Serves the cocky little greaser right, damn him. Call my hand, will he? Take my girl away from me, eh? Not without paying for it, my black-and-tan friend. You'll find that Snowshoe Slade has brains. We'll get along very nicely without you, laddie. Old Julian will win over your band of merry cutthroats to our side. And when I'm through with that old paddle foot, I'll slip the gaff to him. Then, my María, you and I will see the world. London, Paris, Buenos Aires! Lights, music, wine! And the United States can go to the devil!" His well-kept hand caressed an automatic. "And I'll make buzzard bait out of a meddlesome bird named William Douglas!"

CHAPTER
FOUR

Against the moonlit sky showed clearly the gaunt, bare limbs of a Joshua tree. The Devil's Pitchfork, the *peónes* call it, because of the two limbs that branch skyward from the bare trunk, giving it the appearance of a mammoth, three-tined fork. This sole specimen of vegetation but added to the desolation of the desert. Nearby, gleaming silver in the light of the moon, was a water hole. Here converged a score of trails that came from every point of the compass.

Near the water hole burned a tiny campfire and beside it squatted a tall, gaunt form wrapped in a faded serape. The man's lean face showed but dimly beneath the huge sombrero. Only when he pulled deeply at the husk cigarette and the ash glowed were the hawk-like features visible.

A lean brown hand left the carbine on his crossed legs to throw a mesquite stick on the fire. The rekindled blaze revealed a saddled horse, reins dropped on the ground, nibbling half-heartedly at the sparse grass at the edge of the water hole.

"*Diablo*," muttered the man in the serape. "A curse on the sluggards for keeping an old man waiting on a night so chilly. Fools, do they think that Julian Nuñez is but a common *peón* to be kept waiting? Ah!"

He cocked his head sideways like an animal to catch the faint sounds that broke the silence of the desert night. Then, with the inbred caution of a hunted animal, he left the fire to take his stand behind the Joshua tree, carbine ready.

The *swish* of a catclaw limb as it raked against bull-hide chaps, the *pad-pad* of a horse's hoofs in the sand. And the next moment a lone rider loomed against the skyline.

"*¡Buenas tardes, señor!*" called the rider, halting his horse before he came into the radius of firelight.

Julian Nuñez, his bushy brows knit in a scowl, made no answer save to shift his carbine so that the gun covered the newcomer.

"Come from behind the tree, *hombre!*" called the rider pleasantly. "Do you not know that I can see you? And this gun in my hand is cocked. Quick, *hombre*, step out or I pull the trigger. I ask no quarrel, but if you don't move out from behind that tree, I'll shoot. A bullet would pass through its trunk like a pebble through a sheet of paper. Step out! *¡Pronto!*"

"*Madre*," grumbled old Julian as he quit his hiding place. "You would not shoot one so old? You have the eyes of an owl, *Señor Americano.*"

"Sure." Bill Douglas grinned, for it was the Ranger who had ridden up so boldly. "I need to have. Who are you, *señor*, and why do you hide?"

"I am but a weary old man who has halted here to let my horse eat and to take the cramps out of my old bones while I smoke. As for hiding, one must be careful in a country traveled at night by outlaws and robbers who have no respect for gray hairs and no mercy for one whose pockets are as empty as his paunch. Perhaps you are one of these, *quién sabe*? But you will find me poor pickings, *señor*. Look you at my ragged clothes, my worn sandals. Do I look like one who can pay ransom? May the saints . . ."

"Where is your pack horse?" asked Bill suspiciously. "Have you come from so short a distance that you need no food or bed?"

"My serape is my bed. I come from far off, a stranger, chased from his home by the cursed rebels, who have killed my family and run off my stock," he whined.

A liar of no mean ability was old Julian, father of María. Bill found himself in sympathy with this skinny old bag of bones that stood shivering in the chill night.

The tremor in the old man's limbs, however, was not altogether due to the night air. He was nervous in the presence of this strange *gringo* who rode so boldly up to strange campfires and so coolly called one from behind trees. Wise in the ways of that fearless band known as Texas Rangers, Julian drew his own conclusions as to the calling of the fearless *gringo*. A Ranger, surely. What brought him here? "You are riding for cattle, perhaps?" he put his thoughts in subtle question.

"Perhaps," came the answer.

"That is well," returned Julian, hiding his chagrin with a shrug of his lean shoulders. He walked to the fire and, squatting, spread stiff fingers above the blaze. "That is well," he went on. "For if you were, perhaps, a Ranger, I should fear greatly for your safety."

"So? Why, old man? Why should a Ranger be in danger?"

"Because," lied old Julian glibly as he lowered his voice, "you are not the only rider who has stopped at this water hole within the hour. Others ride the trail tonight, señor."

"So?"

"Did not two men halt here for water? They were drunk, those two, and were loose of tongue because of it. They talked of smuggling and of crossing the border by way of the Pass of the White Buzzard."

From the shadow of his great sombrero, the old fox covertly watched the American's face, smiling inwardly as he saw the man grow suddenly stern.

"How long since these two were here? Answer with the truth, hombre, or I'll leave you here for the buzzards."

"A scant half hour before you came. They rode by way of that trail that leads to that pass of the evil spirits that is guarded by the great white bird with head of blood. Madre, but these are terrible times for one who loves peace. Is there no place where an old man can spend his remaining days in quiet? My cattle, my horses, my family taken from me. May the Señor Dios look down upon me this night and have mercy! May the saints — "

But Bill Douglas waited no longer. He interrupted the old Mexican by throwing him a handful of silver.

"Madrone is but two hours from here, old one. The *padre* there will take care of you. *Adiós*."

He whirled his horse and rode on into the night along the trail indicated by the old man.

Once more alone beside his fire, old Julian grinned wickedly as he counted the silver coins in his lap. Two of them he tested with his teeth before slipping them into the buckskin sack that he tied and replaced in his waistband beneath his soiled, ragged cotton shirt.

Before he had finished a second cigarette, he was once more sent scurrying to his hiding place behind the Joshua tree.

Snowshoe Slade, accompanied by three heavily armed Mexicans, halted beside the fire and swung to the ground. Behind them came two more armed riders, each leading a light-burdened pack horse of slender, race-stock build.

"Dammit," snarled Slade impatiently. "Come out from behind that tree, Julian. Your skinny elbows stick out on either side of it like you were wigwagging somebody. Shake a leg, we're late."

With what dignity he could muster, old Julian did as he was bid and took his place by the fire.

"Trail clear?" snapped Slade.

"But for one," announced Julian. "A *gringo*. A Ranger, by his looks."

"You sent him to . . . ?"

"To the Pass of the White Buzzard." Old Julian grinned. "*¿'Sta bueno, no?*"

"Yes, if those blasted guards are on the look-out as they're supposed to be. They'll have him dead and

201

stripped of everything he carries by the time we get there. And they'd better grab him if they want to see the sun of another day."

"Where is Chávez?" asked Julian.

"In jail. The *rurales* grabbed him while he was making silly love to María instead of tending to business."

"Eduardo arrested? That means they will shoot him at sunrise. And we need his protection in the hills."

Julian's voice ended in a wail of misery. The three Mexicans with Slade nodded in sympathy.

"A man would think that that half-portion spick was the president of Mexico," sneered Slade.

He spoke in English, musing aloud rather than addressing his remarks to his companions.

"*¡Sí, sí!*" exclaimed one of them, understanding but a part of Slade's speech. "Our Eduardo would make a damned excellent *presidente! Sí.* Tonight we should ride down on Madrone and tear that jail to dust, no? *¡Viva Chávez!*"

"Aw, dry up," sighed Slade. "We haven't time to pull any grandstand stuff. There's half a million or more of hop in those packs. And it goes across the border tomorrow night, get me? That means we cross the Buzzard Pass tonight while there's a moon and a clear trail. We haven't the time to fool with Chávez. He should have known better than to let himself get trapped."

An angry growl from the Mexicans caused Slade to step back, his hand on his automatic. Across the fire he faced the scowling followers of the imprisoned Eduardo.

"Keep your shirts on," he changed his tactics quickly. "He isn't going to be shot at sunrise. I heard the *rurale* captain promise María that he would not shoot Eduardo till next week at the earliest. He wants to question him regarding the rebel forces and find out how this hop is crossing the line." He paused to let the lie take effect.

"Eduardo will never tell!" said one of the Mexicans proudly. "No torture could make him! Ah, but he will fool them, those stupid *rurales*. He is like that, our Eduardo."

"Of course," agreed Slade easily. "And would he have us play the fool and lose the profits of two weeks' dangerous labor getting the stuff this far? Of course not. He passed within arm's reach of where I stood when they led him to jail. He winked at me and whispered . . . 'Carry on.'"

"*Viva Chávez*," called one of his men softly. "And in three days we can be back. We will have money, too. We will send word to the men who hide in the hills. We will gather all our forces. Then we will take that town of Madrone and that night we will all get very drunk and celebrate."

"Now you're talking sense," rejoined Slade in a relieved tone.

"Perhaps I should go back to tell Eduardo of our plans," suggested old Julian. "I will have María go to the jail and tell him."

"You'll do nothing of the kind," put in Slade hastily. "We need you tonight. Those men in the hills will not let us pass, unless you talk to them. They obey only the orders of Chávez. You, who know them all, can explain and they will let us by. Come, we're losing time. We need every minute of moonlight on that trail over the pass."

Julian obeyed grumblingly. These long rides were little to his liking. He had not planned on so long a journey. His part had simply been to stay at the water hole at the Devil's Pitchfork and see that the trail ahead was clear. Yet, he realized the logic of Slade's argument. Those men of Eduardo's were a faithful lot, and it would need much tact and diplomacy to get the cavalcade past the guards without verbal orders from their leader. There was money to be had from this journey. Much money. Enough to keep him and María in luxuries for many a day. A trip on fine mules, even to Mexico City, and there to parade the streets, well clothed and mounted, to play the *don*.

"'*Sta bueno*. I will go. But mind you, *señor*, I turn back at the pass when they have let you by."

Slade nodded curtly and swung into the saddle. Julian kicked dirt on the fire and followed suit, his thoughts filled with visions of grand clothes, a silver-trimmed saddle and bridle to put on those sleek mules that he would buy. Perhaps, in Mexico City, he could marry María to some very wealthy official who would make him head of the police. The chill of the night air was, for a time, forgotten and under his faded cotton shirt the heart of Julian Nuñez beat happily. He even raised his voice in a cracked baritone until Slade put a stop to the noise.

Ahead, a broken, jagged line against the star-filled sky, were the peaks that marked the Pass of the White Buzzard.

CHAPTER
FIVE

I wonder if that danged old paisano *was lying?* Bill Douglas mused as he pushed his horse to a trot. Carefully he gave the matter thought. And the more he pondered, the more suspicious he became.

There were tracks on the trail, to be sure, but in the course of an hour's travel he had not found a single sign proving that men or horses had traveled it within the past day.

The old Mexican, if he had lied, had acted his part well. The old man's actions seemed sincere enough. Yet something told the Ranger that he had been sent on a false trail. Years of border service had taught the Ranger to trust no man, Mexicans least of all, when he rode the long trail in quest of human quarry.

Why should this old man betray his fellow countrymen to a gringo? reasoned Bill. *If no men traveled that trail to the pass, why had he sent a Ranger in that direction?*

The answer to that mental query was self-evident. Either the men traveled another trail or had not yet arrived at the water hole by the Joshua tree. Bill halted to debate the question.

I've got men watching the line between Black Mesa and Diablo Cañon. Not even a jackass rabbit can cross there without bein' spotted. This White Buzzard trail is the only open lane and I reckon it's up to me to cork that up. Hmm. I'd bet a new hat that there're men a-layin' along this trail somewhere to stop gents like me as I ride along. That old paddle-footed pilau was aimin' to send me into a trap, looks like. All right, old-timer, I'm a-strivin' my purtiest to make your sweetest dreams come true. Trap and be damned, you yaller-bellied hop-runners. I'm as good fer as many as I got shells in my guns. If it's fireworks you're cravin', here's at you.

With a reckless laugh the Ranger pushed on, whistling a Mexican love song to the rhythm of his horse's hoofs.

Men said of Bill Douglas that he was the most foolhardy man in the Ranger force, which was saying a good deal. The *peónes* claimed that this hard-riding, hard-fighting *gringo* bore a charmed life and would quote incident after incident where he had more than proved the truth of their assertion. Did he not hold in contempt even the most feared outlaws south of the line? Did he not cross the border, time after time, on the trail of Mexicans who had fled to those hills that were as home to them? Had he not always come back from those hunts with his man? *Sí.* And more than twice or three times that wanted one had returned lashed to his saddle. Not sitting in it, but lying across it. Dead.

The inhabitants of the towns these dead ones had terrorized had lined the streets, awe-stricken, while this grim-lipped, hard-eyed enforcer of United States law and order had ridden through without paying them so much as a glance. And twice, when he had thus ridden at a walk along their main street, there had been bloodstains on his clothes and his face had been drawn with pain and loss of blood. A Mexican would have died of those wounds. Even a tough *gringo vaquero* who, as everyone knew, was tougher than a piece of jerked bull meat, could not have lived with so many bullets in him. Did not that prove, beyond all doubt, that this *muy bravo* Ranger bore a charmed life?

Had he so chosen, Bill Douglas could have corrected this belief in his supernatural hold on life. He could have told them of probing for those bullets embedded in his flesh. Probing and fishing them out before the blood poisoning had set in. A less nervy man would have ridden those miles to the nearest doctor and no doubt died from poisoning. Likewise he could have told them of ministering *padres* and Indians who had cared for his wounds.

He felt no fear as he rode alone into the jaws of that trap he knew was waiting, only an intoxicating exhilaration that went to his head, like wine. His unsheathed carbine across his saddle pommel, his .45 within easy reach, he rode boldly along the trail, whistling gaily.

"*Santa María*," growled a waiting picket as he crouched in the brush and pinched the coal of his cigarette between grimy thumb and forefinger. "*Santa María*, but someone has grown loco or perhaps drunk to make such a racket. Hear the noisy one, Felipe?"

"Like the yelping of the coyote," agreed Felipe, caressing his carbine. "Drunk, sure. Let us hope that the greedy fool has some of the liquor left. These nights are chilly."

"Supposing this whistling one is an enemy?"

"Shoot first and ask our questions later." Felipe grinned evilly. "Aim for the belly. This light is not so good for careful shooting."

"*Sí.*"

On came the Ranger, carefree as a schoolboy. Yet, for all his seeming carelessness, his eyes were never dull. More than often, he watched the ears of his horse. He was watching them now as he rode along that twisting trail that threaded through the brush.

The horse's head suddenly lifted. The twitching ears cocked forward, furry, sensitive points. Still unbroken came the whistle from the Ranger's lips as he eased his right foot from the stirrup and gripped his carbine. With his horse still traveling at a running walk, Bill slid easily to the ground. The horse went a couple of paces, then halted as if by command. Head erect, eyes and ears pointed toward a dark patch of brush ahead, the animal stood.

Bill unsnapped his chaps and left them on the ground. Then his whistle died away carelessly as if he had forgotten the tune. Carbine ready, he crawled with the swift silence of a mountain lion toward the brush patch.

Seconds passed. A minute. Two minutes. The guards eyed each other in uneasy silence.

"His horse has stopped, Felipe," came a guarded whisper.

"Perhaps the fool has grown sleepy and got off to sleep. *Diablo*, this is not to my liking, *amigo*."

"Nor mine. Suppose you slip through the mesquite toward where the whistling came from?"

"Go yourself, *hombre*. I tell you, something is wrong. In my bones, I feel it. *Diablo* take that loco whistler. Friend or not, he tastes the lead of Felipe's gun."

"It may be that chattering cousin of yours. It would be like him to be playing a joke. Better to hold your fire until we're sure."

"Cousin or not, he'll pay for such loco fooling. Besides, I have more cousins. Ones who owe me no money. Shoot him, *amigo*, if he breaks brush again. *Santa* Clara, what's become of the fool?"

The two shifted farther into the shadow. The silence was growing unbearable. Felipe, backing into the brush with silent caution, suddenly stiffened with horror. Some hard object that felt much like a carbine barrel had jabbed him between the shoulder blades.

"Make a noise, either of you, and I'll shoot!" came the sharp command in Spanish.

"¡*Madre de Dios!*" gasped Felipe, and twisted like a cat. The rifle barrel thudded against his head and he went down in a heap.

"Reach fer sky, *hombre!*" snapped Bill, grinning as he watched Felipe's companion obey.

210

With swift movements, Bill bound his prisoners. Felipe, but slightly stunned from his blow, groaned and opened his eyes.

"Now, *hombres*, me 'n' you will make medicine," announced the Ranger. "Better talk or I'll whittle on you till you do."

He opened his pocket knife and whetted it on his boot.

CHAPTER
SIX

"But, *Padre*," sobbed María Nuñez, tears streaming down her pretty cheeks, "they mean to shoot Eduardo. That captain who has lied to me about those children and that wife, he told Eduardo that he would do the shooting himself. He is a cruel man and one who knows not the meaning of truth, that captain. Has he not sung to me and made his pretty speeches? *Sí.* And not once, not a single time, did he say that he had a fat wife with red slippers, new ones each week. And many children. You should have seen him, *Padre* José, when our Eduardo told him of those things while he was wearing your cloak."

"My cloak? What nonsense is this, child? I myself am wearing my clothes. A *rurale* captain wearing my gown? *Tush*, child."

"Not the captain! Eduardo! The gown that I was mending for you. And Eduardo would surely have killed that lying rascal, too, when he laid sacrilegious hands on such a sacred garment. But I kept him from it. And just where I had mended it, the threads are again broken loose. May *el diablo* take that peddler who said that thread would not break. Twenty-five *centavos* did he charge me for a single spool of it and a

212

blind man with half an eye can see that it is older than the chinaberry tree in the patio, which is over a hundred years old, and was planted by . . ."

"Hush, child, hush. Think you that even a *padre* of my years can make sense of such chatter of thread and chinaberry trees and everyone a liar and no head or tail to the whole thing? Is it for such nonsense that you rouse an old man from his slumber?"

"For my Eduardo, who makes such beautiful love, I should rouse *el presidente* himself and make him . . ." Suddenly abashed at her temerity, María flushed crimson and lapsed into embarrassed silence.

Padre José gave a sigh of relief as he fastened his sandals to his bare feet. He understood now that the gallant Eduardo had been singing love songs and somehow had gotten into trouble. His corpulent frame shook with suppressed mirth. Tears washed the sleep from his eyes as he sat erect, puffed a time or two, and wagged a fat forefinger under María's nose.

"And when do you two think to be married, eh?"

"When we have gotten Eduardo out of jail." Again she broke into a fit of wailing that brought a look of consternation into the good *padre*'s dark eyes.

"My Bible is on yonder table, child. Bring it. And my hat with it."

"You're going to Eduardo?"

"What else. And wipe those tears from your eyes, child. It is not well that a bride should be weeping."

"Bride?" gasped María.

"Exactly. Before you are an hour older, María, you shall be the wife of Eduardo Martínez Chávez, who is undoubtedly the best-beloved rascal that ever strummed a guitar beneath a *señorita*'s windows. This time he shall not fool me."

"Fool you? I do not understand, *Señor Padre*." María was laughing excitedly as she patted her mass of jet hair into place and smoothed her dress.

"Nor did I intend you should, child. That is something between that Eduardo and me."

"You have come to administer the last sacrament to my prisoner?" the captain said.

He looked coldly at María. He was still angry at having been caught.

Padre José shook his head. "It is a far more pleasing task than that which brings the *Señorita* María and me here."

The captain frowned. "So?"

"Eduardo has often told me how you two boys had been raised together." The *padre* smiled. "It will no doubt give him great pleasure to have you present when he marries María."

The captain's frown deepened. "You have come to jest, perhaps."

"Does this blushing child appear to be jesting, Captain?"

"You must know that Eduardo Chávez will be shot at sunrise. What good can come of marrying a man who has but a few hours to say his beads before he dies? A ghastly mockery of marriage, that."

"But surely, *Señor Capitán*," pleaded María earnestly, "you would not shoot the husband of one

214

who you have so often sworn to move the earth itself to please. Set him free and I promise to forget those times when you made so much love to me that you forgot those wives and children at Guadalajara."

"One wife," corrected the captain stiffly. "I would have made mention of it had it come to my mind. Spare that Chávez? That fighting rooster who has done his best to upset our government? You speak the language of the loco, girl. And you, *Padre* José, you know the law."

"All too well, son," agreed the priest. "A law that is written in blood. You are a man of education. Can you not temper this harsh justice with mercy? Can you not see that such an act of generous mercy would do more than a dozen battles toward a truce between the government and these misguided patriots who call Eduardo Chávez their leader? News of such a deed would travel like a prairie fire and men who now hate you would call you friend."

"And the governor would immediately kick me out and replace me with a man made of sterner stuff. You plead well for that rascal, *Padre*, but I must do my duty as I see it. Chávez dies against the adobe wall at sunrise. No amount of pleading can change my mind."

"So be it, *Señor Capitán*," said the old *padre* sadly. "You will allow us to see the prisoner?"

"Most surely." The captain rose, straightened his jacket, and smiled pleasantly. "This absurd ceremony of marriage was but a joke, eh?"

"No. Tomorrow's sunrise makes María a widow."

In uneasy silence, the *rurale* captain led the way to the iron-grilled cell door.

Eduardo greeted the trio with a look of surprise. Yet he made no comment when the girl and the *padre* were ushered into the cell. The captain locked the door, bowed stiffly, and made his way back along the dim-lit corridor to his office. The guard at the door, at a curt command, followed his leader. Eduardo and his guests were left alone.

In the flickering light of a solitary candle, Eduardo faced his guests. "Well?" he said.

"This must be fast," said the *padre*.

María giggled.

CHAPTER
SEVEN

His feet propped on his desk, the captain of *rurales* dozed. An hour passed. Two hours. The battered alarm clock on the desk ticked off the minutes of a third hour. It was a few minutes past three now and still the *padre* and the bride had not come out of the cell.

In the doorway a sleepy guard rubbed flakes of tobacco in his heavy-lidded eyes to sting them into wakefulness.

"Perhaps I should walk back along that corridor to the cell where they still talk, *Señor Capitán?*" he ventured.

"I think not." The captain yawned. "The man dies at sunrise. Let him spend his last hours in peace. When *Padre* José calls, let him and the girl out. I'm off for bed."

His booted feet swung to the floor, spurs jingling. Yawning, he strode out into the starlit night and down the street to his quarters.

The guard waited until the captain was gone, then helped himself to a cigar from the box on the desk. He had just settled himself in his superior's chair when the *padre*'s voice brought him to his feet.

217

With a grunt of impatience, he picked up his gun and strode down the corridor. Inside the death cell stood the *padre*. Leaning heavily on his arm was a mantilla-draped form that trembled with convulsive sobbing.

The guard glanced about in quest of the prisoner. At first glance he saw nothing. Then he perceived a gaily clad form lying face downward on the cot in the corner.

"Asleep," whispered the *padre*. "It is well not to disturb one who has but a short time to live. Unlock the door quietly, guard."

"*Sí, sí,*" whispered the guard, eager to be quit of his visitors so that he might occupy the captain's chair again and tickle his own vanity by playing that he was the commander instead of one who took orders. He let them into the corridor, fidgeting a bit as the sobs became louder under the mantilla.

A moment and the *padre* was outside the jail, escorting his companion, who leaned heavily on his arm.

"These skirts are the devil's own contrivance, *Señor Padre,*" came a muffled voice from under the heavy mantilla. "And these infernal slippers are squeezing the blood from my feet."

The *padre* chuckled. "Hush, Eduardo. We're not far enough away to be safe. You might sob as we pass along the street. Gently, mind you. There are *rurales* in town and they know not the meaning of sleep, those nighthawks."

Not until the two had gained the safety of the *padre*'s house did Eduardo kick off the slippers that had caused him so much agony. The mantilla cast aside, he made a ludicrous figure in his feminine array.

"Are there no men's clothes about, *Señor Padre*?"

"None. Change your clothes when you reach your camp. And remember your promises to me and your bride."

Chávez shrugged resignedly. "Married! Still, it is better, no doubt, than being shot. Time will tell. Eduardo Chávez keeps his word, count on that. And I do love the girl."

"I should hope so, rascal."

"No harm will come to her for this night's work?"

"Rest easy, my son. I shall be there when the guard and the captain open the cell door. I would not miss that for a king's crown. And unless I read men wrong, our *el capitán* will come to my way of thinking when I tell him of our plans. I wish the American Ranger could be here when you return."

"What American Ranger?"

"Douglas. Your friend who was in the big war with you. I forgot to tell you he was here in this room but a few hours ago."

"¡*Santa* Clara! Bill Douglas? Here? What for?"

"He was after news of the drug smugglers. He went on."

"¡*Madre!* Which trail?"

"He took the trail that leads to the Pass of the White Buzzard."

"Alone?"

"*Sí*. I told him to head for the *hacienda* of our friends."

"Tonight?"

"When else? What is wrong?"

"This, *Señor Padre*. Those men of whom we spoke in the cell, they are planning to travel that trail tonight. They are bad men, some of them. *Muy malo hombres* who will kill before they ask questions. Even now he may be squarely into the trap. I must go. *Adiós, amigo*."

"Remember the promises, my son. And do not forget this. The happiness of a woman and the honor of a priest rest with you. Keep sacred those trusts. God be with you. *Adiós*, my son."

Out under the stars, Eduardo Martínez Chávez pushed his horse to a swift gait and laughed joyously. Ahead lay danger, perhaps death, for he rode on a strange mission. Danger never failed to thrill this gay adventurer and the night promised much. Besides, was he not wed to María? The thought of Bill Douglas sobered him. His hand dropped hipward, to pause as it brushed the folds of the skirt he still wore. He realized with a feeling of dismay that he was unarmed. Unarmed and ridiculously clothed in woman's garments.

"*¡Madre!* It is one hell of a fix, no?" he muttered, then laughed at himself. Twisting, dodging along the crooked trail, his finery ripped to shreds by raking catclaw limbs and mesquite thorns, he rode with reckless abandon.

"This happiness of a woman, this honor of a *padre*," he mused aloud, "rests with me, eh? 'Sta bueno. Also, this life of my boddy, Bill Douglas, it is also up to me, you bet. Pray, *Padre* José. Pray like hell. Eduardo is in need of many prayers, sure. But more than that, he needs a gun. It's a damned good thing I ride the fastest *caballo* in Sonora."

He dodged a mesquite limb that missed his head by a scant three inches.

"Who goes?" barked a hoarse voice. Eduardo's horse slid to a halt.

"Chávez!"

"'*Sta bueno, Capitán*." The voice sounded unconvincing. Plainly, the challenger was a bit skeptical as to the rider's identity.

Chávez, speaking sharply, quickly quelled the man's suspicions and a shadowy form came from the brush.

"Undress, *amigo*," commanded Chávez, swinging to the ground. "I have need of clothes and a gun. *Pronto*, slow one. *¡Madre!* Never mind the reason for these silly clothes. Pants. Boots. A shirt, *hombre*. *Pronto*, hear me, or I'll pull them off you like a man skinning a banana."

Speaking as he pulled on the man's clothes, Eduardo explained his method of escape. "Slade? The dream tobacco that is to be smuggled? Where are they, *hombre*?" he asked.

"Well on the way to the pass. They traveled fast. Old Nuñez went along. I stayed back here to cover the trail in case they were followed. We'll need to be careful. A Ranger rides the trails."

"I know. What became of him?"

"Old Nuñez sent him into the trap. A wise old fox, that Julian. He . . ."

Chávez waited no longer. He was in the saddle and away before the astonished guard could finish.

Shivering in his underwear, the guard swore fervently at his leader and with much disgust wrapped the mantilla about his shoulders. Still, it was more than an honor to have one's leader borrow one's clothes. This thought served to comfort him as he sought his serape that he had left on his saddle. Thus garbed, he settled himself as best he could to ponder on the vagaries of his commander, chuckling even as he shivered.

CHAPTER
EIGHT

"Let me ketch either of you *hombres* in a lie and I'll jest nacherally whittle out your gizzards, *sabe?*" Bill Douglas prodded Felipe with the needlepoint of his long-bladed stock knife.

Felipe cringed.

"*¿Sabe?*" growled the Ranger ferociously, suppressing a grin as he saw how frightened Felipe had become.

"*Sí, sí, señor.*"

"Then we'd orter git on plumb pleasant. Where's that hop?"

"No *sabe.*" Felipe looked puzzled.

Bill put the question in Spanish, making it clear. Felipe and his companion exchanged looks of frightened desperation. The Ranger's knife prodded Felipe in the ribs.

"Come clean, *amigo*, and make it fast. I'm a busy man."

"Ees not yet come, thees hop," groaned Felipe.

"No? You're expectin' it soon?"

"Soon, *señor.* Tonight some time. Per'aps . . ."

Felipe went ashen gray. Clear on the night air sounded the nicker of a traveling horse. Felipe's mount, tied in the brush, gave answer.

Without a second's hesitation, Bill acted. Gags were shoved into the mouths of the prisoners, and with a hand grasping the shirt collars of each he dragged them into the brush. With cocked gun and narrowed eyes, the Ranger waited the coming of the smugglers.

The creaking of saddle leather, the jingle of bit chains and spurs. Then the cavalcade swung into view, halting in a little clearing not twenty paces from where Bill crouched. The Ranger nodded grimly as a match flared to light a cigarette and revealed the lean features of the old Mexican of the Devil's Pitchfork.

"Felipe should be here," growled a Mexican impatiently. "The horse nickered. *Diablo* take such guards. Does he think we have eternity to cross the pass?"

The Ranger's glance lit on the slim-barreled pack horses. The light packs could mean but one thing. Opium. Bill counted five Mexicans beside old Julian. He was disappointed at not seeing Slade who he strongly suspected of being the brains of the smuggling band.

Suddenly, from the lips of one of the Mexicans, came a shrill whistle, twice repeated.

Signaling for Felipe and his pardner, Bill thought, and grinned as he shifted his position slightly. Then he raised his gun to cover the group.

"Hands up!" he barked harshly without showing himself. "*Pronto, hombres*, or I shoot!"

"*Madre de Dios*," groaned old Julian, "the *gringo*." He reached skyward without wasting time. His companions followed suit.

"One of you at a time, now," Bill commanded gruffly. "Step off your hoss and shed your guns. You first, old liar of a paddle-footed *pilau!* You, old buzzard, I will kill," he bluffed, "unless you give me a truthful answer to one question. I'll know if you're lyin', so don't try it again. Is Slade the head gent of this gang?"

"He is, damn you!" snapped a voice from the brush. The words were punctuated by the roar of a gun.

Bill Douglas whirled as the leaden slug crashed through his right shoulder. The gun dropped from his hand. Unarmed now, he leaped for a horse. A second and he was in the saddle, flattened against the animal's neck.

A second shot came from Slade's gun. The leaping horse crashed to its knees and pitched over, pinning Bill underneath. A threshing of hoofs as the mortally wounded animal twisted and lay still. Bill's head met a rock and he lost consciousness.

"Drag the dirty spy out from under the horse, one of you brave warriors," sneered Slade, reloading his gun. "You don't need to be so scared of him now that he's knocked out. Lucky for you that I heard you whistle. You, Julian, bring that sorrel horse here."

"The sorrel? Ees bad horse, that sorrel. He keeck like . . ."

"Bring him here, I said. That bird wants to see what the pass looks like, so we'll show him. He'll have one sweet ride along that trail, believe me. With his mitts tied and that white bird gouging at his eyes. The sorrel may take him across the pass, but he'll be a blind Ranger when he reaches the far side of the mountain.

Patch up that shoulder of his so he won't faint on the trip from the loss of blood. I want him to enjoy that little sight-seeing jaunt."

Bill revived soon to find himself lying beside a campfire. In the east dawn was graying the sky. Felipe and the other Mexican guard lay beside him. Both of them were dead, shot between the eyes.

"They got a taste of what it means to be careless," announced Slade who sat, squat-legged, on the other side of the fire. "I'll teach these yellow bellies discipline."

"So that's a slacker's idee of discipline, is it?" said Bill, struggling to a sitting posture. The movement caused him to wince with pain. Both his arms were bound tightly to his sides. Yet he eyed his captor with unbroken nerve. "Just what do you aim to do with me, Mister Snowshoe Slade?"

"I aim to personally conduct you across the Pass of the White Buzzard, my inquisitive friend. Up on the narrowest part of the trail is an overgrown hummingbird that has cute manners. A species of South American condor, crossed with an eagle or buzzard, as near as I can make out. Freak bird with a six-foot wingspread and the disposition of a maniac. Red-headed, too. A rare specimen, no doubt, and worth a pretty piece of jack in a zoo. Worth twice that right here, though. Does the work of a hundred men in guarding the pass. Superstition has kept the greasers from killing it. Nice pet. So affectionate, Douglas. It flies right into your face and makes a meal off your eyeballs."

226

"You're a kind-hearted *hombre*, Slade."

"Thanks. I knew you'd appreciate the attention. We'll start as soon as old Julian makes arrangements with the men at the entrance of the pass. Julian is the congenial old chap. He's figuring on a cut of the hop proceeds. Perhaps he'll get it. Again, maybe he won't. I change my mind oftener than a millionaire changes his shirt. I've almost decided to pass up the beautiful daughter of friend Julian and hog the proceeds myself. Why split it with a pack of unwashed chili-eaters? Eh? As for the girl, well, a man travels fastest and farther when he travels alone. More than one slick gent has been nabbed because of a skirt. It was more to spite Chávez than anything else that I kidded her along. Yeah, I think I'll have to slip 'em rain checks and paddle the canoe alone. I'll take you along for company. Now that I've told you the program for the morning, I'll gag you to prevent your passing the good word on to Julian and the other black and tans. How's that?"

Rising, Slade made a gag of Bill's neck scarf, tying it so tightly behind the Ranger's head that it cut the corners of his mouth cruelly. He had just completed the gagging when old Julian rode up.

"I 'ave made arrangement, *señor*. The guard say to hurry."

"No need of rushing now, old diplomat. We've got the enemy all tied up like a bale of goatskins. If the sorrel don't kill him, he's due for a nice ride."

The sorrel kicked, reared, and fought against his burden. Bill, tied in the saddle, rode as best he could. Dizzy and nauseated from pain, he fought off the blackness of swooning that threatened him. After what seemed hours, the sorrel gave in and one of the Mexicans was able to tie his lead rope to the tail of a pack horse. The pack horse, in turn, was fastened in a like manner to the other pack animal.

Slade mounted, waved a farewell to the Mexicans and, leading the foremost pack horse, rode along the trail. Bill, riding in the rear, helpless as an invalid, felt his hopes sink.

Farther on, they were stopped by heavily armed guards who let them pass. The trail rose abruptly here, and in no time the cavalcade was climbing a narrow trail that threaded its way along the face of a cliff.

Bill glanced downward, then shut his eyes. A sheer drop of 200 feet with jagged rocks below. Death, if a horse slipped. He opened his eyes at an exclamation of Slade. Following the direction of Slade's heavily gloved hand, he saw a great white bird soaring above them in sweeping circles.

"Red-head'll be down in a few minutes, Douglas." Slade laughed harshly.

Bill saw Slade unstrap a slicker tied to the back of his saddle. From it he drew a screen mask, such as fencers wear. This device, he adjusted, smiling mirthlessly at his captive.

"If the bird runs true to form, he'll attack you before he thinks of the horses. I'll let him finish you, then I'll shoot the damned thing before it attacks the ponies."

The gag prevented any answer Bill might have wished to make. On and on they climbed. The bird circled lower. They rounded a jagged point of the cliff and halted. The trail was wider here. Almost the width of a wagon road. Slade slid from his saddle and went back on foot along the trail. He was gone some fifteen minutes and was puffing hard when he returned. Grinning wickedly, he cut away Bill's gag. A moment during which Slade seemed to be listening. Then a muffled roar.

"That's that." He chuckled. "Now, damn 'em, they can't follow even if they want to. I knew the day would come when that dynamite charge would come in handy. It'll take a week to repair the trail where that powder tore it up. Now, Ranger, here's how. Remember the little drinking episode at the *cantina?* You do. Too damned good to drink with me, eh? And you'd give a million for a slug of this brandy. Success. Mine, not yours."

The pocket flask tipped upwards. Bill's eyes were fixed on the giant white bird that was settling lower each minute. Slade grinned widely and mounted, pulling on the mask that he had removed to take his drink.

CHAPTER
NINE

"Speak, *hombres!*" barked Chávez, scowling down from his horse at old Julian and the others who sat about a campfire cooking breakfast. "Have you all gone dumb? Slade? Where is he? And *el tejano?* The Ranger who Julian sent into the trap?"

A few minutes of excited jabbering, all talking at once, and after some difficulty Chávez learned of Slade's departure with his prisoner.

"We planned to gather the men to rescue you, Eduardo," explained Julian. "The *Señor* Slade told us that the captain of *rurales* planned to wait a week before executing you. He said it was your wish that we go on with the smuggling."

"So?" Chávez, quick-witted and far more intelligent than his followers, readily grasped the situation. "And you let him go alone across the pass, eh? But I have no time to give the hell to you now. How long since Slade started with *el tejano* across the pass?"

Unconsciously Chávez called Douglas by the nickname given the Ranger along the border: *el tejano.*

"But a scant half hour ago."

"*Bueno.* I will catch him. No, do not follow, *hombres.* Chávez squares his own accounts in his own way. The *Señor Gringo* Slade thinks he has made one damned smart play, eh? *Madre*, we shall see!"

He gave his black horse its head and was gone like a flash. Past the gaping guards, up the steep trail at reckless speed, the black horse scrambling over loose rock like a cat. No horse in Mexico save Eduardo's black could travel the narrow trail at such a gait. No other rider than Chávez could sit the saddle without throwing the horse off his balance on that strip of trail that fringed the cliff.

Sitting his horse as if part of the animal, balancing easily as he gave the black free rein, Chávez scanned the trail ahead. A bend in the trail hid the men he sought. Then a muffled *boom!* A shower of rock and a dust cloud ahead.

"Son-of-a-gon," groaned Chávez. "Dynamite."

Grim-lipped with anxiety, he pushed on at reckless speed that sent showers of flying gravel down the side of the cliff into the cañon below. Then the black slid to a halt.

Directly in front, the trail was wiped away. A gaping hole, ten feet wide, yawned before horse and rider. With a twenty-foot stretch of narrow, treacherous trail for a take-off, a jump that would test the mettle of a show horse, and death the penalty for failure. Odds enough to balk the stoutest of hearts. Yet, beyond that hole rode *el tejano* — at the mercy of the white buzzard, and Slade.

"*Padre* José pray for miserable Eduardo," muttered Chávez, as he stood in his stirrups. "Pray that I live to save that friend, Beel Douglas. *Caballo*, do your best!

María, let the *Señor Dios* bring your Eduardo back into your arms! Let's go!"

Four flint-like hoofs dug into the trail. The slender-limbed black, in whose veins flowed the hot blood of Arabian sires, leaped eagerly ahead. The horse seemed to know what great odds hung in the balance. Honest to the last drop of blood in his body, brave with the fearlessness that belongs to the thoroughbred, he needed no spur or quirt to urge him on. Eyes blazing, nostrils red as blood, he gathered himself on the brink of that yawning deathtrap. Then up, with the easy, smooth-muscled perfection of a greyhound.

A second in mid-air. Chávez, leaning forward, motionless as a statue, nerves and muscles taut as fiddle strings. Then down with a jolt that would have thrown a less expert rider off balance. The hoofs of the black horse, firmly planted, lit on solid ground. Chávez gathered his reins at the exact second to save the horse from a fall.

"*Gracias, Señor Dios,*" breathed Chávez. His hand stroked the sweat-soaked neck of his horse and they were again under way.

Murmuring soft words of praise into the ears of his horse, Chávez reached for his gun. His hand came away empty. The gun had jolted from its scabbard somewhere along the trail.

"Son-of-a-gon! It is tough luck, no?"

Then his fingers closed around the pearl hilt of a slim-bladed knife that hung in an ornate scabbard from the heavy cartridge belt. He grinned appreciatively.

232

A drunken, high-pitched laugh, demoniacal in tone, rose above the clatter of hoofs. It came from ahead, around the point of the cliff. There was a tone to that laugh that made Eduardo shiver. That laugh was the outlet of long pent-up hatred of this man without honor or country. Hatred of race, of decency, of law. Bitter, venomous hate that had saturated the slacker's being until it filled him with poison and made of him a beast.

A blotch of white against the morning sky. White, spotted with blood. The white buzzard with the blood-red head. And the bird was swooping downward, head outstretched, wings spread motionlessly, huge talons crooked.

With a cry of horror, Chávez urged the black horse on. Fifty feet more and he would be around that bend in the trail. Seconds seemed hours as he set his jaws tightly. They rounded the bend in a swirl of dust and flying rock.

Twenty feet beyond the bend, Slade had halted. Crazed with hatred, drunk from the fiery liquor, he croaked out blasphemous abuse at his prisoner. He had turned half about in his saddle to watch the buzzard attack Bill.

The Ranger, stiff with horror, sat rigidly in his saddle, lips tightly pressed to stifle the groans that surged inside him. Between the two men were the pack horses.

Stupefied by drink, Slade was slow to grasp the import of Chávez's arrival. A sneer on his lips, he was intent on watching that great white bird that was swooping downward. The appearance of Chávez was slow to register on his brain.

"Watch the bird, Douglas!" he yelled tauntingly. "Watch the bird while you have eyes to see, damn you!"

Bill needed no one to tell him that. He could not have torn his gaze from the thing even if he had wished to. With a swishing sound, the bird sped downward. A scant ten feet above his uplifted face now.

A streak of silver light as the pearl-hilted knife shot from Chávez's hand. The bird swerved, its wings flopping crazily, and crashed headlong into the cliff behind the Ranger's horse. The knife lay buried to the hilt in the white breast.

"Chávez!" Slade's voice rose to a hoarse scream as he reached for his gun.

"*Sí*," gritted the Mexican from between clenched teeth. No sooner had the knife left his hand than he had snatched the coiled rawhide riata from his saddle. As he spoke, the oval noose shot out, settled over Slade's shoulders, and tightened with a terrific jerk that flung the American from his saddle.

The automatic in Slade's hand exploded harmlessly, then fell from his fingers. With a shriek of mortal terror, Slade felt himself careening through the air. Then with a jerk that flung him against the face of the cliff, the riata jerked tightly.

Chávez, swung far out in the saddle, aided his horse in meeting the shock. The black swayed, almost lost his footing, then stood leaning against the weight. The riata, wound about the saddle horn, quivered with the impact and held.

"That Julian, ees make damn' good rope, *Tejano!*" called Chávez. "Sit tight, *amigo*. When I 'ave 'tend to thees loco *gringo*, then I ontie the arms on you."

"Chávez," whispered Bill turning his head to see what went on. He was too far gone from pain and horror to grasp the situation fully.

Not until Slade, unconscious from his crash against the face of the cliff, had been hauled up and deposited on the trail, and Chávez had eased Bill from the saddle and held a canteen of water to his lips, did the Texan realize that he had been saved.

A strange reunion, that. On a narrow trail, hundreds of feet high on the wall of the cliff, with a dead bird of prey and an unconscious murderer for company, these two men met. Vastly different in appearance were these two. Yet no brothers were ever more alike in heart, no closer welded in affection. No hatred of *gringo* and greaser here. Only kinship bred and born and matured on torturous trails and by lonely campfires. Comradeship that only death can sever.

"Powder River! A mile wide and a foot deep! Let 'er buck!" Chávez grinned. "Son-of-a-gon, ain't you? Ees like those times when Sergeant Beel Douglas an' buck Private Eduardo Martínez Chávez lay on the bellies een that No Man's Land an' coss *poco* planty when thees star shell bost, eh, *amigo?* Always, you and me find those troble, no? *Madre*, thees trail she ain't so damn' wide like I wish. You got the makeengs?"

Bill fished out tobacco and papers. Soon both were inhaling blue smoke and grinning contentedly.

Chávez ended Bill's attempt at thanks with a careless wave of the hand.

"Ees notheeng, Beel. Me, I do but stick a knife in thees *muy malo* bird an' rope one devil *hombre* of a *gringo*. Thank the *Señor Dios, Tejano*. And *Padre* José and my María, who I marry las' night. *Madre*, here I am, forgetting thees theeng which I mus' do. That Slade *gringo* ees 'sleep long time, no? Ees get one *poco* planty hard bomp on the head. I tie heem on hees *caballo*, then we go, *amigo*. Bimeby he come alive. Son-of-a-gon, I mus' hurry."

"What's the rush?" asked Bill. "Danged if you don't look as solemn as a gent that's goin' to git hung."

"*Sí*," agreed Chávez gravely. "Not hong. Jus' line up weeth the back again' the wall while some *rurales* shoot. Remember *el capitán* of *rurales*, Beel? That one wheech marry my girl when I go to the *gringo* war? Ees bed angry on me, that *hombre*. *Padre* José, ees say he won' make that execution *por* me. An' María say that captain weel shake me by the han'. But me, I know that captain planty long time. He've the bad temper, that pompous one. Always, he 'ave been that way. Did I not know heem long time? Sure, Michael."

Chávez loaded the still unconscious Slade across the empty saddle of the lead horse and they got under way.

Bill Douglas listened while Chávez told of his capture and escape.

"Are you mixed up in this opium smuggling, partner?" asked Bill, waving a hand toward the pack horses.

"*Sí*." Chávez grinned. "Ees bad business, no?"

236

"Danged bad, old-timer. I hate to say it, but I'm plumb ashamed of you."

The cavalcade had come to another bend around the cliff. Bill gasped in astonishment to find, directly ahead, a level mesa, covered with grama grass and brush.

Chávez smiled at Bill's amazement.

"My *rancho*," announced Chávez. "Welcome to my home, Beel."

"Well, I'll be hanged," Bill gasped.

"Not you, Beel. Eduardo, per'aps, but not *Tejano*."

Bill was too astonished to note the gravity of his friend's statement. Nor did he see the look of sorrow in Eduardo's eyes.

CHAPTER
TEN

"¡*Viva Chávez!*" came the cry from a hundred throats.

The little Mexican smiled proudly at Bill. "Ees *bueno* eh, *Tejano?* Thees *hombres* of mine, they like to make fon. Jus' like keeds, no? But wait."

He turned from the Ranger to call in a loud voice that carried to the outskirts of the curious throng that gathered like so many eager children about their mother's skirts.

"¡*Hombres! Caballeros* who for many months have followed Eduardo Martínez Chávez! Be in front of my tent in half an hour. I have that to tell you which is of great importance. Colonel Salvador? Where is he?"

"Inspecting the guard, *Señor Capitán.*"

"Tell him it is my wish that he be there."

"*Sí.*"

"'*Sta bueno.* Now, *Tejano,* we weel tie on those feedbags, you and I. The Slade *gringo* shall sit in the corner of the tent, no? Ees your preesoner, Beel. W'at you weesh to do? Hang heem or shoot heem?"

"I want to take him back to El Paso with me. And those packs, too. But dang it all, you lil' old varmint, them packs is yourn and I'm your prisoner."

"Beel Douglas preesoner? By gracious, no! Son-of-a-gon, no! My guest, boddy. Thees Slade? Those pack? They are yours, *amigo*. You bet top sergeant's mess kit on that."

"Thanks a heap, old-timer," said Bill heartily. "It's white of you to be so danged generous. That hop's worth money."

Chávez laughed softly. "Between old boddies, *Tejano*, money don't count."

A doctor, bearded, clothed in ragged, patched garments, bound Bill's shoulder. The Ranger marveled at the medico's skill and polished manners. The ragged doctor laughed and made reply in excellent English.

"We who follow the leadership of Captain Chávez are a motley crew, *Señor* Douglas. We may be in rags now, but wait! Soon we shall be in power and well cared for."

Chávez made no reply, but the smile was gone from his lips as he studied a lizard that crawled up the side of the tent.

"Doc," said Bill. "You're a medical gent. I reckon you know what a crime against civilization it is to give dope to folks. Why didn't you talk to this danged lil' fire-eater and make him savvy that dope smugglin' was pretty bad business?"

The rebel leader laughed softly. "The doctor ees know notheeng of those Slade and the dream tobacco, Beel. Which remind me, Doctor. That *hombre* een the corner, see heem? Ees w'at you call play 'possum, mebbyso. Ees pretend he ees sleep, I theenk. Twice

239

now, I see heem open one eye leetle bit. So." Chávez
gave a ludicrous imitation of a man feigning sleep.

The doctor rose, selecting a sharp lancet from his
bag.

"You think it might be well to bleed him a bit,
Eduardo?"

"Oh, *sí*," came the careless reply.

"Keep your paws off me, damn you!" snarled Slade,
opening his eyes.

"See?" Chávez grinned. "That *gringo* ees sleek one,
no? Ah, *Señor Gringo* Slade. You theenk I am but poor,
foolish *peón* of a greaser, no? Like that card game we
'ave. Those seven-down game when you ween. *Sí*."

Slade made no reply save to scowl at his captors.

"High jack and the game, you say. Remember? You
play Eduardo for one beeg fool. There ees one more
game where they play thees high jack, *Señor Gringo*.
Ees that smuggling game, *sabe*? And een *that* game, eet
ees Eduardo Martínez Chávez who play those high
jack. How you like thees low end, *amigo*? That one who
teach to you thees smuggle game mus' be loco, *señor*."

Slade cursed incoherently, flopping on his other side
so that his back was to the men at the table.

"Doctor," said Chávez earnestly, "for many years you
'ave been good frien' for me. Now, I weesh to ask the
favor."

"Granted before it's asked, Eduardo."

"*Gracias, amigo*. Ees this. You weel take two men
and escort the *Señor* Beel Douglas to the border. Slade
goes as *Tejano's* preesoner. Also go those horses weeth
the packs. *Sabe*?"

240

"You ask an easy task, Eduardo. It will be a pleasure."

"Per'aps. I 'ave 'ope so. Stop at the *hacienda* of the old wood hauler. You *sabe* wheech one. To that *hombre* I send one letter."

"Why can't you come, buddy?" asked Bill, sensing that Chávez was hiding something.

"Because *Padre* José and María would not have eet so."

"Look here, buddy," Bill put in, "didn't the *padre* say there would be a conference with the *jefes* of this country and that you would be put at the head of the federal troops?"

"*Sí*," conceded Eduardo resignedly, "but what does a priest know of what lies in the minds of those *jefes*? He means well, that man of rosaries, but of fighting and the brains of army men he knows but less than a child." Unconsciously Eduardo spoke his native tongue, but Bill followed him with ease.

"Don't be so sure that *Padre* José don't *sabe* what he's doin', buddy. He's a mighty wise *hombre*."

"*Sí, Tejano*, but me, I don't 'ave so moch 'opes. Even eef my Salvador do not 'ave me shot for one traitor, *el capitán* of *rurales* weel do so when I go back to Madrone."

"Then why the devil are you goin' back?"

"Because, *Tejano*, when Eduardo Martínez Chávez geeves hees word, that word he ees keep. *¿Sabe?*"

"I savvy." Bill nodded.

"You are one damn' brave man, Eduardo," said the doctor.

241

"Per'aps. Per'aps jus' beeg fool. *¿Quién sabe?* Now, *amigos*, you shall say *adiós* to Chávez and go while you 'ave the clear trail."

"Go? I reckon not, old *compadre*. I'm stickin' here to back ary play you want to make. How about it, Doc?"

"Till the end, *amigo*," came the doctor's quiet reply as he examined the Luger in his hand.

"Where do I come in?" asked Slade, rolling over to face the three. "You leave me tied up and shot full of holes?"

"To be shot ees too good for you, *gringo*," said Chávez. "Look you, *Tejano* and *Señor* Doc! Salvador, at the head of hees new army!"

Across the stretch that lay between the tents and corrals rode a big-framed bearded man in the faded uniform of the federal army. Behind him, on foot, in a crude effort at company front came the ragged, unkempt soldiers, chattering, laughing, cursing good-humoredly as they played at being soldier.

"Poor *hombres*," sighed Chávez. "They 'ave seen but notheeng of those spoils of war wheech I 'ave so many times promise them. Weeth new uniforms and good guns, Beel, those *peónes* could do moch."

Salvador drew rein, barked an order for silence in the ranks, and saluted stiffly as Eduardo and his two companions stepped outside the tent.

"¡*Caballeros! Hombres* who call Eduardo Martínez Chávez your captain!" he addressed them in a steady voice. "Listen. You see here a captain who has lied and cheated and stolen to help the cause and to give you

242

clothes and food. One who would not do those things for his own gain. Am I not right? Does not Chávez tell the truth? *Sí.* Yet I have failed to make good my promises to you. Always, I have told you to wait until the time came to strike. That time has not come. *Hombres,* it never will come!"

A gasp went up from the soldiers. Salvador went a shade pale, then flushed crimson. "What loco talk is this, Captain Chávez?" he barked in a hoarse voice.

"It will never come," Chávez went on, unmoved, "because the federal forces are too strong. *Padre* José himself told me. Doubt you the word of that man? You dare not, *hombres,* for you know that he does not lie. New armies are marching from Mexico City and Guadalajara. Those armies have clothes, guns, food, and the law behind them. *Hombres,* our cause is lost!"

"Never!" shouted a gray-haired soldier. "*¡Viva Chávez!* Lead us, my captain, and we will wipe a dozen such armies off the earth!"

The cry was seconded by a shout from many of the soldiers. Others made no sound, watching Salvador for some sign.

"Thank you, *amigos,*" said Chávez, his dark eyes moist with emotion at the display of loyalty. "A thousand times, *muchas gracias.* But that can never be." He paused, his voice choking with emotion. "I can never lead you again, my *caballeros.* Why not? Because, faithful ones, I am but a prisoner on parole. I have given my word to disband my men, then return to the prison. Chávez keeps such promises."

"Keep a promise to those federals!" sneered Salvador. "You are loco!"

"The promise was to our good *Padre* José, Colonel Salvador. And remember this. Until I ride away from here, turning my back on this camp, I am still in command. It is not well, *Señor* Colonel, that you call your commander loco. Tomorrow, call me what you will. Today, until I and my friends ride away from here, hold your tongue between your teeth. *¿Sabe?*"

"Say the word, buddy," assured the Ranger, "and the show is on." His gun glistened in the sunlight.

"Company, attention!" snapped Chávez sharply, his words popping like a whiplash. "Stack arms!"

"Hands off your guns, Salvador," called Bill, "or I plug you between the horns! Go careful, you yaller-hided son-of-a-work-ox, or you'll be buzzard bait! *Tejano* shoots straight!"

"*¡Tejano!*" The sinister name passed from lip to lip. "*Tejano*, he of the charmed life!" Salvador's arms reached skyward.

"Son-of-a-gon!" breathed Chávez as rifles rattled into piles. "'*Sta bueno.*"

"But we are not yet clear of the camp, friends," warned the doctor in a low tone. "Watch for treachery."

"You tell us," grunted Chávez. "I 'ave 'ope to spit in your mess kit, we watch. Eh, Beel?"

CHAPTER
ELEVEN

"But surely, *Señor* Captain, you would not put the good *Padre* José in the cell? Myself, I do not care. Shoot me if you wish. But it is very wrong to so mistreat one of the Church and the *Señor Dios* will avenge this wrongdoing. No one but a very evil man would put a *padre* in prison."

"Can you not stop the woman's tongue, *padre?*" The red-faced captain appealed to the priest.

"Peace, María," calmed *Padre* José. "The *Señor* Captain does but his duty. It is you and I, daughter, who have done wrong. Submit with good grace to the punishment. Light enough, goodness knows, considering our crime." He turned to the captain. "Were I a man who was wont to lay wagers, Captain, I would bet that our Eduardo returns as I have promised."

A superior smile twitched at the captain's mouth. "Chávez come back here? One had better expect the eagle to fly into the cage. The adobe wall and a firing squad awaits your Eduardo and well he knows it. Return? Not him!"

"Hear the peacock, *Señor Padre!*" María burst out scornfully.

"Some wine, *Señora?*" the captain asked. "It is of the best. Come, be reasonable, María. Consider yourself my guest as does the *Señor Padre.*"

"I am a prisoner and all your sly-worded lies cannot make it otherwise, untruthful one. I want none of your wine or food. It is my wish that I be put back in Eduardo's cell and feed upon the husks you throw to the *peón* prisoners!"

"May the saints come to my aid," muttered the captain. "Was ever a soldier in such a mess? *Padre* José, are you laughing?"

"Sobbing, son," gasped the *padre*, who was partaking freely of the chicken. "See you not the tears in my eyes?"

"Tears of mirth, I'm thinking," grumbled the captain. "*¡Madre!* What's that? Did you hear?"

He leaped to his feet, his hand on his gun. From outside came the faint sound of rifle fire. A breathless guard slid his horse to a halt at the open doorway of the house.

"A battle, *Señor* Captain! On the mesa but a mile from town. A running fight. Many rebels are chasing a dozen others toward town! *Santa* María, but they ride fast, those running ones. Even now they are at the end of the street and the big band has turned back!"

The captain, *Padre* José, and María at their heels ran into the street. A man on a sweat-drenched black horse rode at a run down the street, followed by three other men and two pack horses.

"Eduardo!" cried María. "My Eduardo! Did I not tell you he would come, *Señor* Peacock?"

Chávez slid the black to a halt, swung to the ground, and took María in his arms. For a long moment he held her closely, then with his arm still about her, faced the captain and *Padre* José. A circle of *rurales* surrounded the group.

"*Señor Padre*, Eduardo has kept his word. To you, Captain, I surrender."

Bill and the doctor, shaking off the *rurales* who sought to detain them, had ridden up with their prisoner.

"Call off your gun-toters, Cap!" called Bill. "Call 'em off afore I spank 'em with their own guns. Is this the way you welcome international visitors in Madrone?"

"Bill Douglas! *Tejano* himself! Let him and his companions pass, men. Welcome, Douglas. But I don't grasp the meaning of all this. Is it possible that the *Señor* Slade is a prisoner? What happened?"

"I'd hope to tell you, he is. Doc, here, is my friend. What's the idee in corrallin' Eduardo? He's done as he promised, Cap. Even when his hull danged army wanted his scalp fer doin' it. Lay off the boy."

"Once before, my friend," reminded the captain, "you saved the life of this law-breaker. But this time he pays the penalty. My orders are to execute him. I shall carry out those orders despite all opposition. You are an officer of the American law. You know full well that a man in my position must carry out orders."

"Ees like I tell you, eh, *Tejano*? Always, he ees been like that. Son-of-a-gon, eet most be 'ell to 'ave soch fonny ideas. Come, María. *Adiós*, Beel and *Señor* Doc.

You, I weel see later. *El capitán* ees good about visitors."

"Come, gentlemen," said the *padre* sadly. "My home is yours. You found that Pass of the White Buzzard, *Señor* Douglas?" he asked as he led his guests down the street.

Bill waved a farewell to Chávez, who, with María, was being ushered into the prison. Then he turned to his host. "I shore found it, Father. In fact, Slade here acted as guide so I wouldn't git lost. And it looks like the hop-smugglin' business was fallin' off in these parts, due to Eduardo. Say, Father, how we goin' to work it to git the boy outta the hoosegow?"

"*¿Quién sabe, señor*? That plan of mine, as you see, has failed. We must not blame that captain too much. He but does what he sees to be his duty. Had I foreseen such a stubborn attitude on his part, I would never have asked that great sacrifice of Eduardo. *Señor*, I had faith in my plan, believe me. I would never have acted so, otherwise."

A barefooted *rurale* came after them with a question.

"*El capitán* wishes to know if you would care to place your *gringo* prisoner in the jail?" he announced.

"*Hmm*. Good idee. He's kinda on my hands like one of these white elephants folks talks about. Sure. Take him along, *hombre*. If he makes a break, shoot him where his suspenders cross."

"*Sí, señor*." The guard grinned as he prodded Slade and started him off for jail.

The kyack boxes, rawhide-covered and sealed with intricate leather lacings, had been removed from the pack horses and placed in the *padre*'s living room. Slade's covetous glance rested on them for a moment — they were visible through the open door — as the guard marched off with him. He had risked all for those boxes. Risked it and lost. Years of imprisonment lay ahead of him. A living death, worse even than dodging like a hunted animal faced him.

With the money that hop would bring, I could live like a king in South America, mused the slacker bitterly, his bloodshot eyes fixed on the little *rurale* who trotted at his side with ready carbine.

The street was dark. Ahead of them stood the black shadow of the *rurale* prison. A gleam of cunning flashed into Slade's eyes.

"The butt of your cigarette, *señor*," pleaded Slade, halting and smiling down into the eyes of the Mexican, visible in a ray of light that shone from the *cantina* across the street. "It has been hours since the smoke of a cigarette passed my lips. You will be rewarded. In my pocket is money. Help yourself." Slade's tone was pleading. The smile on his lips deceptively guileless. "Ten *pesos* for a half-smoked cigarette. What harm in that, *hombre*?"

What harm, indeed? The pay of a *rurale* is not so great. Was not this *gringo* bound? The guard nodded and held the stub of a cigarette to the prisoner's lips.

Slade's knee shot upward, every ounce of strength in his body behind it. The blow was vicious, unexpected. Slade's knee caught the guard in the groin and the guard sank to his knees with a moan of agony. Slade's boot heel caught him as he fell. Caught him on the point of the jaw beneath his left ear. Not content, three more deliberate, well-placed kicks thudded against the unprotected face of the motionless figure that lay in the dust.

A grin on his thin lips, his hands still bound behind him, Slade slipped around the corner of a building and was lost in the shadow.

At the end of the street lived one Pedro Mendez, who would slit a man's throat for the price of a drink. Toward the house of this man, Slade sped swiftly. A cautious kick against the heavy door.

"*Pronto*," whispered Slade as the heavy door swung open a few inches. "It's Slade and I'm in a hell of a rush. Work quick, Pedro, and you and I will be rich by morning."

The door swung open, admitted Slade, then closed once more. A thick bolt shot home. Snowshoe Slade was among friends.

CHAPTER
TWELVE

The tinkle of glasses, the strumming of a guitar, voices. The proprietor of the *cantina* yawned openly and swore beneath his breath at the handful of patrons who sang much but bought so few drinks. A dull night, truly. He looked up from his business of polishing the bar to scowl into the eyes of Pedro Mendez.

"Not so much as a drop, *hombre*, until you pay those two *pesos* you already owe," announced the dispenser of tequila coldly.

"So?" Pedro Mendez swelled out his chest and twisted the end of a ratty mustache. "Then take it out of this and put tequila on the bar."

He tossed over a $10 bill, American money, and in a loud, domineering tone, called everyone to the bar.

"You have killed some rich *gringo*, perhaps?" suggested a crony in a whisper. "Always you are so lucky, sly one."

Pedro and his companion edged to the end of the bar, out of earshot of the rest of the crowd.

"How came that money into your possession, Pedro? An hour ago you left this place broke."

"Our old *amigo*, *Señor* Slade, gave me money to buy drinks. All because I dragged a dead *rurale* out of the street and hid his body. These *rurales* are a beggarly lot, *amigo*. Not one *centavo* in the fool's clothes and he tried to cut me with a knife as I searched his pockets."

"You said he was dead?"

"So I thought when I found him lying in his blood. But the treacherous rascal came alive, I tell you. He was quite dead, however, when I dragged him off to the brush. The miserable wretch had seen my face and I was forced to stick him with my knife. Such treacherous swine are better dead, *amigo*."

"*Sí*," agreed the other, taking a pull at the bottle, which he had thoughtfully carried with him to the end of the bar.

"Who is the stranger yonder, *amigo*? The one who is talking to the bartender. He wears two Luger guns and the loops of his two belts are filled. A follower of Eduardo Chávez, no?"

The heavily armed Mexican downed a drink and took a hitch at his belts. Then he stalked boldly to the door and was gone. A moment later there sounded the beat of a horse's hoofs galloping down the street.

"Who was that *hombre*?" called Pedro to the man behind the bar.

"*¿Quién sabe?*" came the laconic reply. "He was asking about the *rurales*. He said he had news of importance for them regarding the rebels. I told him to go to the prison, where the captain was. Yet the fool rode the opposite way, by the sound of his horse's hoofs."

Pedro nodded sagely. "If he had news, he would have gone at once to the captain without stopping here. Oh, well, it is none of our business. More tequila, *hombre*. Tequila for all. Pedro Mendez pays."

He tossed another bill on the bar and went on talking to his companion in a low tone.

"*Amigo*, we must lose no time. There is trouble coming. Did I not once ride with those ragged, starved troops of Chávez's? Do I not know their methods? *Sí*. That was a spy, that armed one." He again turned to the bartender. "When that *hombre* asked regarding the number of *rurales* at the prison, you told him the truth?"

"Why not?" growled the seller of liquor. "What use to lie, eh? I told him that there were but thirty at the most. The rest are out hunting that Chávez who gave himself up. I had no reason to lie to the man. He paid for his drinks."

Pedro nodded carelessly and went on with his conversation.

"It is as I thought, *amigo*. Mark my words. There will be an attack by morning. You saw the men that chased that Ranger and Chávez to the edge of town? Bet on this, *hombre*, those chasers are close by. There will be an attack. Let them come . . . you and I and the *Señor* Slade will be many miles from here, with good horses between our legs."

"Pedro, you have the brain of a general."

"Don't I know it? *Vámonos*. *Pronto*, *hombre*, for we have not more than time enough."

CHAPTER
THIRTEEN

Bill Douglas, the rebel doctor, and the *padre* heard it. María and Eduardo heard it. The captain of *rurales* heard it. That pop-pop-ping like exploding corn over hot coals. And even María, who knew more of tortillas than of bullets, understood. That far-off popping was the distant sound of rifle fire.

"If you'll kinda ride herd on this hop, I'll lope over to the jail and make medicine with the captain," Bill told his two companions. "Sounds plumb like our friend Salvador was givin' somebody a glorious Fourth celebration out yonder on the mesa. And I ain't puttin' it past him to carry on into the town."

A worried-looking *rurale* captain met him at the prison door.

"Bad business, Douglas. Come inside, where we can talk."

"How strong is the town guarded, Cap?" asked Bill as the door was closed and bolted.

"Little better than if there was no guard at all, *Tejano*," came the reluctant admission. "My men are still out hunting Chávez. You see, I put little stock in the *padre*'s belief that Eduardo would give himself up. So I sent out men to scour the country. There is a mere handful of men to guard the town. If we are attacked?" The captain's hands went out in a gesture that spoke louder than shouted words. "We will fight to the finish, of course, Douglas."

Bill nodded, brows knit in deep thought.

"I might have expected that those men would try to rescue their leader," said the captain grimly.

Bill swung about impatiently. "Sufferin' horn toads, man! Don't you git the idee a-tall? This ain't no rescue party. It's to be an attack on the town. Chávez is in Dutch with his men. Didn't you see us runnin' from 'em when we hit town?"

"I thought it was only part of the ruse to free Eduardo," put in the captain lamely. His cocksureness was gone now.

"Well, it wasn't," snapped Bill. "Take it from me, pardner, you'd better start in trustin' one or two folks around here. *Padre* José and Eduardo, fer instance. They ain't liars, neither of 'em. Chávez and the gal still locked up?"

The captain nodded.

"Send a man to let 'em out and make it snappy," ordered Bill impatiently.

"Never! My duty is —"

"To hell with your tin-soldier duty! Let Eduardo out afore I lose my temper and pull this two-bit hoosegow to pieces. Dang it all, man, can't you see that you've got the only man that kin save your dinky town locked in a cell?" Bill turned to a gaping guard. "Lope in there and unlock that cell, *hombre!* Rattle your hocks, afore I kick you into action. Atta boy." Bill grinned as the guard

255

sprang to do as he was bid. Then he faced the captain who was white with anger. "Now keep your shirt on, pard. No use to go gettin' ringy about it. But time's worth a heap right now and we gotta make it snappy. Got ary machine guns?"

"Two Lewis guns with plenty of ammunition. But nobody here . . ."

"*Bueno*. We're settin' purty. Send word out to every human in town to cluster here. There's women and kids and old folks here in town that might git hurt if they ain't close-herded. Them, we'll lock up. And when Salvador starts fer to take this town, he'll find out he's stuck his bayonet into a hornet's nest."

"*¡Buenas tardes, señores!*" Eduardo Chávez, holding María's hand, stood in the doorway.

Bill and the captain nodded. María's eyes showed red from much weeping. Otherwise, she was calm and collected. Briefly, in a few words, Bill outlined the situation. Chávez smiled and nodded.

"Ees w'at I expected, *Tejano*. Colonel Salvador ees w'at you call it, rearin' to go. For that *hombre*, every day ees Fout' of June, no?"

"Fourth of July," corrected Bill. "Yeah. But this time we're makin' it April Fool's Day fer him. Reckon it's any use to try fer a compromise with Salvador? Then we gotta fight it out with him. Cap, where's them Lewis guns?"

"There, behind the desk. But as I tried to say before, they are useless to us."

"How come?"

"Not a man here that understands the mechanism."

256

Bill and Eduardo grinned at each other.

"That's where yo're wrong, Cap. Me and Chávez kin handle them babies on the darkest night ever made. How about it, Eddie?"

"You 'ave said one head full, Beel. *Madre*, Captain, were that *Tejano* and I not een the beeg *gringo* war, side-by-side? Did we not geeve those enemy one 'ell of a time? I 'ope to 'ave told you! Son-of-a-gon, we *sabe* those machine gon from those 'ard-fried instructor who make us put those gon together weeth blindfold on. You bet! Powder River! A mile — "

"Let 'er buck!" Bill cut in on what he anticipated would be a lengthy sketch of the Great War. "Come on, kid, we'll give those guns the once over."

Like two boys assembling toys, they went at it, María and the captain standing by in open-mouthed amazement at the rapidity with which two cased guns were lifted from their packing and set up on short-legged tripods. It became a race. Bill won by the fraction of a second.

"Son-of-a-gon!" panted Chávez, grinning widely.

"Send men out to herd in the town people, Cap," said Bill.

The captain, with surprisingly good grace, submitted to the leadership of the Ranger and dispatched men to summon the people to *rurale* headquarters. In the excitement of the new danger that threatened, Slade was forgotten.

Came the clatter of hoofs and a dust-caked, bloodstained man slipped from his saddle and staggered into their midst. It was old Julian Nuñez.

"The old paddle-foot," grunted Bill.

"*¡Padre mío!*" called María, and took the old man in her arms.

Bleeding from two slight wounds, disheveled and thoroughly frightened, the old man poured out his tale. Accompanied by four companions, he had started for home. Not knowing of Salvador's presence, they had run squarely into the outposts of the band that lay hidden in the mesquite-covered mesa. It was a mutual surprise. There had been shots fired. Old Julian, running like a frightened coyote, had reached town, not knowing who had shot at him, or for what reason. Burdened by a guilty conscience, the old maker of ropes and plots had run. And that was that. It took Bill the better part of five minutes to quiet the babble of explanations that threw the excitable Latins into an uproar.

"Fer the love of mud, can the chatter!" he bellowed at last, and sighed with relief at the hush that followed the command.

Men, women, and children were pouring into the streets now, headed for the prison. Soon they were filing into the place. Bedlam reigned until the crowd was forcibly shooed into the corridor and locked in.

"You savvy this Salvador, *poco* plenty, Eduardo," said Bill as he and Chávez mounted their machine guns on the flat roof of the prison. "How d'you reckon he'll plan his attack?"

"One beeg charge. Down the main street. He ees theenk that only few *rurales* guard the town, *sabe?*

Always, he like to play to thees gran'stan', that Salvador. Sure Michael, that ees w'at he do."

It was dark on the roof. All lights, at the Ranger's command, had been extinguished. Eduardo's gestures and grin were lost because of the dark, but Bill chuckled as he pictured the excited movements of his little partner.

A scuffling sound and a low-called word announced the approach of the captain of *rurales*.

"What's wrong, Cap?" called Bill.

"*Padre* José just came," whispered the captain excitedly. "He has been badly beaten and but a moment ago got free from the ropes that bound him. That Slade *gringo* and some *peónes* attacked him and the doctor. They killed the doctor and made off with the opium."

A moment of silence, then Bill spoke. "Well, it can't be helped. Means another chase, I reckon, but I'll git him again. Dang the luck. Poor Doc. He was a regular guy and a brave man. Where is the *padre?* I thought I saw him a while ago."

"Quieting the people in the corridor. They are like frightened rabbits. Perhaps Slade and his men are not yet out of town. I have guards at every trail and nothing has been reported. I have big hopes that those murdering ones have not gotten away."

"I hope not. Slade needs killin' and he'll shore git it. Well, let's fergit that now."

"*Sí*," agreed Chávez who had attempted to put in a word without success. "About those hop, Beel, I weesh to — "

"Never mind the hop, now, pardner. Cap, didn't I see a tin Lizzie parked around here somewhere?"

"Lizzie? Ah, you mean Elizabeth, no? The daughter of old Francisco Cordero who — "

"No, no," Bill interrupted impatiently. "I'm referrin' to an automobile I seen around somewhere."

"Oh, *sí, amigo*. But it does not run. I have had much trouble with that machine since that fast-talking *gringo* sold it to me. The handle on the front of it does not work as it should. One tire is not capable of holding air for more than an hour. He cheated me, that *gringo*. I can assure you that the lights are the only thing about that cursed machine that will work."

"And the lights're all we need, Cap. Listen. Push that Lizzie to a place a hundred yards down the street. Hide it behind the brush or a building so that it can't be easily seen. Leave one man with it."

"But . . ."

"Lemme finish, Cap. Leave a man with it. Tell him to lay low till Salvador and his men start their charge down the street in the dark. Then he turns on the lights, square in their faces, and beats it. Get the idee? There will be that chargin' gang, lit up fer fair. Us in the dark. We fire a low volley with the Lewis guns that'll kick dust in their faces. If they keep comin', we aim higher and get ourselves a few men."

"*¡Bravo!*" burst out the captain. "*¡Viva!*"

"Can it," grunted Bill. "Git goin'. Have your boys shove that Lizzie into place. It'll take a nervy gent to stay with it."

260

"That, my friend, will be *my* job," insisted the captain. "I myself will turn on those lights. When you are ready, you will say."

"Atta boy." Bill turned to Chávez. "Got your gun set up, buddy?"

"I 'ave 'ope to tell 'em."

"All right. Let's go below and drag ourselves up a few hundred rounds of ammunition."

But the captain had anticipated their wishes and sent two *rurales* up the ladder, each laden with a case of ammunition. Bill relieved them of their burden, and he and Chávez pried the lids off the wooden boxes.

A squeaking noise from the street below told of the moving of the automobile to its point of vantage.

"Listen," hissed Eduardo. "Hear? Beyond the edge of town? That, *Tejano*, weel prove to you that Salvador ees one 'ell of a bum general. The fool does not make hees men take off those noisy spurs and bit chains and wrap the hoofs of the horses een pieces of blanket. Such noise as they make! And that fool colonel imagines he ees sneak up like the pack of wolves! Bah!"

Chávez had exaggerated the sounds. Yet Bill could distinguish the faint rattle of bit chains and other sounds of traveling horsemen. The squeaking of the flivver could no longer be heard. The captain had reached his goal. The trap was set.

Bill broke open a cartridge box and commenced feeding shells into the magazine.

"Damnation!"

"Eh?" whispered Chávez.

"These shells," groaned the Ranger. "They're the wrong caliber! Buddy, the joke's on us!"

"Son-of-a-gon! W'at we do, *Tejano?*"

"Grab rifles and make fer the flivver! *¡Pronto!*"

They grabbed rifles that lay on the roof beside them and scrambled down the ladder. Both were panting when they reached the machine.

"Better gather your men, Cap," panted Bill. "We'll make it shore hot fer them birds while we last."

"*Sí.*" And the captain was off like a shot. The sounds of approaching troops were plainer now.

Then, straight down the street, traveling at a run, rode Slade and two Mexicans, leading pack horses. Shadowy, uncertain blots in the night.

"Let 'em go," whispered Bill when Chávez raised his rifle. "They're runnin' square into Salvador's gang. It'll be a kinda shock fer Salvador and his gents when these fools come chargin' into 'em. And it'll be curtains fer Slade."

Bill was right. A minute of silence. Then a volley of shots. Salvador's men, thinking themselves attacked, had opened fire.

"*Adiós, Señor* Slade," grunted Chávez.

Came another volley, shouts, clatter of running horses. The charge was on! "Lights!" snapped Bill.

The headlights of the little machine blazed into the night, a white tunnel in the inky blackness. Square in the glaring light, a mass of horses was jerked to a halt. Riders, white and drawn, stared with wide-eyed fright. Men and horses piled up in wild confusion as the front rank of the charging rebels halted too abruptly.

Ten feet ahead of his men, Colonel Salvador stopped, blank amazement stamped on his set features.

Eduardo Chávez squinted along the sights of his rifle. A spurt of flame. Salvador, a black hole between his eyes, swayed in his saddle and fell, face forward in the dust.

It was then that Chávez did the thing that Bill Douglas, reckless as he was, called an act of sheer madness.

The little Mexican, the smoke still curling upward from the barrel of the rifle that he held in the crook of his arm, stepped from behind the shelter into the path of light. With the easy swagger that made him the idol of the *peónes*, he strode toward those men who had broken faith with him. A cigarette hung from his smiling lips. He had reached the spot where the body of Salvador lay.

Squatting, he shoved a hand into the pocket of the dead man's coat. It came out again, holding a match. Chávez, with a cool insolence that brought a murmur of admiration from the gaping rebels, pulled the match across the sole of Salvador's boot and lit his cigarette. Then he stood erect.

"¡*Hombres!*" he called, a cloud of smoke rising from his lips as he drew deeply at the cigarette. "At my feet lies a traitor and a liar. I, Eduardo Martínez Chávez, killed him. Why? Because, *hombrecitos*, it is not well that so many brave men should follow such a coward and a liar. Have I ever lied to you? No. And I am not lying now when I say that your Chávez is ready, this night, to keep his promises made to you. Clothes,

263

tobacco, food! All are here in Madrone, waiting for you. There shall be a barbecue and *fiesta* for you. Tequila for all. *¡Hombres, caballeros!* Do you want these things?"

There was a moment of silence. Then a great cheer from those ragged followers of misfortune. "*¡Viva Chávez!*"

"*¡Madre!*" panted a voice in Bill Douglas's ear, and he turned to grin into the startled face of the *rurale* captain who was followed by what few men he could muster.

"Does our Eduardo win?" asked *Padre* José, who had appeared as if by magic.

"*¡Santa María!*" gasped the captain. "*Sí, sí, padre.* Chávez wins. What else can one say after such an act of heroism. We owe that rascal our lives. We — "

"Then come with me."

Padre José, gasping the arm of the dazed captain, waddled to Eduardo's side. On the *padre*'s bruised face was a smile of extreme happiness.

"One 'ell of a gran' bloff, no?" Chávez grinned. "Captain, I 'ave promised these men moch. Do they get it?" He spoke in a low tone as the men, whipped into rough formation by the faithful followers of Chávez, awaited the command of their reinstated leader with a humility that was all but ludicrous.

"Eduardo," said the captain in a tone that showed his respect for the other's bravery and generalship, "I salute you. One so brave should be at the head of the Mexican army."

"And that will be the fulfillment of my fondest hope," said *Padre* José earnestly. "You think these men can be persuaded into loyalty to the government, Eduardo?"

"When their bellies are full and they have clothes," came the ready answer. "Not until then."

Padre José spoke to the ragged throng, vouching for the word of Chávez. The *rurale* captain added his promise. Chávez gave orders to stack arms and care for the horses. He ordered men off to get ready.

The men worked swiftly, visions of food and drink speeding them to quick action. Fifteen minutes later a laughing, carefree army trudged down the street to the *cantina*, singing the marching song that had to do with the many virtues of one Eduardo Martínez Chávez.

CHAPTER
FOURTEEN

"Well, I'll be teetotaly, plumb dad gummed!" Bill Douglas stood, open knife in his hand, staring wide-eyed at two rawhide-covered kyack boxes, their lacings cut, flaps thrown back to expose their contents of small cans. Several of the cans lay on the ground, contents spilled carelessly into the dust. Bill held an open can in his hand now.

"Chávez," he said in a puzzled tone, "somebody has shore gypped you and Slade. This ain't opium. It's salt!"

Eduardo Chávez, standing beside the blanket-wrapped body of Snowshoe Slade, flashed the Texan one of his wide smiles. "Sí. Me, I 'ave know that all the time, *Tejano*."

"The devil you have?"

"Sure Michael. Een Guadalajara ees old frien' of mine. One Chinaman. One time I save that Chino's life and Chino don't forget. So, *Tejano*, when thees *Señor* Slade ees make bargain for opium weeth Chino, and make the smuggle talk weeth me, Chino and I play one game. You know that game, *Tejano*. Ees call high jack."

"Well, dog-gone me! You and the Chinaman framed him, eh? And Slade paid out his good, dishonest money for a lot of salt, eh? Buddy, I shore owe you one darn' big apology."

"'*Sta bueno*, Beel. And me, I make to you one of the same kind. Remember las' night on the roof? When you find those shells which don't fit those Lewis gon?"

"Uhn-huh. What of it?"

"Well, *Tejano*, I am know about those shell. But only a few weeks ago, I own those gun and those shell. I buy them from one gun-runner, *sabe*? Then, when I find the shell don't fit, I sell them to that foolish peeg-head captain. That father-in-law of mine, Julian Nuñez, he make the sale *por* me, onderstan'."

"Go on, kid. This is gettin' good," said Bill, grinning in spite of himself.

"Ees like this, Beel. Long time, I 'ave sospec' thees Salvador ees bust up morale of my men. Some of those *peónes* ees fall for that beeg stiff, you bet. Others but pretend that they do. For every man who go to Salvador, two stay loyal to Eduardo. *¿Sabe?*"

Bill nodded.

"So, *amigo*, think you that Eduardo Chávez ees soch a bad *hombre* that he would turn loose a Lewis gun on those men, some of who are hees frien's? No, señor. Especially when those *hombres* 'ave come to save their Eduardo from that firing squad behin' the adobe wall!"

"Then that grandstand play of yourn last night was jest a frame-up?" gasped Bill.

Chávez shrugged, smiling. "Partly, *Tejano*. Ees like this. *Por* those *caballeros* who were faithful, eet was a rescue party. I 'ave leave the orders weeth them to save their Eduardo from the firing squad. But, *amigo*,

Salvador was not weethout a following, *sabe*? For that colonel and hees men, eet was to be one gran' battle, onderstan'? You bet, Beel, know you that when I lit the match on the boot of that Salvador, no less than six of those *peónes* took aim at poor Eduardo. *Sí*. Only for the fact that those faithful ones of mine were queeck like 'ell weeth the knife, Chávez would be dead like that Slade *gringo* yonder." He turned to several men who stood waiting, shovels in hand. "Plant the *gringo* deep, *hombres*. He and the Colonel Salvador, side by each other. Two snakes een the same hole, no?"

"Here comes *Padre* José to pilot 'em across the Big Divide."

Chávez nodded. "Wasted prayers, *Tejano*. And listen. Say notheeng to the *Señor Padre* about my *hombres* coming *por* rescue me. I weesh not to 'ave heem theenk that his Eduardo had doubts about that peace plan he try to make. Per'aps eet make heem feel bad to know that I was . . . w'at you call eet? . . . play safe."

Bill nodded, then grinned widely as he saw old Julian Nuñez, who accompanied the *padre*, show signs of agitation when he saw the Ranger who he had been avoiding carefully.

"Tell your daddy-in-law that I ain't goin' to hurt him, Eduardo."

Chávez called reassuringly to old Julian, then shook his head sadly.

"Ees bad crook, that Julian, but, *Madre*, ees make strong riatas. And *por* that wife of mine, *Tejano*, I would put up weeth moch. Even soch a father-in-laws.

Wait, *amigo*, until you 'ave taste her chicken and chili. Then you weel onderstan' why I do not let even my good *Tejano* keel that old buzzard of a Julian. Ah, Beel, you 'ave seen my María! Tell me, *amigo*, 'ave you ever seen soch beautiful one? No. I am tell you now, my frien', my María ees the only *señorita* that your miserable Eduardo has ever love. Soch eyes, *Tejano!* Soch hair! Soch chicken and chili! Son-of-a-gon, to theenk of soch food makes me hongry. Let's go!"

About the Author

Walt Coburn was born in White Sulphur Springs, Montana Territory. He was once called "King of the Pulps" by Fred Gipson and promoted by Fiction House as "The Cowboy Author". He was the son of cattleman, Robert Coburn, then owner of the Circle C ranch on Beaver Creek within sight of the Little Rockies. Coburn's family eventually moved to San Diego while still operating the Circle C. Robert Coburn used to commute between Montana and California by train, and he would take his youngest son with him. When Coburn got drunk one night, he had an argument with his father that led to his leaving the family. In the course of his wanderings he entered Mexico and for a brief period actually became an enlisted man in the so-called *gringo* battalion of Pancho Villa's army.

Following his enlistment in the U.S. Army during the Great War, Coburn began writing Western short stories. For a year and a half he wrote and wrote before selling his first story to Bob Davis, editor of *Argosy All-Story*. Coburn married and moved to Tucson because his wife suffered from a respiratory condition. In a little adobe hut behind the main house Coburn practiced his art and for almost four decades he wrote approximately 600,000 words a year. Coburn's early fiction from his Golden Age — 1924-1940 — is his best, including his novels, *Mavericks* (1929) and *Barb Wire* (1931), as well as many short novels published only in magazines that now are being collected for the first time. In his Western stories, as Charles M. Russell and Eugene Manlove Rhodes, two men Coburn had known and admired in life, he captured the cow country and recreated it just as it was already passing from sight.